# DEAD RINGER

## A GRIPPING CRIME THRILLER WITH A KILLER TWIST

### JAMES D MORTAIN

MANVERS PUBLISHING

# BOOKS BY JAMES D MORTAIN

## DETECTIVE DEANS SERIES
1. *STORM LOG-0505*
2. *DEAD BY DESIGN*
3. *THE BONE HILL*

## DI CHILCOTT SERIES
1. *DEAD RINGER*
2. *DEATH DO US PART*
3. *A WHISPER OF EVIL*
(All formats coming in late 2021)

## DETECTIVE DEANS PREQUEL
*THE NIGHT SHIFT*
(Visit www.jamesdmortain.com to download a free and exclusive copy)

DEAD RINGER

A DI CHILCOTT MYSTERY
BOOK ONE

*In my 50th year, I dedicate this book to my lovely mum.*

# CHAPTER ONE

Friday 21st February

5:45 p.m.

'Are you doing much this weekend, Sammie?' Jeremy Singleton asked as Samantha Chamberlain raced through her last-minute Friday afternoon office duties.

Re-assembling the stationery on her desk that was clear for the first time that week, she placed the customised *Single-ton's Accountancy* embossed pens, correcting fluid and stray treasury tags inside a small metal mesh pot beside her computer terminal. She acknowledged the question from her boss with a nod and smile, but didn't answer.

Samantha had been with the company for only a few months, having moved back to Bristol following university to be closer to her family, but especially closer to her father who she missed through her formative years when he was always away. At first, she found the attention from Mr Singleton quite flattering – he may have been about the same age as her father, but it was nice to be noticed and welcomed so enthusiastically into a new job. Soon though, it became blatantly clear that he was nothing but a lecherous old sleazeball of a boss and she was his latest *"play-thing"*. The other girls in the office knew it too. Oddly, they all looked remarkably similar to her: long dark hair, slim athletic builds and well spoken in an educated way. There were times, several times in fact, when she wanted to mention in passing what her dad used to do. You know, just throw it out there and watch Singleton's face change. She already knew how it would play out; it would be the same reaction as every other male who strayed a little too far over the line, but he was her boss and she needed this job. She'd just have to stomach the flirting, for now. Singleton was married of course and by all accounts had three children aged between three and seven.

'I'm actually meeting an old school friend and we're having a good old-fashioned boogie in town,' she finally answered, placing a Post-It pad onto the top of a stack of three other sealed packs of the sticky yellow labels.

Jeremy perched the butt of his Italian cloth suit onto the edge of Samantha's desk, managing to trap the tips of her fingers beneath the material and the desktop. She tugged her hand away and placed it into her lap with a short measured smile. He returned the smile with interest and shuffled himself into a more comfortable seated position so that his right thigh was only inches away from her.

Samantha coughed behind closed lips and wheeled her chair back by an inch or two.

'Oh, I'm in town tomorrow night,' Jeremy crooned, widening his legs in a deliberate show of confident masculinity.

Samantha's eyes darted towards his now open groin area and she inwardly flinched. *Was that an erection beneath his trousers?* She blinked nervously and swiftly turned away, her cheeks flushing.

'Where will you be going?' he asked with his affected velvety tone.

Samantha smiled falsely. 'We haven't decided.'

'Is it…' he leaned towards her conspiratorially. 'Just… the two of you?'

Samantha caught Michelle's eyes staring wide at her from across the room. Michelle flashed an urgent look of caution, wobbling her head from side to side and then ducked low when Jeremy quickly turned in her direction.

'I may bring my boyfriend… and his rugby friends,' Samantha replied. 'I haven't decided yet.'

'Well,' Jeremy drooled, now leaning his weight through a hand placed directly in front of her. 'You've got my number.' He looked over at Michelle's desk just as her head disappeared behind the computer monitor once again. 'We could get together separately, if you like. I could…' he hesitated and then parted his lips looking intentionally down at her mouth with doe-eyes. '…I could thank you properly for all of your hard work since Deborah left.'

Samantha glanced again over at Michelle, who again ducked behind her screen as Jeremy followed Samantha's line of sight. He stood up from the desk and put a gentle hand on Samantha's shoulder. 'I'll wait to hear from you,' he whispered. 'It'll be fun. I promise.'

As he walked away from the desk he glared over at Michelle who stayed low until he had left the room.

'Bloody hell, Sammie! Stay well away. Do not meet up with him under any circumstances.'

'Don't stress, I'm not going to. He's totally gross.'

'Is your boyfriend really going out with you?'

'No – at least, he wasn't. I might ask him along now though.' She laughed and turned to the door. Singleton was standing on the other side of the half-frosted glass looking directly back at her.

Samantha blushed and lowered her head.

'Right, that's me done,' Michelle said pushing her chair tight up to the desk. 'Thank God it's Friday! Do you want me to wait for you? We can walk to the station together.'

'No, it's alright. I need to pop to the shops, but thanks.'

'Okay, hun. Well have a lovely time tomorrow, sounds like it could be *interesting*.' She flashed her mascara-painted eyelids and they both sniggered.

'Thanks, Miche. And you. Take care and see you on Monday.'

Michelle wrapped a vibrant coloured silk scarf around her neck, pulled on her rain jacket and left the room with a breezy wave. Samantha took her iPhone out of her clutch bag and typed a quick message to her boyfriend before leaving the office.

*Just leaving. I'll pick up some Choo Choo. Home in about an hour xxxxxx*


Corkers wine shop was just a five-minute walk from the office along Cotham Hill and a further thirty-minute walk downhill to Temple Meads train station where she caught a sprinter to her flat, which she shared with her boyfriend, Dan. Samantha could have used any of the dozen convenience stores on a more direct route to the station, but none of them stocked her favourite brand of wine: Bacchus Rosso Piceno Ciu Ciu, or *Choo Choo* as it was pronounced and more easily referred to. She first tasted the moorish red at her favourite Italian restaurant and it had become a staple favourite since.

Bottle in hand, she turned into St Michaels Road and began the long descent towards Bristol city centre. The cool fine drizzle that had clung to her face like a second skin just moments before, was turning into something more persistent and overtly annoying. She pulled the hood of her canary yellow mac up over her head and pulled the belt a little tighter around her waist as the rain began to bite. She enjoyed the changing seasons, but couldn't wait for the first hints of spring to arrive. It had been a long drawn-out winter. Samantha loved photography and would often visit the Downs with her digital SLR camera, or her swanky new iPhone 11, taking photos that she would share with the rest of the world on social media. Hashtag *naturepic* and hashtag *ourplanet* being her two personal favourites to tag to her images.

Although this route took longer to walk than the more direct pavements of Whiteladies Road, Samantha much preferred the solace this offered as opposed to the throng of pedestrians escaping their weekly office routines. Of course, a few people still attempted the steep incline of St Michael's Hill, but today with the penetrating rain, they were clearly only here if they had to be. As she approached the lower end of the road, she looked back over her shoulder. She was alone, but an inner voice was telling her to move a little quicker between strides. She didn't get easily spooked, but began to quicken her pace. Nearing the disused church on the high section of raised pavement, she became aware of a dark figure hovering near to a row of trees in her path. She knew the area well, walking it most days. A hot spot for the local graffiti artists trying their luck at becoming the next *Banksy*, but even they would be lying low in this weather.

She reached the corner of the abandoned church building and the first evergreen tree, from which she'd spied the lurking figure. Now walking briskly, she removed her mobile phone and put it to her ear.

'Yeah, that's right,' she said loudly. 'That's me by the church...' She paused to get the effect of someone talking back to her on the phone. 'You can see me? Great!' She waved high in the air as if acknowledging someone ahead on the lower, far side of the road. 'I'll be with you in a second.' She put the phone down to her side, but kept the screen active. The dark hooded figure stepped out into her path looking down to the opposite pavement below them – the way she'd just waved. She tightened her grip around the white recycled paper wrapping the neck of the wine bottle and hugged the metal railings at the side of the tall pavement as she passed the trees. The figure countered the movement and the gap between them swiftly closed. Samantha was now upon him, but he was still facing away. Seven feet, six, five... her breath became shallow and she took a deep gulp of air. Simultaneously and with one smooth, fluid motion, the stranger swivelled to face Samantha and with a sudden sharp thrust of a hand, grabbed her throat forcing what little air she had out of her mouth as her feet were literally swept up off the floor and she found herself 'floating' backwards at speed through the trees and towards the church building. She clawed at the hand gripping her throat. She wanted to scream but the force of pressure around her windpipe was preventing any noise from escaping. A second hand joined the first and the pain and fear intensified. She became aware of her feet bouncing and bumping off rubble and debris left by years of damage to the old church, before being slammed down backwards onto a hard stone surface, forcing the remaining capacity of her lungs to escape in one massive surge. Her mobile phone spilled to the ground. The wine bottle was no longer in her grasp. She looked up desperately at the kneeling attacker, unable to see anything of his face other than two intense cold eyes peering down upon her through the narrow slits of a balaclava. He said no words. There was no heavy breathing. No sound of exertion whatsoever. The hands around her neck were pressing tighter and tighter, the thumbs pushing down like crushing vices on her windpipe. The pain was unbearable, but the shock and fear cast that far into the shadows. Samantha's eyes rolled backwards and she noticed the high fractured and open roof of the derelict church. Rain dribbled down and patted gently onto the stone floor around her. She couldn't call out. Couldn't scream. Couldn't fight back. Darkness filled the periphery of her vision, until slowly, uncontrollably the darkness closed in like an old TV set shutting down to a final, faint, hazy circle of vanishing light. And then everything went black.

· · ·

He stood astride his victim and assessed his work. It was a shame: she was a fine looking young woman, but a job was a job. The day he saw it as anything other than that would be the day he'd get sloppy and make mistakes. And he didn't make mistakes.

He had watched her every Friday for the last three weeks, waiting for the conditions to be just right. He almost had to abort again today, but the weather app on his mobile phone hadn't let him down. He needed the rain and it had come just in time. He lifted his right foot over the body, paying attention to the watery footprint disappearing away on the stone floor leaving no trace. A quick glance back outside satisfied him that nobody had noticed and even if they had, he'd be out of here long before any police could arrive. His escape route was well planned. Twenty-three seconds and he'd be back on his motorcycle and soon after that he'd be in amongst the heavy commuter traffic and able to take one of four different directions away from the scene. No one would be any the wiser. No one would bat an eyelid. This was what he was trained to do. Blend. Execute. Blend. He leant down and felt for a pulse through latex-sleeved fingers. She was dead. The job was done.

# CHAPTER TWO

Saturday 22nd February

9:00 a.m.

The detectives gathered in the large open plan briefing room with a palpable buzz of excitement and anticipation, despite their weekends being cut short. There was nothing quite like the initial thrill of a "proper job" to get the investigative juices flowing. Detective Chief Inspector Julie Foster entered the room at a strident pace with DI Jasjit Chowdhury not far behind the DCI's purposeful wake. DCI Foster took a front and centre position and addressed the assembled detectives.

'Thank you for coming in today. I appreciate you would have had to make last-minute alterations to your home lives, but that's what we get paid for.' She took a moment to peruse the faces of her team. 'For those of you who haven't already heard, early last night the body of a twenty-three year-old woman was discovered inside the disused church on St Michael's Hill. She was strangled and left for dead.' She glanced around the concerned faces staring back at her. 'The body was discovered at approximately 9.15 p.m. by a homeless vagrant taking shelter from the poor weather. I was notified shortly after 10 p.m. by the force incident manager at Comms and I have been on duty since.' DCI Foster blinked moisture into her gravelly eyes. 'We've identified the victim from her bank cards thanks to her purse and mobile phone being found on the ground near to her body and we have already notified her next of kin.' Her eyes became heavy. 'This wasn't a robbery gone wrong and neither does it appear to be sexually motivated, unless the perp took the time to redress the victim fully, once he'd had his wicked way.' The DCI noticed heads turning to one another. 'This was a cold-blooded murder. This is a real-time manhunt, people. There is somebody out there with callous intent. I want the area swamped with officers and that means you too. Let's reassure the public with our presence. I've decided DC Fleur Phillips will be the officer in the case for this one. I will be Senior Investigating Officer and DI Chowdhury will be Deputy SIO. Forensics are still in-situ at the crime scene conducting an extensive sweep of the building and general area. Crime Scene Manager, Nathan Parsons is overseeing the forensic recovery and uniformed officers are keeping the scene contained from all access points until we are certain there are no more forensic opportunities.'

DI Chowdhury stood forward. He was relatively new to the Central Major Crime Investigation Team, or more widely referred to by its acronym CMCIT, having been recently promoted from District.

'This murder was brutal and clinically executed,' he said. 'There are no obvious defence wounds on the victim's body, suggesting the attack was sudden but sustained. Early indications would suggest the victim was strangled, but we must keep an open mind to all possibilities. We need this offender off the streets. I cannot express that enough. This was a determined assault—' The DI stopped talking and looked over at DC Sasha Elliott who was having her own conversation with the officer sitting alongside her.

'Elliott? Something you wish to share with us?'

'Sorry, boss. I was just saying, this smacks of déjà vu—'

DCI Foster furrowed her brow and took over from Chowdhury, controlling the room with an outstretched arm. 'I know,' she said. 'I can appreciate the unusual similarities, but let's put all thoughts of Op Fresco out of our minds. We must approach this crime in isolation and not be distracted by assumptions and what-ifs.' She searched the faces staring back at her, all of them with the sort of *who are you trying to kid* look that her own voice was screaming over and over again inside her head. Most murderous attacks ended in the theft of property, sexual assault or as a result of some kind of disturbance or dispute – in other words, there was always a tangible motive that led to a death. It was highly unusual to literally drag someone off the street and leave them for dead, as appeared to be the case now. Highly unusual – but not unheard of. Just seventeen months before, the department investigated the murder of another young woman in Glastonbury, Somerset under very similar circumstances. She was sexually intact, had all of her identification and property still on her person when discovered and it appeared the perpetrator made no attempt to conceal the crime. Operation Fresco was still very much a live investigation, but it had come at a cost to the department. The SIO at the time had to be relieved of duty having suffered a breakdown of sorts, and the department was still reeling from his departure.

'Anyone else have a comment to share at this time?' Foster asked, quickly scanning the twelve officers in the room not really giving anyone the chance to respond. 'No? Good. The body has been removed to the mortuary and a detailed post mortem will follow in the coming days.' Foster pointed to an officer seated in the front row. 'Johnno, you were the first detective on scene. What can you tell us?'

Detective Sam Johnson rubbed a hand down his fatigued face. He'd been on duty since five on Friday afternoon and was unfortunate to have become embroiled in the incident before he was due to knock off.

'Ma'am, although the attack site is located on a relatively busy road, it seems the attacker chose his timing well. So far, no independent witnesses have been identified. The derelict church, as some of you will know, is set up high off the road and is therefore not easily overlooked. It's a magnet for graffiti artists and drug takers, but nobody we've spoken to so far is saying a word about the attack.'

'Not talking through fear, or they didn't see anything?' DCI Foster asked.

'The latter, I suspect, Ma'am. Although they're not the most pro-police individuals, as we know.'

Several officers affirmed acknowledgement of the statement and Johnson continued.

'There was absolutely no attempt to conceal the body, yet the early indication from CSM Parsons, is that they will struggle to get much from the environment due to the water contamination from last night's rain, which as those of you who have been there will know, leaks through the damaged roof.'

'Do we think the attack happened there or elsewhere?' a detective on the second row asked.

Johnson scratched the side of his neck. 'There are scuff marks on the floor, potentially heel marks from the victim's shoes as she was dragged inside. It is possible the attacker waited for the victim to approach and then dragged her from the pavement before killing her inside the building. If this is the case, then the attacker likely chose the site rather than this being a completely spontaneous or impetuous act of violence.'

The DCI thanked DC Johnson. 'We've spoken to the next of kin and we know that Samantha would regularly take this route from her office on Whiteladies Road towards Temple Meads train station on Fridays.'

'Why not take the most direct route down Whiteladies towards the train station, Ma'am?' A question was voiced from the rear of the audience.

'That's what we need to find out. We believe this attack happened around rush hour yesterday evening from the text messages that were sent and received on the victim's phone and from the first calls to the police at around 8 p.m. from the victim's boyfriend reporting that she hadn't arrived home. Her boyfriend states that she was buying wine en route to the train station.' Foster exhaled loudly. 'This attack was blatant. Unbelievably savage and completely foolhardy.

13

Whether we like it or not, this is going to be big news, especially given the similarities to Operation Fresco. Make no mistake, the media will draw their own assumptions about this crime, so don't be surprised to see this on the main TV channels in the coming hours. If you are approached for a comment, refer them to the press officer. I do not want to see any of your quotes flashing across the bottom of the screen while I eat breakfast tomorrow morning.'

A hand went up from the back of the room.

'Yes, Charlie.'

'Sorry, so the victim was in a relationship?'

'Yes, Charlie. We are not looking at any family links at this present moment in time, but we must keep an open mind. Uniform officers are with them at the moment, but we'll need departmental Family Liaison Officers to take control of that situation.' She looked across to two detectives seated at the end of the front row. 'Stephie and Nigel – take over FLO duties immediately following briefing. DI Chowdhury will give you the necessary information.'

Both officers nodded willing acceptance of their task.

'Use your subtle sensitivities to find out what you can from the family.' The DCI turned to the large blank white board that hung behind the briefing podium and doubled as a background for the digital projector. 'We need a timeline of the victim's final hours. I want volunteers for a CCTV trawl—' She pointed into the middle of the seated officers. 'Yes, Reeves – thank you. You are now in charge of all high-tech evidence. Do whatever is necessary to get the job done. That goes for all of you. As detectives, you know what is expected. Budget isn't a factor. If it needs doing, make it happen. Let me deal with the pen-pushing purse-holders still enjoying their weekends of leisure. Let's close this one out early and show the general public of this great city that they are all in safe hands.'

The word, 'Ma'am' repeated throughout the room.

'I'm going back to the crime scene with DS Skinner. Let's reconvene at 4 p.m. and see where we are.'

The officers stood and slowly vacated the room, some in muted conversation, others already texting loved ones to say they wouldn't be home – yet all of them wide-eyed and in no doubt about the challenge that lay ahead.

The DCI and DI watched in silence as the final officer left the room.

The DCI waited until the soundproofed door sucked closed and then she faced Chowdhury. 'They've got a point,' she said emptily. 'It looks like "Fresco" is up to his tricks again.'

# CHAPTER THREE

11:17 a.m.

A uniformed constable welcomed DCI Foster and DS Skinner to the crime scene. Police tape was tied around the metal railings of the high pavement and attached to the corner of the building line nearest the church. A further string of tape was located at the rear of the church and again at the steps that dropped down onto the road that Samantha Chamberlain would have used, had she made it that far. They signed their names in the incident log book with the officer keeping record and ducked beneath the tape, taking slow steps at a wide arc towards the building entrance. The Crime Scene Manager met them and handed them paper coveralls to put on before they entered the inner cordon of the crime scene.

The DCI stepped cautiously into the damp red-brick building. The pews had been removed and recycled years before and now it was just a roofless shell. Sections of the vandalised stained glass windows of St Michael and the high vaulted beams were all that remained of the original features. Numbered yellow plastic marker flags signalled areas of forensic interest and there were a lot of them. The DCI had directed that every blob of phlegm, every man-made stain, every fag end, discarded syringe and every fibre of material be catalogued and lifted. They would probably end up with a veritable who's who of the local ne'er-do-wells, but maybe, just maybe, they'd strike lucky and get a match on somebody they weren't expecting to see. Then they might be in business. It was a painstaking and unpleasant task for the CSIs, but it was vitally important to the investigation.

Foster looked out through the open front entrance and watched her team of officers going about their duties.

'Why did nobody see what happened?' she asked aloud, not really expecting an answer.

'The weather?' DS Skinner suggested.

'It wasn't that bad at six. It didn't get really bad until gone eight,' Foster pondered.

'Did she come in here willingly?' Skinner asked.

'No, not with these scuff marks on the floor.'

They both looked down at the dozen or so short, black, skid marks running inwards from the entrance.

'*If* they belong to our victim,' DS Skinner said.

Foster unzipped the forensic shelter covering the area where the body had been recovered and stepped carefully inside.

'They do,' she said adamantly. 'Parsons took photographs of the body in-situ. The black scuffs lined-up with the final resting place of the victim and the trajectory she would have been dragged; the forty-three feet from the pavement to this very spot.' She crouched alongside a collection of small yellow flags where the body had been and shook her head. 'I'm sorry, but no homeless bum has the strength to do that.'

'Agreed.'

'So we're looking for someone of considerable strength,' she pondered.

'Probably.'

'A boyfriend? An ex with a grudge? Her father?'

'Why not a strong woman?'

The DCI scratched through the side of her dark bobbed hair. 'It could be, but it'd have to take some effort, especially not to alert others to the ongoing attack.'

CSM Parsons came into the forensic tent to join them and together they peered down at the forensic flags dotted around the floor beside their feet.

'How much longer?' the DCI asked him.

'We are more or less done with the ground swabs and impressions. Another couple of hours and we'll have this area completed,' Parsons said.

'What about the rest of the building?' Skinner asked.

'There's nothing to indicate the victim went any further into the building than right here.'

'What about the offender?' Foster asked.

'We can't go through the entire building. We'd be here all week.'

'Secure the building once you're done,' Foster said. 'Get boarding arranged and secure this place. We can always apply for a warrant to search the areas we are leaving this time around if we think there's potential for more evidence.'

. . .

3.53 p.m.


DCI Foster watched the detectives file one by one into the briefing room, having broken away from their various enquiries. Most had been placed into teams of two. Each team would be given a number of enquiries to follow-up. When these were completed, the results would be fed into the HOLMES 2 database, which in turn would generate further enquiries such as tracing and interviewing named persons, who may or may not have witnessed the victim or suspect prior to, during, or after the incident. This would be the process throughout the early stages of the investigation and would continue until all enquiries were completed or no longer required. Some of the detectives' faces were already looking jaded. Not a good sign for day one of a murder enquiry.

Foster stepped forwards.

'Okay, settle down everyone.' She scanned the room and could sense negativity coming from her team. 'This has been a tough day at the office,' she said. 'We may be no further forward with tangible results than we were when we started out this morning, but we have achieved a lot. The forensic examination of the crime scene has been completed and the body is awaiting expedited forensic pathology. I'm told the results of the scene will be back with us on Tuesday morning, if not sooner, and that will tie in nicely with the post mortem.' She paused and assessed a few of the dejected faces, mostly from the officers who had been in a similar situation with the Operation Fresco investigation. 'We can't always have results on day one, people. The effort we put in over the next few days will reap dividends in the weeks and months ahead of us, so buck up.' She looked at DC Reeves who had been allocated the high-tech crime elements of the investigation. 'Reevsey, you had CCTV – an update, please.'

'We've secured CCTV from every business premise on the Cotham Hill section that leads to the attack site.'

'Give me an indication how many?'

'Uh,' he turned to his colleague DC Donna Woods who mouthed *eleven*. 'Eleven, Ma'am.'

'Good. What about CCTV at the attack site?'

'Nothing, Ma'am. The pub opposite the church has been closed for some time and the business premises on the other side of the road have proved fruitless. In between the crime scene and Cotham Hill are mainly domestic residences, but we are still working our way through these.'

'Alright. What about the route from the victim's work place on Whiteladies Road to Cotham Hill?'

'We're working backwards, Ma'am – taking the route in sections from the crime scene due to the large number of business premises, particularly on the Whiteladies Road area.'

'Fine. Right, house to house – who has that?'

Two hands went up.

'Yes – progress?'

'No positive sightings yet, Ma'am. A bit like Reevsey; we're making our way backwards along the route taken by the victim.'

'Okay.' The DCI sucked in her bottom lip and chewed it

for a second or two. 'Okay… can anyone tell me what we do have?'

DC Stephie Byron held up a hand.

'Stephie, you've been with the next of kin.'

'Yes, that's right, Ma'am. Speaking with the victim's boyfriend, it's clear that the victim wasn't doing anything out of the ordinary at the time of the attack, in fact, it was a route she took every Friday at around the exact same time.'

The DCI narrowed her eyes as DC Byron continued.

'She would leave the office around six most days and each Friday would stop off for a bottle or two of wine from Corkers on Cotham Hill.'

'Yes, we know she was there prior to the attack.'

'She sent Dan, her boyfriend, a text message which again I think we've identified…' she looked at the DCI who nodded. 'But he didn't hear from her again. Her train would normally arrive at their local station around six fifty and then it's a short five-minute walk to their home. Quite frankly, Dan is a mess and that is putting it mildly.'

'Thank you, Stephie. Did Dan report anything unusual in the victim's behaviour recently, or anything else that might raise a flag – any financial debts for example?'

'Well, he did say that they'd had a few conversations about her boss at work—'

'Her boss?' Foster interrupted.

'Yes, apparently he was paying her quite a lot of unwanted attention.'

'Go on.'

'She started her job on the nineteenth of January. Her boyfriend said she was really happy at first, but then would complain in the evenings about her, and I quote, "pervy boss". Sounds like he wouldn't leave her alone.'

The DCI squinted further. 'Any physical contact?'

'Not that he mentioned.'

'Did you get that information in statement form?'

'Yes, Ma'am. I submitted it to the reader recorders earlier.'

Detective Constable Sanna Wainright raised a hand to elbow height.

'Yes, Sanna.'

'I was tasked to trace and interview the victim's work colleagues, Ma'am. I completed the interviews this afternoon. I agree with Stephie, sounds like the boss is a right perv.'

'Go on,' DCI Foster encouraged, standing taller.

'By all accounts, he was laying it on pretty thick before the victim left for home on Friday evening.'

'Pretty thick? Come on, Sanna, give me details.'

'Yes, Ma'am.' DC Wainright straightened her seated position. 'He was overheard by one of Samantha's colleagues attempting to meet up with her on Saturday night in town.'

'Saturday night? Were they an item or something?'

'No, Ma'am. Apparently, he tries it on with all of the new girls. Those that have been there the longest are wise to his tactics and are pretty much left alone.'

The DCI offered an inquisitive nod. 'Sounds like it might have legs. Got a name for this perv?'

'Jeremy Singleton, Ma'am.'

'Anything else?'

'Just before Samantha left the office, Singleton was seen

loitering in the corridor. The witness said he must have been waiting for Samantha because he had no other reason to be there.'

The DCI grabbed a red marker pen and hovered it over the black horizontal timeline drawn onto the large whiteboard behind her. 'What time did she leave?'

'Between five fifty and five fifty-five, Ma'am.'

The DCI scribed 5:50 onto the board near to the beginning of the timeline. 'Have we got her on CCTV at this time?' she asked DC Reeves.

'Haven't got to the CCTV covering that area yet, Ma'am.'

'Get it done as a priority following briefing. I want to know if this Singleton character is a potential suspect or just a sad tosser.'

'He *is* an accountant, boss,' someone commented to stifled giggles of those around.

'Okay – settle down,' the DCI said writing *JEREMY SINGLETON* beneath the recent time entry on the time line. She put a circle around his name. 'Reevsey, do you need anyone else to assist you with CCTV collation?'

'An extra pair or two of hands wouldn't go amiss if I'm honest, boss.'

'Volunteers, please?' The DCI scoured the room with a keen eye. 'I'll pick someone at random unless I have two volunteers. Need I remind you that this is imperative to our progress?'

A hand went up.

'Yes,' Foster said pointing to the officer. 'Thank you...' she hesitated, 'sorry, I don't know your name?'

'DC Mark Sparrow, Ma'am. I've been seconded across from District to help out this weekend.'

'Well thank you for assisting us. It's very much appreciated, Mark. One more?' she said casting her eager net. 'Yes, Warwick. You tie up with Detective Sparrow after briefing and Reevsey will tell you where to start looking.' DCI Foster glanced at Chowdhury for half a second as if she was seeking his approval. She wasn't. She took a black marker pen and in capitals wrote *CCTV* and alongside it wrote *JEREMY SINGLETON*. She tapped loudly on his name three times with the butt of the marker pen and turned back to the room. 'Right, I've decided. Let's get him in for questioning.'

Chowdhury coughed quietly and shifted on his feet. The DCI noticed and shot him a fierce stare.

'Reasonable grounds to suspect involvement is all we need at this stage, people. Singleton was with her moments before her death. We've got unusual behaviour on his part, and potentially, we also have sexual interest. Get him in.'

'I'll notify custody to keep a space,' Chowdhury said.

'I want three teams,' the DCI said. 'One to effect the arrest alongside uniform. Another to conduct a search of the property and a final team for interview. Those of you on CCTV duties secure that footage ASAP. I want to see our victim leaving her place of work. I want to see her walking down Whiteladies Road, Cotham Hill, entering the wine shop, the works. I want all that footage until we can see her no more.'

# CHAPTER FOUR

5:43 p.m.

Jeremy Singleton was at home with his wife when a loud knock came at the door.

'Are you expecting someone?' his wife asked, pausing the TV with the remote control. She was addicted to *Game of Thrones* and was watching the boxed-set for the umpteenth time.

Singleton didn't take his eyes away from his iPad and shook his head.

'What time did you say you were going out later?' she asked him.

'Doesn't matter what time I'm going out,' he said, still not looking up from his tablet.

'But didn't you say you were meeting work colleagues – could it be one of them?'

Singleton gave his wife a disinterested glance and peeled

himself up from the seat and dragged himself to the door. The last thing he wanted was for his wife to finally meet one of *his* girls, not that they were remotely likely to come directly to his house. The door knocked loudly again.

'Alright. Fucking hell, give me a chance,' he said beneath his breath, opening the front door.

'Jeremy Singleton?'

A large man in a grey suit flanked by two police officers in uniform who looked as if they were ready for a war stood on the doorstep.

'Ye… yes.' He looked beyond the officers and saw two others in suits and another three officers in uniform standing in his front garden. He glanced quickly left, then right to see if any of the neighbours had noticed. Suddenly, he felt a strong grip on his right wrist.

'Jeremy Singleton, I am arresting you on suspicion of the murder of Samantha Chamberlain on Friday the twenty first of this month. You do not have to say anything but it may harm your defence if you do not mention when questioned, something that you later rely on in court. Anything you do say may be given in evidence. Do you understand?'

Before he knew it, his arm was being twisted and he was forced into a spin, his face planted against the hallway wall as his second hand was wrenched from his side and forced up his back. He suddenly felt a sharp pain as cold metal clamped down hard around his wrists.

'Who is it?' his wife called out from the living room.

Snapping back into reality, Singleton turned his face to the arresting officer, one cheek pressed firmly against the cool wall. 'Wha…' he whimpered. 'W… w… what's?' He was too stunned to speak.

'Who else is here?' one of the uniformed officers asked.

'M… my… w… wife. My wife. Jesus! What are you doing?'

Two of the suited detectives entered the property and headed towards the female voice.

Singleton was bundled unceremoniously outside of his property, down the steps to the front garden where another uniformed officer began rummaging through his pockets.

'Got anything on you that may harm you, me, or any of my colleagues,' the officer said as he patted the outside of Singleton's trouser pockets before stuffing his gloved hand inside to double-check he hadn't missed anything.

'What's happening?' Singletons voice broke with emotion. 'I don't know what you're doing? You've got the wrong person!'

'Afraid not, mate,' the detective who was still holding on firmly to Singleton's bicep said, nonchalantly. The detective spoke to one of the other officers standing nearby. 'Inform custody we're one up and coming in.'

'Custody?' Singleton repeated hysterically. 'What?' He wept as he was forced to walk away from his garden by two officers on either side of his incapacitated arms. They walked towards a waiting police van and the rear doors opened outwards.

'Watch your head getting in,' one of the officers said moving Singleton towards the rear cage of the van.

'I don't know what this is?' Singleton wept, his tears no longer holding back.

'You are being taken to Patchway Custody Suite, where you will remain until interview,' the first officer said. 'You can arrange to have legal representation once we get there.'

'Interview? You've got the wrong the person…'

Singleton was forced to sit down onto the wooden bench and the double doors closed tight with a clattering bang.

# CHAPTER FIVE

11:49 p.m.

It was hard to tell who was more surprised at the arrest, Singleton or his wife. He had come as willingly as possible, for a murder suspect, his wife, on the other hand, was nearly brought in herself for obstruction. Singleton came from a nice home in the Clifton area of Bristol. He was a local man running a family business that his father began back in 1981. A struggling enterprise at first during the market recession, the business boomed during the "yuppie-years" of rising house prices and wages, when more people were encouraged into enterprise and in turn, needed sound financial advice. Singleton was a man who knew every step and raised paving slab of the neighbourhood. That meant he also knew every camera location, escape route and hidey-hole if he needed to.

Jeremy Singleton was a wiry forty-seven year-old man with longer than average dark hair slicked back away from his forehead. He had a pox-marked jaw, partially disguised by five-day-old growth around his top lip and at the point of his chin. Small wispy hairs on his cheeks disclosed he probably struggled to grow a full beard. His small beady blue eyes looked cold against his navy *Ralph Lauren* polo shirt. He appeared overtly anxious as he stared furtively between the interviewing detectives seated opposite him; Fleur Phillips, the OIC, and Penny Chiba the number two interviewer. It had been decided that two female officers would interview Singleton. They weren't at any particular risk. Two other burly detention officers were waiting on the other side of the closed interview room door and the girls themselves were known to mix it up with the best of them, when required. It was anticipated that two things might happen as a result of facing his female interrogators; either, his chauvinistic qualities would shine through and he'd feel less threatened by their presence and potentially open up more than if two male officers interviewed him, or, they might get to see the *real* Singleton in the face of two attractive young females. He was also accompanied by the duty solicitor, Mr Franklin, who had only left the station a couple of hours earlier having dealt with a robbery detainee for the preceding six hours. That one hadn't gone his way; the young man was being remanded to the next available court on Monday. This wasn't turning out to be his day.

As DC Phillips commenced the interview following the standard legal introduction, a shimmer of perspiration glistened on Singleton's forehead from the fluorescent strip lighting above their heads.

'We are here about the murder of your employee,

Samantha Chamberlain early yesterday evening,' Phillips said plainly.

'Yea…yes.' Singleton dabbed around his hairline with the back of his index finger. 'It wasn't me.'

'Tell us about Samantha.'

Both officers waited, eyes fixed on their subject as he squirmed in the seat and his face made all manner of contortions.

'Um…'

'Start by describing her,' Detective Chiba asked.

'Uh… you mean how tall she is…?'

Both officers picked up on the nuance of the word *is*.

'When did you last see Samantha?' Phillips asked.

'On Friday. At work. She… she, she——'

'Take your time,' Phillips gently soothed.

'She left before me.'

'Who else was left in the office between Samantha leaving and you closing up?'

He looked nervously between the two officers. 'No… no one.'

Phillips massaged her lips together in response to the answer, ensuring Singleton noticed her reticent reaction.

'I promise… it wasn't me,' he said despairingly.

'Ah ha,' Chiba uttered making a note in her interview book.

'Seriously,' he bleated looking between them anxiously. 'I wouldn't hurt a fly.'

'Do you know how many times we've heard that, Mr Singleton,' Phillips came back.

'Oh God!' Singleton began to shake.

Mr Franklin leaned forwards and handed his client a

plastic cup of water. 'Take your time,' he whispered. 'Remember, you don't have to answer any of these questions—'

'No – I... I want to,' Singleton answered back. 'I didn't kill Samantha.' He stared at both officers. 'I didn't kill her.'

'Image is important to you, isn't it, Mr Singleton?' Phillips asked conversationally.

'Um...' he shook his head.

'You're wearing a nice designer top around the home. Your staff say that you always dress in smart, expensive-looking suits and I can smell that you care about your hygiene.'

'Y... yes.' Singleton looked confused and then peered at his solicitor.

'I'm sorry,' Mr Franklin intervened, holding out a calming hand towards his client. 'I was under the impression my client was under arrest on suspicion of murder, not because he takes pride in his appearance.' Franklin glared at Phillips over the top of his rimless spectacles.

Phillips smiled thinly at the solicitor. 'I'll get to the point,' she said. Her smile dropped instantly. 'You are a player, Mr Singleton. You prey on the female members of your staff. You employ attractive young women so that you can fantasise about them. You proposition them, you give them unwelcome attention and you bully them, don't you?'

Singleton wiped a quick hand across his mouth. 'I—'

Phillips didn't give him a chance to speak. 'We've got statements here from your current employees.' She looked up from the pages and stared at him. 'All pretty young women. And we've got a statement from a recent employee who left as a result of the sexual harassment she was suffering at your hands.'

'Deborah was a trouble maker,' he threw back quickly.

'How did you know I was talking about Deborah?'

Singleton's eyes flickered and he looked down at the table.

'And so, Mr Singleton... we know you fancy your chances with the ladies.'

He shook his head but didn't answer.

Phillips separated one of the statements away from the others. 'Michelle has provided us with a statement specifically relating to the Friday just gone. The Friday that Samantha Chamberlain was murdered.'

Singleton looked up briefly enough to catch Phillips' eye.

'You were *trying it on* with Samantha moments before she left the office, weren't you?'

His mouth opened, but no words came out.

'Asking her to meet you over the weekend. Getting unnecessarily close.' Phillips leaned back against her chair and allowed a few seconds of silence to magnify what was coming next. 'She spurned you. Didn't she? You didn't like it, so you followed her out of the office and took your opportunity to teach her a lesson—'

'No.' He pleaded with red and despairing eyes.

'No?'

'I... I...'

'Yes...'

He dabbed at his wet cheeks. Detective Chiba tossed a box of tissues across the table towards him. He took a fist full and rubbed at his eyes.

'I didn't follow her,' Singleton breathed. 'I left at least ten minutes later.'

'So?'

'I didn't see her again.'

'Do you have CCTV at the office?' Chiba asked.

'Yes.'

'Where exactly does it cover?'

'Uh… by the safe. Uh… the entrance.' He wiped beneath his nose and flicked her a glance.

Phillips narrowed her stare and cocked her head. 'And?' she asked after a deliberate three-second pause. She could see from his lack of eye contact he was holding back. 'Where else?' She asked, her voice stern and demanding.

He looked down and away from everyone including his solicitor.

'Okay,' Phillips said. 'We've got officers there right now. They are seizing all computer equipment and CCTV recording equipment. What else are they going to find, Mr Singleton?'

He swung around to face her. 'There's…'

Phillips raised her eyebrows and gestured with her hands for him to continue.

'There… there's recording of the ladies changing area.'

Phillips' brows dropped. 'You'd better tell us more.'

Mr Franklin lowered his pen to his lap. 'You do not have to answer any of these questions,' he repeated in a calm, reassuring way.

'Agh… um… there's a camera in the toilets.' He blinked and stared down at a spot half way between himself and the officers. 'They'll find… recordings.'

'Okay,' Phillips encouraged. 'Recordings of Samantha?'

Singleton scratched the side of his face. 'All of them. Uh… all of them.'

Phillips and Chiba exchanged a tight look. Phillips continued. 'Thank you for offering that information, Mr Singleton. We'll deal with those matters separately.'

She waited until Singleton looked up directly at her.

'Did you kill Samantha Chamberlain?'

'No,' he said immediately.

'Did you follow her from the office and strangle her?'

'No.' His face warped and he began to weep loudly.

The officers waited until his emotions subsided. Neither of them spoke encouraging Singleton to speak next.

'Yes, I recorded the girls,' he suddenly blurted out. 'I… I did have thoughts about them, well, some of them, but I didn't kill Samantha.' He covered his face with his hands and broke down in wailing tears.

'I think my client needs some time,' Mr Franklin said. 'I'd like a private consultation with my client if you don't mind.'

Phillips turned to Chiba and then looked back at the small video camera above the door that had been recording their conversation. 'The time is zero seventeen hours on Sunday the twenty-third of February. This interview is being suspended to allow Mr Singleton to seek further legal advice.'

Phillips watched Singleton with pity as he was assisted from his seat and taken back to his cell.

Mr Franklin came back from the cell block to find the officers talking in the corridor.

'Will there be another interview tonight?' he asked.

'No, I don't think so. We've obviously got some CCTV to review from your client's office.'

Mr Franklin gave a pained expression. 'You'll appreciate my client didn't have to answer any of those questions. The information he has volunteered has assisted you with your investigation. May I assume that this will be fed back to the Crown Prosecution Service when a charging decision is made?'

'Yep.' Phillips agreed. 'He didn't have to tell us that, I agree.'

'For what it's worth,' Mr Franklin said as he secured his aged brown leather briefcase with a click of a metal buckle. 'I don't think he's your man.'

Franklin left the officers with a nod and walked out of the unit.


The DCI was waiting for Phillips and Chiba beside the charge desk. 'I heard everything from the satellite room,' she said. 'Let's wait for the results on the office search and scene forensics before we go at him again.'

'What do you think, Ma'am?' Detective Penny Chiba asked.

'Argh! It's early days, but that's as compelling a denial as we are likely to find.' DCI Foster's mind drifted off briefly and then snapped back into focus. 'Thanks for your efforts today, girls. Get yourselves home and try to grab some sleep. I think we're in this one for the long-haul.'

# CHAPTER SIX

Sunday 23rd February

5:12 p.m.

It had been another long and painstaking day at the Central Major Crime Investigation Team. DCI Foster had let everyone go by 4 p.m., and now she was alone in the large silent incident room looking up at the timeline. Not much had changed since this time yesterday. They were still waiting on the results of the forensic examination at the church and the post mortem was due to commence in the morning at ten. Both could be game changers. She'd taken the bold move of releasing Jeremy Singleton on police bail regarding the murder – on the proviso that a district CID officer would take on the voyeurism case separately. That gave twenty-eight days to prove or disprove his involvement in Samantha Chamberlain's murder, or up to three months, if they obtained a superintendent's authority. Deep down, however, she believed he wasn't their killer. Nobody of his fragile emotional state was capable of such a cold-blooded, calculated killing, unless he had a schizophrenic side like *Dr Jekyll* and *Mr Hyde*.

These were the worst moments of a major crime investigation; the delays she couldn't control. Her team were keen, but needed small results to feed from. They were like a pack of wolves hunting down the killer, but even wolves needed a scent to keep them hungry.

She drew a deep despondent lung full of air and flicked off the light switch. Her car was parked in the front open plan car park. Apart from the utility vehicles used to conduct enquiries, hers was the only other car present. She waved to the security officer at the barrier as the large blue metal gates retracted on their wheels allowing her to exit the compound. She turned right onto the avenue and waited at the main road as a procession of Sunday drivers pootled past. Indicating, she pulled out and began her thirty-minute drive home.

DCI Foster lived alone. Never married and hardly in a relationship during the last eight years as she rapidly progressed up the ladder from district DS to central major crime DI and then to her goal as detective chief inspector, a position she had occupied for almost two years. At just turned fifty, she still had time to hook some lucky guy, but cases like these had the habit of removing any desire to chase men. It wasn't unknown for her colleagues to try it on with her, however; one district inspector in particular had designs well above his station only a few months earlier. He seemed quite put out when Foster pointed out to him that he was married with three teenage children, and perhaps, should be paying more attention to them than her.

She lived on the edge of Frenchay Common, in a four-bed detached home left to her by her late parents. It was a sizeable property and she only used a portion of it being on her own, but she'd grown up here and had never considered moving. Looking at her watch, she estimated the time before they'd know more. Monday Lunchtime would be the next key stage of the investigation. The crime scene forensics were anticipated in the morning giving them time to digest the results and action the next stage of the jigsaw. Just shy of twenty hours. Twenty more hours without knowing their killer's identity. Twenty more hours for a victim without justice. Twenty more hours with a dangerous lunatic on the streets of Bristol.

# CHAPTER SEVEN

Monday 24th February

11:12 a.m.

Home Office Forensic Pathologist, Simon Leonard was leaning over Samantha Chamberlain's body at Flax Bourton Mortuary Unit. He had put up a meritable display of disappointment at the news of the cadaver laying in his 'office' over the weekend, but the reality was quite the opposite. His wife, Susan had arranged a day of haberdashery shopping at Cribbs Causeway, the two things that drove him to near distraction; shopping for his wife's needlecraft hobby and Cribbs Causeway. He silently welcomed the call from DCI Foster on Saturday booking in the post mortem for this morning. Dead bodies were always a good excuse to avoid the humdrum boredom of retail park shopping.

The mortuary unit was a modern purpose-built forensic

examination suite replacing the dated hospital-based mortuary. Boasting remote viewing and video recording facilities
south west of Bristol and not too far from the police headquarters near Portishead. His wife would be only a few junc-
tions up the M5 motorway and he promised he'd join her as
soon as he'd finished with the examination. Detective
Constable Tanya Greenslade had been on the twilight shift
with DC Johnson and therefore also one of the first detectives on scene on the night of the murder. As a result, she
had become the forensic continuity officer for the body, and
now, she was back at the mortuary viewing the post mortem
examination on the screen above her head. The victim had
already undergone the external body examination; swabs for
the attacker's DNA, fingernail cuttings and scrapings in case
she'd scratched the attacker in the process of fighting him
off, both of which could yield matching DNA to the crime
scene, and now, they were moving on to the invasive exami-
nations. First off, Leonard was conducting vaginal and anal
investigations for signs of sexual assault. He came with a
reputation for unerring accuracy and detail in his findings
of such matters.

DC Greenslade watched the monitor from the viewing
room as Leonard's commentary continued through the wall
speakers.

'Examination of the vagina and surrounding tissue does
not appear to show signs of entry wounds or the type of
marks associated with forced penetration, however, I can
confidently report that the victim was sexually active prior to
death. I can see no indication of external fluids although this
cannot be ruled out by sight alone. A more detailed examination of the swabs will be required to discount traces of semen

completely. I understand that the victim has a partner. Trace semen, of course, could be present from consensual unprotected intercourse with her partner and I would expect to see his DNA present in this instance. I must therefore concede at this moment in time that sexual gratification would not appear to be the motivation for this particular crime.'

DC Greenslade stood up from her seat and looked directly through the wall of glass into the examination room. 'Mr Leonard, can you identify the cause of death?'

Leonard looked up from his subject with a confident expression. 'Yes, of course.'

DC Greenslade waited patiently for his verdict.

'Asphyxiation, as a result of a collapsed trachea.'

Greenslade stared wide-eyed through the glass at the body, as Leonard continued his verbal analysis.

'There is a mild misconception that a great deal of force is necessary to crush one's windpipe; in fact, just five pounds of pressure per square inch is required to achieve this. A sustained pressure greater than five pounds PSI for just three minutes would be enough to cause a person to firstly fall unconscious, and then to die as a result of oxygen starvation to the lungs and then in turn, to the brain.'

DC Greenslade scratched above her eye. 'How much force is that in terms of an adult male?'

'Most adult males, depending on age and fitness, can exert pressures of between approximately seventy and one hundred and twenty pounds per square inch. Of course, some will be higher and some will be lower.'

'So we can't narrow it down any more than that? Effectively any male could have done this?'

'Indeed. As could any female.'

Greenslade shook her head.

Leonard leaned in over his subject. 'You see these marks,' he said identifying faint spots around the lower jaw line of the victim.

Greenslade looked closely at the TV monitor. 'Yes, I can see them.'

'These are an indication of petechiae, or broken capillaries beneath the skin, often seen above the point of strangulation. I would suggest, given the faint tendril marks on either side of the victim's neck below this area of mottled skin that strangulation was bare handed, rather than assisted with the use of a ligature. Of course, our victim was young and fit, so it goes without saying that the assailant was at least her equal. I can confidently say that her suffering was probably only half the time it took for her death, as the pressure on her carotid artery here would result in unconsciousness far sooner than death.'

Greenslade fumbled for her mobile phone and immediately dialled the office. The phone was answered by one of the murder team.

'Get me the DI, now,' she breathed anxiously.

Greenslade shifted side to side on her impatient feet until DI Chowdhury finally answered the phone.

'Boss,' she shouted impatiently on hearing DI Chowdhury's voice in the background asking *Who is it?* 'Boss, you need to hear this—'

'Hello,' Chowdhury answered with a tone that was more of annoyance than anticipation.

'Boss,' Tanya repeated exasperatedly. 'Listen, the

victim's windpipe was collapsed by strangulation causing death.'

The other end of the line went silent. Greenslade could hear Chowdhury's laboured breath.

'Boss, are you there?'

'Yes,' Chowdhury said quietly. 'Okay, Tanya. Thank you for letting me know. Any suggestion of sexual assault?'

'None at this time.'

'What is the current state of the autopsy?'

'We're about to slice and dice, but I thought you should know sooner rather than later about the cause of death. Do you have any messages for me to pass on to the pathologist?'

The DI didn't answer to start with and then uttered a sombre reply. 'No. Just get back here as soon as it's over, we're going to need all the help we can get.'

2:00 p.m.

DCI Foster stood at the front of the packed briefing room. This was no longer an exclusive domain of the 'suits' and the assistant chief constable was now taking an active interest in proceedings, as was the detective chief superintendent who had dragged himself away from a lunch with the crime commissioner in one of the swanky hotels in town. Both senior managers stood silently against the back wall out of immediate sight, but very much keeping a watchful eye on proceedings.

Julie Foster had been up most of the night. She didn't sleep well at the best of times, but the interview of Singleton hadn't done anything to assuage her gut feeling that he wasn't their man. She studied the faces in the room gazing back at her in a quiet moment of contemplation before she spoke. It was understandable that the brass were showing an interest, especially given the failings of the "Op Fresco Fiasco", as the managers had dubbed it.

'Thank you all for joining us,' she began. 'I won't keep you any longer than is necessary, as I know you are all working tirelessly on this case. But I'm afraid to say this meeting *is* necessary. I can report progress, of sorts, from the forensic examination of the scene and from the post mortem examination, both of which have been completed in a very professional and timely fashion.' She lifted her head and saw the silhouette of the detective chief superintendent moving restlessly on his feet. 'I'm afraid to say that the crime scene at the church indicates a certain forensic awareness. Seventy-two samples were recovered around the immediate vicinity of the body and from a wider ground floor radius. Mostly spittle, phlegm and other fluids. At least, half of these come back to Warren Jacks, who I am sure most of you from the city would have come across on numerous occasions. Warren is a vagrant with barely the ability to keep his own eyes open let alone murder someone who is much younger and fitter than him. We of course need to trace Warren to see when he last dossed down in the building and we certainly have some of his bedding, for want of a better word, stored inside the premises. The other marks, stains and discarded gum are being processed, but I'd suggest the killer was careful in his selection of this building, knowing how contaminated it was with other potential forensic possibilities. The body of Samantha Chamberlain has failed to offer up an identity of the suspect at this time. Skin swabs have been obtained, however, Pathologist Leonard suggests that the attacker more than likely wore gloves. Fibres found beneath the victim's nail on her right hand are still being processed and may still take some days to come back. One thing we can now confirm is the victim was not sexually assaulted, as was the initial assessment on scene due to her intact clothing.' The DCI stopped talking as a hand went up. 'Yes,' she said.

'Ma'am, are you suggesting that the killer specifically chose this building knowing it would contain a high level of contaminants?'

'Yes, I am.'

'Suggesting the killer was well versed in police methods of evidence gathering?'

Foster cocked her head and licked her top lip with the tip of her tongue. 'Potentially, yes.'

Murmurs spread and the DCI looked down at a white sheet of paper she'd placed on the lectern containing just one word: *Fresco*. The Major Crime Unit had nicknamed the suspect of the Glastonbury murder after the operation of the same name. To most in the room who had worked on that unsolved operation, the similarities to this case were stark and there had been mumblings even back then that the offender could be linked in some way to the police.

'CCTV has provided us with information we already knew. We can see the victim leaving her place of work, continue down Whiteladies Road to the Cotham Hill turning where she attends Corkers Wine Shop. We have continuity from the victim entering the wine shop, until she leaves and continues her journey. She is then lost to sight some two hundred metres short of the attack site.' Foster blinked and folded her arms like she was hugging herself. 'House to house has proved fruitless,' she pressed on, 'though we still have a number of properties to return to where there has been no reply, so we'll try to remain positive. A press release has been compiled and will be disseminated to the media later this afternoon to hit the tea-time news requesting witnesses to come forward. Social media statements to the same effect will be tweeted, posted and pinged at the same time.'

'Has cause of death been confirmed yet, Ma'am?' a question fired from somewhere in the room.

Foster paused and found she was looking down at the name on the paper once again. 'Yes,' she answered solemnly. 'Cause of death has been confirmed as asphyxiation, due to a collapsed trachea as a result of strangulation.' As the mutterings returned, only this time louder, Foster spoke up over the numerous conversations being had. 'This investigation will be known from this point on as Operation Boundless. It is important that we do not get distracted by the similarities...' She coughed behind a clenched fist noticing the detective chief superintendent heading through the centre of the room towards her. '...uh, distracted by other investigations that may or may not...' She stopped as her superior came to the front of the room sharing her space.

Detective Chief Superintendent Carl Prideaux stopped alongside Foster and leaned in close to her right ear, his back to the rest of the room.

'Get him back,' he whispered.

Foster cut him a challenging stare.

'Set aside your differences and reinstate him – now,' Prideaux ordered.

DCI Foster stood tall and took a half-step backwards from the lectern. She noticed the detectives in the room hanging on their not-so-private conversation.

Prideaux took two steps to the side and turned to face the assembled detectives. He had the appearance of a pitbull who hadn't been fed for three days.

Foster touched the side of her face before shooting Prideaux another sideways glare. She bowed and heaved a loud breath in submission. 'Let's run Operation Fresco alongside Operation Boundless as if we are treating this as the same offender. I want all information from the previous investigation available by the close of play today. The OIC choose four officers to take responsibility for this and just get it done.' She stared at a spot on the floor for an uncomfortable minute of silence. She cut Prideaux another stare. 'I won't be here… I've got something else to do.'

# CHAPTER EIGHT

---

3:42 p.m.

The tarmac road had ended ten minutes before and they were negotiating a deeply rutted one-vehicle track. The surface was soft and muddy beneath the tyres and now they were inside the deeply grooved tracks, there was no going back. The BMW slewed and scuffed off the slippery surface until the narrow track widened into an open field and they could finally see what they had come for; a solitary and sad-looking run down caravan.

DI Chowdhury, who was driving, looked over at Foster. 'His Jeep's here.'

Foster closed her eyes and drew a long slow breath through her nose as she anticipated the *welcome* they were about to receive.

'I've been dreading this day,' she breathed.

Chowdhury parked alongside the mud encrusted Jeep

Cherokee and killed the engine of the Beemer. He stepped out and felt the bonnet of the much larger 4x4 vehicle.

'It's warm,' he said.

Foster nodded blankly, unbuckled her belt and stepped out into the fresh, damp air of the countryside. She scoped around the field and pursed her lips together. 'I have to admit, this isn't a bad spot.' And then she looked down at her shoes, sinking slowly into the muddy turf. 'Come on,' she groaned. 'Let's get this over with.'

They approached the side door of the old caravan, neither speaking. It was clear from the flat perforated tyre, tufts of long grass growing around the wheel, and green algae growing on the seams and window frames that this vehicle hadn't moved for some time. Foster gave Chowdhury a twitched brow and rapped her knuckles against the thin-skinned door of the van. They waited. There was no noise from inside, but a low light was clearly visible through the cracks in the drapes. An increasingly deafening whirring sound of easyJet engines made the job of listening all the more difficult as a large orange and white aircraft screamed upwards within a few hundred metres above their heads on its ascent from the nearby Lulsgate airport on the south westerly fringe of Bristol.

'Come on,' Chowdhury said, shouting above the thundering wash of the aircraft. 'This is a waste of time.'

Foster held onto Chowdhury's arm to keep him alongside her. 'Okay,' she said loudly towards the window of the van. 'You want me to apologise? Fine… then I apologise.' She clamped her jaw and listened for a response in the once again silent and peaceful setting of the open field.

'Oh, this is hopeless,' Chowdhury grumbled.

'Wait,' Foster whispered. 'He's here. I know it.' She began to walk around to the front end of the van, her feet squelching in the mud as she went. A dark brown curtain was pulled across the large window at the front of the caravan. She spoke louder. 'He's just being an arsehole for a change.'

She circumnavigated the van looking down at her ruined shoes and re-joined Chowdhury who had by now lost complete patience with the situation. *He's inside*, she mouthed. *I saw him move.* 'It's a shame he's not in,' she said loudly, encouraging Chowdhury to walk with her away from the caravan towards the BMW. 'I'm sure he would have wanted to know that Fresco has killed again.'

They reached the car and looked back towards the caravan. The door remained resolutely shut. Foster heaved a breath and shook her head, and just as she was about to climb back inside the car, the door to the caravan groaned as rusty springs were called into action and the door slowly swung open.

Foster stood upright and gestured with a beckoning hand for Chowdhury to get back out of the car.

'What do you mean?' a gravelly voice came from within the darkness of the caravan.

'He's killed again,' Foster called out blindly. 'But you won't want to know the details... being *retired* and all.'

A dark shape emerged in the doorway. Chowdhury stood taller, puffing out his chest and folding his arms.

'Come on,' Foster uttered beneath her breath to Chowdhury. 'Let's eat some humble pie.'

In unison, they stepped slowly forward.

'Stop,' a loud voice directed. 'You. Not him.'

They did as they were told and Chowdhury waited ten feet short as Foster continued forward.

A face appeared from the shadows.

'You're looking well,' Chowdhury called out behind the mask of a spluttering cough.

Foster turned and shot Chowdhury a barbed glare. She looked back into the van and standing defiantly in the doorway was a dishevelled man she knew well, possibly too well. Before her, in an off-white hoody top and baggy blue joggers stood one of the finest DIs she'd ever had the pleasure and displeasure of working with.

'Chilcott,' she acknowledged him.

'Julie,' he answered in low tones. 'Brought the muppet, I see. Or should it be puppet?'

'Prick,' Chowdhury retorted, this time not attempting to hide his comment beneath his breath.

'I like what you've done with the place,' Foster said. 'Noisy neighbours though.' She prodded a finger towards the sky.

'What do you mean… *"He's killed again?"*'

Foster gave Chilcott a once-over. His hair hadn't seen a wash in days and the wild growth on his chin aged him by at least fifteen years.

'I need your help,' she said.

Chilcott guffawed and ducked back into the darkness of shadows.

'I mean it. I can't do this without you.'

Half of Chilcott's face came back into view.

'Nobody knows Fresco better than you,' Foster continued.

'Who was she?' Chilcott asked simply.

Foster and Chowdhury shared a glance.

'Don't you watch the news?' Chowdhury asked with a sarcastic bent.

'Don't have a TV.'

'You'd probably only get to hear it every other ninety seconds anyhow,' Chowdhury joked sarcastically looking up to the sky at the sound of the next approaching aircraft.

'She was called Sammie. Samantha Chamberlain,' Foster replied. 'Twenty-three year-old personal assistant from Singleton's Accountancy, on Whiteladies Road.'

'When?'

'Friday evening.'

'Witnesses?'

'Not yet.'

'Evidence?'

'We're working on that.'

Chilcott ducked slowly away. 'Well, I suggest you come back when you have something to tell me.'

'Will you help us?'

'The question,' Chilcott's voice said from inside the void of the caravan, 'should be, will you help yourselves?'

'Prick,' Chowdhury said again under the guise of another cough, but surely loud enough for Chilcott to hear.

Chilcott leaned forwards into the fading light, stared at Chowdhury and grabbed the edge of the door tugging it from the magnet housing it against the side of the van. 'You know the way out,' he said and slammed shut the thin-skinned door causing the entire side of the van to shake.

Foster turned angrily. 'Why did you have to say that?'

The whirring noise of the next easyJet began to deafen them.

'Because he is a prick,' Chowdhury shouted over the top of the jet engine noise.

Foster shook her head and groaned. 'Come on. Let's get back to the office.'


Chilcott clamped his hands around the lip of the sink and looked at his faded reflection in the dust encrusted and, of late, obsolete shaving mirror. He flipped the small mirror around making his face appear five-times larger. He leaned in to the glass and wiped a diagonal line in the dust with his fingertips. He stared with abhorrence at the blood vessels criss-crossing the whites of his eyes and clamped his wire-bearded jaw tight together and slowly ran a hand down his face. Standing upright and backing away from the tiny bath-room he looked around his ten-by-six *prison*. Was this really who he had become? The DCI had just offered him a chance to turn his life around, to seek redemption, to right the many wrongs. For nearly fourteen months, he'd lived and breathed Op Fresco. It had become his waking and sleeping obsession, but it had cost him. It had cost him dearly. His wife couldn't bear the anger, the arguments, the mood swings, the drinking, and in the end it was one job too many and she took the house and the kids, and in time, she'd be taking half his pension to boot. But more than just turning his life around, the DCI was offering him a chance to get even with a killer who Chilcott blamed personally for his sudden and unceremonious demise.

# CHAPTER NINE

Tuesday 25th February

8:45 a.m.

DI Chowdhury looked at Chilcott with unfettered disdain from behind his office desk. 'Don't you know how to knock?'

'I never felt the need to knock before entering my own office.'

'Well, as you can see, it's no longer *your* office.'

Chilcott tossed a worn black leather wallet onto Chowdhury's desk. 'This says differently.'

Chowdhury picked up the weathered flip-wallet, opened it out displaying the Force Constabulary Crest and a warrant card photograph of a far more youthful Chilcott. He guffawed and slid the wallet nonchalantly back towards the edge of the table like it was a worthless, disposable object.

'You got it back, so?'

'*So*… that says you're in my seat.'

'Bollocks! Says who?'

Chilcott smiled insincerely for a second. 'Let's just see who's there at the end of this investigation, shall we?'

'Right gentleman,' the DCI said passing from behind Chilcott and standing alongside Chowdhury's desk. 'Just so there's no ambiguity or misunderstanding, you are rein-stated on a temporary basis, or until we solve these murders.' She shot Chilcott the kind of stare he used to get when caught talking in class, both as a child and during police training. Foster handed him a blue document ring-binder.

'What's this?'

'The initial forensic report from the post mortem, and images.'

Chilcott sniffed and opened the cover.

'Look it over,' the DCI ordered. 'Tell me what you conclude. I need to know if we're dealing with the same attacker.'

Chilcott took the file and found an unoccupied seat on the end of a long white work station capable of housing ten detectives at once – five either side of a central divider. The Central Major Crime Team occupied the first floor of a specialised CID unit on the outskirts of Bristol city centre. Nothing gave it away as police property, other than tall blue-spiked railings surrounding the entire site, the security oper-ated barriers and the occasional visiting marked police unit. He knew the building well. He'd been seconded from the

Glastonbury and Wells CID, as a DS at first, during a lengthy murder enquiry almost twelve years earlier. He returned to District, before landing a plumb position as a detective inspector and then an opportunity several years on brought him back to Bristol, and that's when it happened – the murder of Jessica Asher, on his old patch. He became the SIO, partly due to the fact that he knew the Glastonbury area so well, but Chilcott could never erase the niggle that constantly ate away at him; that if he had still been running the ship at Glastonbury, the murder of Jessica Asher would never have happened.

Glastonbury was a small town located in the West Country, with a history steeped in medieval Arthurian legend and with the majestic looming presence of the iconic Tor and the remains of the monastic tower of St Michael's church rising high above the Somerset Levels like an island of hopes and dreams. Attracting New Age followers from across the globe to the mystical and potentially magical location, Glastonbury was also world renowned for its music festival, which was actually held in the nearby village of Pilton. Despite its charm and mystical allure, everything about the town changed for Chilcott when he took on the only case in his career he'd been unable to solve.

He started on the papers Foster had given him and ignored the odd glance and stifled conversations that were being had around him. His return to the unit seemed to be generating just as much interest as his sudden and dramatic departure a number of months before. He had been in the wrong, he knew that, but his stubborn pride wouldn't allow anyone else to hear his guilty plea that had plagued him since. He didn't blame DCI Foster for taking his warrant card away from him. He had punched a goading and gloating Jaz Chowdhury square in the face when his application for the new department DI was overlooked in favour of the younger, better qualified man. In a way, he was lucky Chowdhury hadn't pressed for assault charges, but he suspected that was more to do with Foster's diplomatic skills rather than Chowdhury's forgiving heart. But now he was finally back where he belonged, he had no intention of screwing it up this time – he had a killer to get even with.

As he pored over the photographs, both from the scene and the victim's post mortem examination, he thought about everything that had gone before; everything he'd come to lose. He wasn't fazed by the more gruesome aspects of the job. Death and tragedy were part and parcel of life as a cop and dealt with by wit – the kind of black-humour that most police officers possessed, or diving into the bottom of a bottle. No, that didn't trouble him – what bothered him was losing. And to his mind, he'd lost, twice over.

As he read the forensic report and initial police accounts, the similarities to the previous attack were stark. There were few, if any details about the suspect. Both attacks took place in brazen locations. There was the same apparent modus operandi – asphyxiation from a crushed trachea, and most worryingly, an apparent forensic awareness. He scooped the papers together and entered the DCI's office without invitation.

'It's the same attacker, has to be,' he said dropping the file onto the corner of the DCI's desk.

Foster stopped typing leaned back in her chair and chastised Chilcott's rude interruption with darkened eyes. She saw determination in his rigid stance.

'Okay – good,' she finally said.

'Good?'

'At least we know we've only got one lunatic on our patch.' She stood up and quietly closed the door. 'I'm going to give you complete freedom to do whatever is necessary to secure a conviction, Robbie. There's a shit storm of media interest in this murder and I need a result.'

'I saw a report.'

'I thought you didn't have TV?'

'I've got a smartphone – I'm not that archaic, you know.' He dropped her a nod. 'You'll be famous.'

'Just make sure I'm famous for all the right reasons, Robbie. Tell me what you need; equipment, resources, whatever… just get this bastard off our streets.'

'What about Chowdhury – where does he fit into the equation?'

'You two just need to work together on this. Chowdhury isn't your replacement, Robbie. Nobody could take your place. I just wish you could have seen that for yourself.'

Chilcott groaned. 'If it wasn't bad enough—'

'What, having a woman for a boss?'

'No… you know what I mean. I worked bloody hard to get to where I am, and he waltzes in full of *ologies* or some other useless degree, and suddenly that makes him a better cop than me—'

'Jaz got the DI's seat on merit, Rob.'

'Bollocks, he ticks boxes and you know it.'

'Like me? Do I tick boxes too?'

'No, that's not what I'm saying… I've got absolutely nothing against the bloke, his ethnicity, or his religion, but I do take issue with the system—'

'Then take it up with the brass, Robbie. Don't take it out on Jaz.' The DCI looked at Chilcott like he was a toddler refusing his greens. 'Remember, if you hadn't had such a hissy-fit you might have stood a chance at another DI position here at Central.'

Neither of them spoke for a brief moment and then the DCI ushered him closer with a twitch of her finger. 'Rob, full disclosure now – do you really think you can catch this bastard?'

He hesitated, just a beat. 'As we're talking *openly*… if I'd been allowed to investigate Op Fresco the way I had wanted to right from the off, this latest victim would still be alive.'

# CHAPTER TEN

9.30 a.m.

Chilcott had spread both sets of case papers out on the DCI's desk and together along with Jaz Chowdhury, they were looking over them with a new perspective.

'Let's look at the victims,' Chilcott said, placing Samantha Chamberlain's victim profile alongside that of the existing Op Fresco victim profile. The faces of two young women stared back at him. 'Sammie Chamberlain, aged twenty-three. Murdered by strangulation. February the twenty-first, two thousand and twenty.' He touched the image alongside and spoke with reverential tones. 'And Jessica Asher, aged seventeen. Brutally beaten and murdered by strangulation – October the nineteenth, two thousand and eighteen. Something must link them to our killer, but what?'

The DCI picked up Samantha Chamberlain's file and spoke down to her photograph. 'Both died of strangulation.

Both had their windpipes crushed in exactly the same manner. Both girls were murdered in daylight hours, broadly speaking, and both were left in the open to be found—'

'They are attacks of extreme violence. Brutal, angry even,' Chilcott cut in.

'Angry about what?' Chowdhury questioned.

Chilcott rolled his eyes and slowly turned to face his younger peer. 'Are you trying to tell me you didn't learn the basics of police work on your needlecraft degree?'

'Robbie!' Foster barked. 'That's enough.'

Both men reacted to the chastisement in their own individual way: Chowdhury standing taller, shoulders pinned back; Chilcott curling Chowdhury a surly lip.

'You're right,' the DCI said bringing the focus back to the task in hand. 'There certainly has to be a link, but what and why?'

'Glastonbury and Bristol,' Chilcott grumbled. 'That's twenty-five-miles as the crow flies.' He paused in thought as he calculated simple arithmetic in his head. '…or nearly eighty miles in circumference.'

'Do you think there could be more victims we don't know about?' Chowdhury asked.

*At last, a sensible question.*

'I suppose it's possible,' Foster replied placing Samantha's file back onto the desk. 'We only know about the attacks within the boundaries of Avon and Somerset. What if he's doing this elsewhere?'

Chowdhury tossed Chilcott a smug expression. 'I'll get an enquiry team on it,' Chowdhury said. 'What else do we need to do?'

Chilcott put one file on top of the other and scooped

both from the table pulling them tight into his chest. 'I don't know what you're going to do, but I'm going back to speak to the next of kin.'

Chilcott attended the home address of Mr and Mrs Chamberlain, along with the Family Liaison Officer assigned to the case. It was always challenging speaking to the bereaved. There were no hard and fast rules about how it should be done – other than with utmost care and respect. Each encounter was different; there were often tears, or vehement anger, or a sheer refusal to acknowledge the news. He'd even known stifled laughter, followed soon after by one or all of the previously described emotions. The FLO had the toughest of jobs – they had to deal with the constant expectation that the police would soon bring someone to justice, but it sadly didn't always work out that way, as Mr and Mrs Asher could testify, and, of course, the liaison officer had to field the biggest question of them all – *Why?*

Chilcott was asking himself the exact same question throughout the journey across the city. The Chamberlains lived in a comfortably-sized detached house in the Pucklechurch region of Bristol. The FLO introduced Chilcott to the mother, father and sister and then perched on a Union Jack decorated footstool in the corner of the room to allow Chilcott to engage with the family.

'Thank you for seeing me and may I extend my deepest sympathies on behalf of all of my colleagues working hard on this investigation.' Chilcott looked at each of them in turn as he spoke and then lingered on the father's face. His emotions, or apparent lack of, took him slightly by surprise.

Chilcott twitched a smile. 'Before I continue, have any of you got any questions for me?'

'Have you got any suspects?' the father asked bluntly.

Chilcott paused momentarily as he thought about his response. 'No, not yet… but trust me, we're working on it.'

'When can I bury my daughter,' the mother asked.

It was a natural question, but one of the hardest to answer given the circumstances. Samantha Chamberlain was technically a crime scene and one that might potentially require further examination. Her body wouldn't be released until they were certain it had given up all its secrets. Chilcott bit down. 'We'll let you know the moment you can put your daughter's body to rest.' In the corner of his eye, Chilcott noticed a framed picture on a tall mahogany lamp table. He studied the picture for a second or two and then raked back to Mr Chamberlain in recognition of what he was seeing. 'You're in the military?' he asked.

Mr Chamberlain stalled. 'I was.'

Chilcott stood up from the dining room chair that had been brought in for him sit on by the FLO and looked with more purpose at the photograph. 'Afghanistan?' he asked.

'It was.'

'May I?' Chilcott asked hovering a hand beside the photograph for permission to look closer.

Mr Chamberlain nodded.

Chilcott brought the frame closer to his face, aware all the time that he was being scrutinised by several pairs of watchful eyes.

'Doesn't look like you were a regular soldier, going by this picture.'

'I was just one of the lads,' Mr Chamberlain downplayed.

Chilcott returned the frame and adjusted it to line up perfectly with the faint dust tracks marking its original position on the shiny red wooden plinth. 'Can I ask what regiment you were in?' he asked turning to Mr Chamberlain.

'What does that have to do with the death of my daughter?'

'I'm sorry – it's just for interest's sake.' Chilcott saw the FLO rising hesitantly from the low foot stool in the corner of the room, ready to intervene. 'I respect what you guys went through and for the many sacrifices you made.' That should be enough flattery to divert the growing air of hostility.

'I was a Para.'

'But not in this picture,' Chilcott answered quickly.

Mr Chamberlain looked at Chilcott with dark searing eyes that didn't hide his inquisitive and questioning mind. 'That's right,' he said, but fell short of asking, *what's it to do with you?*

Chilcott waved air away with the back of his hand. 'My nephew is a Para,' he clarified giving Chamberlain what he needed to hopefully satisfy the growing curiosity. Chilcott leaned in and looked closely again at the image. 'But he doesn't have that kind of kit.'

Chamberlain stooped his head and kept his eyes widely trained on the detective. 'That's because I was a *blade*.'

An overwhelming itch forced Chilcott to scratch behind his ear. 'Okay,' he said not pushing it any further. 'Well, I'm very pleased to have met you all, and once again, I'm deeply sorry for your loss.' He stood once again from the seat. 'I think it's important to be more than just a name or a voice at the end of the phone, but I've taken enough of your time already. You have your FLO, Nigel to ask any questions of, but here's my card if you'd like to speak with me directly.' He smiled politely again. 'Call at any time, no matter how small you think the question might be – I'm here for you, so use it.'

The others all stood from their seats, except the young daughter who remained on the sofa, her knees tucked tightly to her chest, her expression full of fear and misunderstanding. Mr Chamberlain shook Chilcott's hand with the firmness expected from a military veteran and held a steely, intense gaze until their hands parted. The handshake with Mrs Chamberlain was far more flaccid.

Chilcott left them in the living room and made for the door alongside the FLO, whose own expression was somewhat bemused. Chilcott patted him on the shoulder, winked and made his purposeful way back to the car.

From the secure confines of the pool car, Chilcott looked out through the passenger side window to check that he wasn't being watched from the house and then he dialled the number.

DCI Foster answered almost instantaneously. 'Chilcott!'

'I may have found a link between our victims,' Chilcott said quietly, despite his solitary surroundings. 'But I need to speak to Paul Asher again.'

'What – why do you need to speak Jessica's father?'

'Because Samantha Chamberlain's father was in the SAS.'

# CHAPTER ELEVEN

2:10 p.m.

The long terrace of houses on Avalon Parade pointed like a finger directly towards the huge conical 'island' supporting the spectacular tower remains of the 15th Century church, also known in modern times as the Glastonbury Tor. Chilcott waited beside his open car door looking up at the magnificent monument. He wasn't a believer in all that mystical mumbo jumbo, but he did feel *something* different here. Maybe it was melancholic emotion he was experiencing as a result of the long hours he'd worked as a bobby on these very streets, or perhaps during his stint as the most senior detective on the district? Either way, he felt warmth in his heart.

He peered over the roof of the white BMW toward the Asher house with pondering reflection. The last time they made this same visit they were bringing Mr and Mrs Asher back from the mortuary at Flax Bourton having identified the battered body of their one and only daughter, Jessica. The palpable grief of that case would live with Chilcott for the remainder of his days, and so began his obsession with catching the Operation Fresco killer. Jessica was just a child and her murderer had used her body to exert a level of unimaginable violence Chilcott and the rest of the team had rarely, if ever, seen. Every long-serving cop had a case that *stuck* with them, that made them wake with consternation or regret in the middle of the night, that made them question the very humanity they strived to protect. Jessica Asher's murder was Chilcott's.

Foster and Chilcott paused momentarily on the doorstep and exchanged a cautionary look before the DCI pressed the doorbell.

Angela Asher opened the door with a warm, welcoming face, which immediately dropped on recognition of who was standing before her. A year and a half of placing dark memories inside a fragile box were unleashed in an instant. No one spoke at first and then instinctively, Angela grasped for the edge of the door to shut out the memories once again.

'We just want a quick word, Mrs Asher,' the DCI said as the door began to close on them. 'We won't keep you long, I promise.'

'What do you want?' the breakable voice asked from behind the door.

'Can we come inside for a moment – please?' Chilcott asked.

Angela Asher peered out at them through the narrow

gap in the door, her eyes wide and wild. Her choice was simple, but the internal debate raging inside her mind was clear for Chilcott and Foster to see. Suddenly, she lowered her head and ducked back behind the door, leaving a gap just wide enough to get a foot between.

Foster prodded Chilcott in the ribs and he stepped respectfully into the void. He smiled, apologetically at Angela, who was now leaning back against the hallway wall her head towards the ceiling and Foster followed close behind and gently closed the door.

'Is Paul here?' Foster asked.

'No,' Angela said quickly. 'No. He's… working.'

'At the engineering plant?' Chilcott asked.

'No.' She looked directly at him, the pain in her face just as he'd remembered. 'He was dismissed for taking too much time off during the…' her voice broke away.

Chilcott bowed his head and Foster smiled painfully. Unresolved murders were long, drawn-out affairs. If they were frustrating for the cops, they must have been unbearable for the families left behind. A long silence followed, the three of them standing uncomfortably inwards like strangers stuck in close proximity on a tube train.

'Was Paul ever in the Special Forces?' Chilcott asked directly. After all, that was why they had come.

Angela's twitching and questioning eyebrows told Chilcott that he was.

'Why didn't you mention this before?' he asked.

'What does it matter? Paul's past military service is a part of our lives that is private to us. We don't talk about it. That's the way he wants it.'

'Angela,' Foster said calmly. 'This is important.'

Angela stopped glaring at Chilcott and faced Foster.

'Was Paul in the SAS?' she probed gently.

Angela turned away, breaking the triangle. 'I can't talk about any of this.'

She began making along the corridor away from them.

'Angela, we think there could be a connection between your daughter's death and the murder of a young woman in Bristol last Friday,' Foster called out.

Angela stopped walking away and turned about to face them, a hand covering her mouth.

'Angela, can we sit down somewhere, please?' Foster said.

They went through to the living room, Angela taking the armchair closest to the door. Foster dipped her head at Chilcott and they both followed suit, perching down on the lip of the sofa alongside Angela's chair.

Angela stared into space. 'I saw the news about that poor girl. It brought it all…' Her voice tailed away.

'Yes, it was a vicious attack,' Foster said. 'We believe this crime could be linked to Jessica's death.'

Angela looked with desperation at the two officers.

'It's still early days, but DI Chilcott has a theory, which is why we're here. Angela, we really need to know if Paul was a member of the Special Air Service.'

Angela gripped her knees and stared, eyes fixed to the floor in front of her feet. Her arms began to shake and then she twitched her head, just twice, but enough to affirm the question.

Chilcott sat back in the sofa and exhaled loudly, slapping

the sides of his thighs in exuberant recognition of finally establishing an avenue down which he could pursue the killer.

Foster glared at him, correcting his insensitivity and brought the focus back onto Angela. 'How much can you tell us about his time in the forces?' she asked.

'You really need to speak with Paul,' Angela said. 'All I know, it was a difficult and uncertain time... for both of us.'

'Do you know what company he was attached to?' Chilcott asked re-engaging with Angela.

She shook her head. 'Um...'

'It's okay, Angela,' Foster reassured her. 'You can tell us.'

Angela emitted a stifled groan. 'It was "D" Squadron.'

Chilcott and Foster shared a look.

'When will Paul be home?' the DCI asked.

'Around four.'

Angela began to weep and the DCI passed her a tissue from a nearby box on the coffee table.

'Okay, can we come back again?' Foster asked.

She agreed and dabbed tears from her eyes and cheeks. 'Shall I say anything to him?'

'No,' Foster said gently. 'I don't want him to worry unnecessarily.'

DCI Foster stood up and offered Angela her hand. 'Nice to see you again, Angela. I'm very sorry if our visit has caused upset. Here's my card,' she said handing Angela her business card. 'Call us if you think of anything else that might assist.'

Chilcott and Foster left Angela seated in the lounge and made their own way out of the house. They didn't speak again until they were back in the silent security of the BMW.

'I think you've got it,' Foster said. 'The link between the two girls.'

'There's only one way to find out,' Chilcott said. 'Let's see if Chamberlain knows Paul Asher.'

# CHAPTER TWELVE

5:17 p.m.

Chilcott and Foster were once again face-to-face with Stephen Chamberlain. They had managed to prize him away from his wife on the premise that they would only be a short while in the other room. Mrs Chamberlain reluctantly agreed, but only on the basis that she wasn't kept out of the loop with any information. In retrospect, it probably looked highly suspicious to his wife and perhaps could have been managed differently, but they needed Chamberlain on his own.

'Do you know a chap by the name of Paul Asher?' Chilcott asked him directly, negating any unnecessary waffle.

Creases formed in Chamberlain's brow like the life-lines of a recently felled oak tree, and this particular oak had seen some life that was for sure.

'Sit down please, Stephen,' the DCI told Chamberlain and she sat down on the leather sofa next to him. She moistened her lips and glanced at Chilcott. 'We think we may have found a link between the victims of these horrible crimes.'

'Crimes?' Chamberlain searched between them, a look of confusion crossed his face. 'There's another?'

'I'm afraid so.'

'And you didn't catch him after the first one?' Chamberlain's tone was now hostile.

Chilcott stepped closer towards the sofa. 'How long have you lived here, Mr Chamberlain?'

Chamberlain's jaw rippled as he bit down.

'How long have you lived here?' Chilcott asked again. 'It's potentially important to the case.'

'About nine months,' Chamberlain seethed through a clenched jaw.

'Where did you live before?' Chilcott asked.

Chamberlain stared at Chilcott with the kind of no-nonsense look that could unsettle an individual with a weaker constitution. 'We lived in Gibraltar for a while. What's that to you?'

Chilcott squinted ignoring the provocative question. That explained why Chamberlain didn't appear to know anything about Jessica Asher's murder. He looked deeply into Chamberlain's calculating eyes. 'Paul Asher's daughter, Jessica, just seventeen years old was murdered in a similar way to Samantha. We suspect the crimes are connected through your *particular* line of work.'

Chamberlain didn't move. Not so much as a flinch.

'You do know Paul Asher, don't you?' Chamberlain dipped his lids in an accepting gesture, but still refused to confirm the fact.

'Were you all in the Gulf War together?' Chilcott asked not letting up.

'Amongst others,' Chamberlain huffed.

'Are you still in contact with Paul?' the DCI asked.

'No,' he said immediately, 'otherwise I'd have…' He searched the DCI's face and started breathing heavily through his nose. 'When?' he asked. 'When did she…?'

'About eighteen months ago,' Foster answered.

'October the nineteenth, two thousand and eighteen,' Chilcott said. 'His daughter was strangled, beaten to a pulp and left in the street,' he said bluntly.

Chamberlain's mouth dropped enough for both officers to notice his apparent dismay.

'Something about your squadron links your daughter's murder to that of Jessica Asher,' Chilcott said. 'And we need to establish what that is.'

Chamberlain's face screwed up into a jumbled mixture somewhere between intense ferocity and utter confusion.

'Do you know if any other members of your squadron live in this area?' Foster asked, picking up on his increasing loss of composure.

Chamberlain sank his forehead into his hands and Chilcott and Foster waited in silence as he processed the information. He looked up at the DCI with a pained expression. 'I don't know. When I came out of the last mission, I wanted to leave it all behind.' He scratched the side of his neck. 'For Anna's sake.' He looked down at his left hand and twisted the silver ring on his wedding finger in a subconscious display of troubled times between himself and his wife. 'I didn't make an effort to keep in touch with anyone specifically. Does Paul live in Bristol too?'

'Glastonbury,' Chilcott said. 'That's also our patch. That's how we've been able to connect the crimes.'

'Can you think of anyone who may bear a grudge against you, or Paul?' the DCI asked.

Chamberlain spluttered. 'Seriously?' He stared hard at Foster and then at Chilcott. 'Pretty much everyone we ever came across in a professional capacity bears a *grudge*. We did what we had to do. We got it done.'

'Would you be willing to help us?' the DCI asked.

'Help?' He cocked his head. 'How exactly?'

'We need to know who else was in your squadron – they may be the next targets.'

'I can't betray the boys; some of them are still in active service.'

'It won't be betrayal,' the DCI countered. 'We can't do this without inside help. The Ministry of Defence won't feed us information relating to service personnel, let alone SAS operatives – past or present.'

'We're going to have to work on this together,' Chilcott reinforced. 'Help us catch your daughter's killer.'

Chamberlain stared through Chilcott like he was focused on something a thousand yards behind him.

'The photograph?' Chilcott said moving across to the lamp stand. 'Is this your unit?'

'Three teams from my squadron, well, most of them…' Chamberlain hesitated, '…some of the boys aren't with us anymore.'

'I'm sorry,' the DCI offered sympathetically. 'Do you have any photos of your squadron teams we can take away with us?'

Chamberlain pouted and rubbed a thick finger under

the bony part of his eye socket. He considered the question for a moment and then signalled acceptance.

'Would you be willing to come with us back to the office and talk through a few things?' Chilcott asked.

'Can't we talk here?'

'No,' Foster said. 'We're going to take the unusual step of sharing some of our confidential information with you, and for that, you'll need to come with us.'

A little over an hour later and Chilcott, Foster, Chamberlain and Chowdhury were back at the station. Chamberlain had somewhat reluctantly provided the names of those persons in his unit still alive, and now it was down to Chilcott and Foster to work with police intelligence systems to see what materialised.

Police work wasn't just about catching baddies, preventing disorder, managing the aftermath of serious car wrecks, or dealing with death, it was also about intelligence gathering. Every time a name, address or contact detail was taken and input onto a database, it could be re-captured in the future, but it didn't stop there – a person's description, vehicles they drove, places frequented, known associates etcetera, the list goes on. Absolutely any detail no matter how small or insignificant submitted on an intel report, could be sitting somewhere in the background of a data-base. But as with anything to do with data protection, there were rules and regulations and that was why teams of offi-cers worked in specific intelligence departments to ensure the police acted within the laws of data protection.

The DCI gave Chamberlain a guided tour around the

Major Crime Team offices and introduced him to members of the investigative team. It was clear that if they were to catch the killer, Chamberlain was potentially going to play a vital role. Pleasantries over, they went through to the DI's office where Chilcott and Chowdhury were already waiting for them.

Lying alone on the DCI's desk lay Samantha Chamberlain's murder file.

Chilcott watched Chamberlain with interest as he hovered near to the desk, his eyes transfixed on the buff folder bearing his daughter's name. It was highly irregular for a civilian to have access to the Major Crime Team offices, let alone look at case files, but Chamberlain was no ordinary citizen. Of course, the file had been sanitised; the forensic post mortem images had been removed; details of the police log of enquiries were also missing, but Chamberlain stared with rigid silence down at the CSI flip-folder wallet containing images of the crime scene. He looked back at Foster for permission to take a look inside the wallet and she gave him a silent nod. His hands trembled above the blue plastic cover, but stopped short of taking a hold and he returned his quaking hands to his sides.

'You won't see any images of Sammie,' the DCI said. 'We can't show you those – it'd be wrong of us to show you those at this time.'

Chamberlain sucked in a shaky deep breath and reached forward again, this time lifting the wallet from the table. He blinked a tear from his eye and tentatively opened the cover, bringing the folder closer to his face. 'Should have brought my specs,' he quipped with a nervous laugh.

Foster smiled understandingly. Chilcott watched with dead-pan concentration.

Chamberlain turned the pages with a slow, unsteady hand. This was the first sign of *weakness* Chamberlain had shown. Nobody spoke until the CSI wallet was closed again and returned to the table.

Chamberlain turned directly to the DCI. 'Tell me what I need to do. Tell me how I can help you.'

'We have to be very careful,' Foster said. 'One sloppy move on our part and the entire investigation could be compromised. It's not usual for this to be happening, you have to understand that. You are here because you might… *see* things differently to us.'

Chamberlain looked at Chilcott and then at Chowdhury and then back to the DCI. 'But you are…' He stopped himself short.

'We are doing everything we possibly can,' the DCI confirmed. 'But the simple fact is, at the moment without evidence, we don't have a suspect.'

'But…' Chamberlain looked confused. 'You've got CCTV, haven't you?'

'We have secured CCTV from all available cameras on the route taken by Samantha and these are currently being reviewed,' Chowdhury said. 'But sadly, there are no cameras at the crime scene and it appears the incident isn't captured on camera.'

Chamberlain shook his head. 'What about the other murder?'

'What about it?' Chilcott asked.

'Do you have CCTV there?'

'Sixty-three hours worth of closed circuit television.

Seven hundred and twenty-three still images, but not of the crime scene or the crime.' Chilcott fixed his stare on their guest and noticed his eyes moving from side to side.

'What about facial recognition?' Chamberlain asked.

Chowdhury spoke. 'We don't have that technology, and even if we did, we'd need a suspect to cross reference it to and there'd be far too many hoops to jump through—'

'No, you wouldn't need a suspect.'

Chilcott kicked his head back. 'Go on. You know otherwise?'

'You play all of the footage and wait for a cross-match from the two locations. The chances of the same individual appearing in both sets of CCTV must be hundreds of thousands, if not millions to one.'

'No. No, no,' Chowdhury said. 'That would be impossible to do. It would take hundreds of man hours—'

'If the images are digital, it takes a fraction of that time.'

'You are talking as if this technology exists,' the DCI said.

'It does.'

'Hold on,' Chilcott cut in, his hands raised to pause the conversation. 'You are saying you can access equipment that can review CCTV from different locations, dates and times, that will identify faces of people who are shown at both scenes?'

'Exactly that.'

'That's brilliant! If we could link an individual or individuals to both crimes scenes, we'll potentially identify our suspect.' Chilcott turned hopefully towards Foster.

'Have we already forgotten about what I said? One sloppy move…' She thinned her lips. 'We can't use software like that. Imagine the fallout if the public discovered their privacy had been so blatantly violated. The civil rights group, *Liberty*, would have a field day. Not only would we compromise our investigation, but we'd be the focus of Christ knows what backlash—'

'You might not be able to, but I could,' Chamberlain offered.

'No,' the DCI said defiantly. 'It doesn't matter who does it, or where. Human Rights Laws are there for a purpose and we must uphold them.'

Chilcott caught Chamberlain's eye and they shared a brief *connection*.

'Or, maybe we should be asking ourselves how much we want to catch this killer?' Chilcott said.

'No,' DCI Foster snapped. 'I said, no.'

Chamberlain took a while to look away from Chilcott.

'This bloody snowflake world drives me mad,' Chilcott mumbled beneath his breath.

'And it's that kind of attitude that keeps dropping you in the shit,' Foster retorted.

A loud knock at the door from one of the detectives interrogating the intelligence databases made them all turn and she rushed into the office. 'Sorry to interrupt, Ma'am. Uh, Sirs.'

'Yes, go ahead,' Foster said to the breathless officer.

'One of the list lives about twenty miles away, Ma'am.'

'Christ almighty! We should be safe from any terror attacks with all the Special Forces living nearby,' Chilcott muttered.

'Who've you got?' Foster asked the detective.

'Brian Kershaw. 76 Maple Grove, Chepstow.'

'Chepstow's in Wales isn't it? Chowdhury asked.

'See, that degree wasn't all wasted on you,' Chilcott said sarcastically.

'It's just the other side of the Severn Bridge,' Foster said and eyed Chamberlain.

'Yeah. Brian was one of us,' he confirmed.

'Okay, we will need to do this bit alone,' the DCI said to Chamberlain. 'Jaz will drop you home and we'll be in touch again soon. Thanks for your help today.' She took the Chepstow address from the detective. 'Get the keys, Robbie, we're going for a ride.'

# CHAPTER THIRTEEN

Chepstow, Wales was situated on the western side of the River Severn and could be driven in less than forty minutes from Bristol. Although they were entitled to continue their investigation in another constabulary's geographical area, Foster had called ahead to her counterpart informing him of their enquiries in the Chepstow area. It was better to be courteous, especially if for whatever reason they needed some local back up. After all, they had no idea what they were going in to. Foster said she'd never visited before, but Chilcott knew the area well, having dated a pretty little native from Wales back when he could be bothered to make an effort with the opposite sex, or rather, back when he still had a chance with the opposite sex.

They found the address with ease, but had to park in a pay and display carpark several hundred yards away as a result of recent resurfacing work on local roads. Both sides of the street were coned off in readiness for dressing with lines. They had already decided not to make the visit a formal Osman warning – official police warnings to potential targets of imminent death by murder – because there wasn't any evidence or intelligence to suggest they needed to go that far, today. They waited a good few minutes on the step before the door inched open. Chilcott immediately clocked the man's rugged appearance. He was no more than six feet tall, Chilcott's height, but he seemed a whole lot larger. He had a forehead like a mallet, or perhaps a meat tenderiser would be more apt a description. Small blue sunken eyes seemed to accentuate the impressive feature even more. Chilcott's mind immediately took him back forty years to his school days and an image of primeval man. The person in front of him didn't quite look Neanderthal, but he didn't appear too many evolutions along either. As the cold blue of his eyes pierced through the two visitors on his doorstep, Chilcott couldn't help but have the impression the man had lived; seen a little action.

DCI Foster spoke first. 'Brian Kershaw?'

The man looked down at her, as if she was something shitty he'd just trodden in.

'Mr Kershaw, I am Detective Chief Inspector Julie Foster and this is my colleague, Detective Inspector Robbie Chilcott. We are based at Bristol Central Major Crime Investigation Team.'

He studied them both with an unnerving interest, but showed no urgency to engage them in conversation.

'Would it be possible to come inside, please? We have something rather sensitive to discuss with you.'

'How long will this take,' Kershaw's deep voice rumbled. 'I'm busy.'

'Not long, Mr Kershaw,' Foster said.

He looked Foster up and down in a purposeful manner

and then repeated the same for Chilcott. He faked a smile and stepped to the side forcing them both to squeeze beyond him in the narrow gap left between his barrel chest and the hallway wall. Kershaw held out an arm pointing towards an open door at the end of the short hallway.

As Chilcott shimmied through the tight space, he caught Kershaw's eye and smiled. *You might be built like a brick shithouse*, he thought, *but I bet you'd still go down if your nuts were in a vice.* He continued through the hallway behind Foster and stopped just inside the living room entrance. There was a single piece of furniture; a large black leather reclining chair placed in the middle of the room, facing a wall-mounted television that was large enough to be seen from space. Two huge speaker columns stood on either side of the massive flat screen. It reminded Chilcott of that old *Maxell tape* advert where the man sits in a chair, his hair and clothes flapping in the turbulent resonance of audio excellence.

'Does anyone else live here?' Chilcott asked, secretly impressed by the simplicity of the decor.

'No,' Kershaw said, folding his arms.

Chilcott couldn't help but notice his granite forearms, which were not far off the thickness of his own thighs. He smiled, making a point of looking around the extremities of the room rather than at the hulk standing a few feet ahead of him. In the corner, behind the door entrance, a white rectangular metal cage the size of a microwave oven hung suspended on a chain from a ceiling hook. Chilcott focused through the bars and could see two small green and yellow budgerigar huddled together on a thin wooden rod that crossed from one side of the cage to the other. *Poor little sods. That's no existence.*

'What's this about?' Kershaw asked, his voice deep and vibrating.

'We're investigating a series of murders in the Bristol area,' the DCI responded. She waited several seconds for a reaction – there wasn't one. She caught Chilcott's raised brows as he took in another sweep of the room. Kershaw appeared to notice Chilcott's reaction and stepped in the space between the officers and his chair, closing the gap between them. Instinctively, Chilcott mirrored the movement, partially blocking his boss from the man. They were now within touching distance, and in reality, Chilcott knew he stood no chance against the younger, fitter man if he decided he wanted to play up.

'We know you were in the SAS,' the DCI said. 'Trust us; we're not here to cause you any problems.'

Kershaw tipped his head slightly and looked menacingly over the top of Chilcott's shoulder at the DCI standing behind him.

'The murders involve family members of your old team, "D" Squadron,' she said.

Kershaw straightened up and stared at her with a rigid intensity.

'Stephen Chamberlain's daughter is the latest victim,' Chilcott took over. 'Samantha, or Sammie. Twenty-three years old.'

Kershaw squinted with one eye and peered between Foster and Chilcott like he was getting them in his sniper sights. 'Latest? Who else?' he boomed.

Chilcott looked back at Foster for permission to answer and she bobbed her head.

'The other victim was called Jessica Asher... Paul Asher's daughter,' Chilcott said.

Kershaw's mono-brow dipped in the middle and he broke eye contact momentarily.

'Do you have any dependants, Mr Kershaw, any sons, daughters?' the DCI asked.

He shook his head and walked over to the window and appeared to look outside through a grubby mesh net curtain.

'Are you in contact with any of your old squadron?' Chilcott asked.

Kershaw shook his head, still facing away from the officers.

'Bristol and the south west in particular, appear to be a common denominator,' the DCI said. 'Can you think of a reason why that might be?'

Kershaw rocked on his heels and he turned about. 'You tell me. You're the cop.'

'Did you know that Stephen Chamberlain and Paul Asher's families lived within a short distance of the Bristol area?' Chilcott asked.

'How would I know that?'

Chilcott raised his hands in front of his face in a non-accusatory, open-palmed gesture that belied his gut feelings. 'It's alright; I'm not suggesting you did.'

Kershaw glared at him with disturbing potency.

'Thank you for your time,' the DCI said gesturing for Chilcott to head back out to the hallway. 'Please remain vigilant, Mr Kershaw. We don't have any suspects at this time but we're keeping an open mind. If you have any questions or information, please call me directly.' She handed him her business card and made a quick exit with Chilcott.

'Well then,' Foster said back inside the dark security of the BMW. 'What do we make of that?'

'Friendly chap. I think he liked me,' Chilcott quipped.

'Quite different to the others, wouldn't you agree?'

'Completely.'

'The house was also conspicuous in its absence to any reference of military service.'

'Conspicuous of anything, apart from the two quietest caged birds in the UK.'

'I mean, who can live like that?' the DCI continued.

Chilcott scratched the back of his neck. 'Yeah, I mean, it's quite a step up to a knackered and decrepit two-berth caravan isn't it.'

Foster chuckled and shook her head. 'Why *do* you live in that caravan, Robbie?' She asked the question as if it had been burning away at the back of her brain for a while.

'It's just a stop gap.'

'A stop gap is meant to be a short-term affair; a week or two surely, not the months you've been living in it?'

Chilcott rocked his head. 'Well, Patricia made certain I couldn't afford to get back on the property ladder, thanks to her ridiculous divorce demands.'

'You were always going to get done over, Rob. Look at your salary, your pension. What have you got left, five years?'

'Four and a half, and I'll be lucky if I can afford a bottle of propane gas for the van, let alone put aside a deposit for anything remotely half decent on the property market.'

'Anyway, your divorce was over a year ago. You should be more settled by now. It's not good for the young in service to see you like this. That's all I'm saying.'

Chilcott huffed despondently. 'Are we going, or have you got something else you'd like to counsel me over?'

'I'm just saying… you need to start sorting out your affairs. Get yourself back to the old Robbie we all miss.'

'Yes mother.' Chilcott keyed the ignition and began the journey back to Central.

# CHAPTER FOURTEEN

Wednesday 26th February

11:00 a.m.

The incident room of the Central Major Crime Investigation Team was alive with purposeful and determined activity. DCI Foster had called her chiefs into her room and they were speaking behind closed doors.

'No suspect forensics from victim or scene? No useful CCTV? No witnesses? Is that what you're telling me?' the DCI barked on hearing an update from DI Chowdhury. 'This has the hallmarks of a well planned and clinical killing.'

'Professional, you might say,' Chilcott offered in a provocative manner, his thoughts already racing away with him.

The DCI leaned her elbows onto the desk top and rested her face in her hands.

'You make it sound like the work of organised crime,' Chowdhury said, rebutting Chilcott's ridiculous comments.

Foster looked up over the top of her despairing hands. 'No, it's not. Not organised crime in the traditional way we may know it.' She turned to Chilcott with fire in her eyes.

They were on the same wavelength.

'Am I missing something here?' Chowdhury said.

Foster tapped a fingertip against the side of her temple like it was stimulating her brain synapses into action. 'Where have we got to with the rest of "D" Squadron, Jaz?'

Chowdhury opened his day-book and flicked back a page or two. 'Pretty good, considering. Stephen Chamberlain has been extremely useful. There's no way we would have got anywhere without his cooperation.'

'Any more of his old unit living in our jurisdiction?'

'It seems unlikely, Ma'am. The rest are dotted around the country, simply off the radar, or dead.'

The DCI clamped her jaw and bounced back and forth on her swivel chair giving herself time to think. 'It's the ones off the radar I'm concerned about, but we need to warn the ones we can locate.'

'We're already doing that,' Chowdhury said. 'We've requested urgent send-tos at the addresses we know about outside of our force area.'

'I want to speak to Chamberlain again,' Foster said. 'Ask him to comment on the members of his old team, not just give us their names.' She stared ahead with a blank expression. 'I just can't shake the feeling we made a big mistake yesterday.'

'Maybe. Maybe not,' Chilcott put in. 'We can't predict what's going to happen, or who we're going to run across in the course of our enquiries—'

'I know. I know,' Foster countered. 'You both go back to Mr Chamberlain and see what you can establish about specific team members—'

'I can't,' Chowdhury said. 'I've got—'

'Just do it,' the DCI glared. 'As of this moment, there's nothing more crucial than this task. Have you got that, Jaz?'

'I'm happy to go on my own,' Chilcott mumbled.

'You are both going together. I want a detailed profile of "D" Squadron by the end of play today. Also, build a profile of our victims, and their parents and see if we can prevent the next attack.'

'The next attack?' Chowdhury said.

Foster stood up, marched to the door and held it open. 'Are you both still here? The report isn't going to write itself.'


They hadn't been in the car long before Chilcott had his first dig at Chowdhury. 'Has the milk run out then?'

'The milk?'

'You *are* the station cat. I'm surprised you know the way outside of your office?'

'Finally, you acknowledge it is *my* office.'

'Not for much longer.'

'Don't bank on it, Chilcott. Policing has moved on since your heyday. The *old-boys-network* is well and truly in the past.'

'Ah, that's right – we can't be any good at our jobs anymore unless we've got a degree. That's right isn't it?'

'If that's the criteria for jobs, then I suggest you apply yourself and get one.'

'Apply myself?' Chilcott bit back angrily. 'You can have ologies coming out of your arse for all I care. I've got a degree in life, sunshine. I don't need a university certificate to prove I'm up to the task and capable of doing my job.' He laughed sarcastically. 'What do you know? You've only been in the job five minutes.'

'Long enough to get the plum DI position at Central.'

'Don't flatter yourself – you're a tick in the box. In fact…'

'Go on…' Chowdhury encouraged with an angry sideways stare. 'Finish what you were about to say.'

Chilcott glanced in the rear-view mirror and caught his own disapproving face peering back. 'I wasn't going to say anything else.'

The remainder of the journey was swathed in prickly silence. Chilcott didn't dislike Jaz Chowdhury, or the fact that he was in the role that he felt was rightfully his – no, what he hated was the system; the new way of policing. It was more important for officers of his rank and above to be a politician rather than a leader of highly skilled detectives. In this era of social media, they were given training on engaging the 'customer'. Christ! It wasn't a retail business, it was police work. The *fun* of the job had long gone; not the turning up for work half-pissed and topping up alcohol levels with a lunchtime meeting down the local boozer – those days were ancient history, and just as well – it was the constant pressure to meet government targets set by some bureaucratic civil servant who had never seen a night shift, let alone dealt with the increasing threat of violence towards officers up and down the country because their numbers had been so significantly hacked away. There was one thing all these politicians seemed to be overlooking; crime didn't follow a business plan. Crime was an animal; a living beast that had to feed. And Chilcott was happiest when he could hunt down crime on his own terms.

He killed the engine outside of the Chamberlains' house and turned to Chowdhury. 'Look, we both know the score; you know I was stitched up. This isn't personal in any way against you and I'm sure you'd feel the same if you were in my boots.'

Chowdhury sighed loudly and looked out of the side window as he gave his reply. 'You got shafted, I'll acknowledge that.' He swung back around to face Chilcott. 'But you know nothing about prejudice.'

Chilcott looked around Chowdhury's face for a moment. He knew his background was a tough one. He was a local kid done good, but born into a society of ignorance and racial discrimination. Chilcott held out his hand. 'You got me there, kiddo.'

Chowdhury accepted his hand, but his grasp was half-hearted.

'I'm sorry that I punched you,' Chilcott said gripping his hand a little tighter. 'I've had a lot of time to reflect and I know it wasn't you who I should have been angry with... I'm sorry.'

Chowdhury faced away.

Chilcott let go of his hand. 'Come on, Jazzy. Let's both catch some baddies.'

.  .  .

Mr Chamberlain's wife and daughter stayed upstairs while Chilcott, Chowdhury and Chamberlain sat around the kitchen table looking at Chamberlain's photographs of "D" Squadron.

'Tell me about the guys,' Chilcott said.

Chamberlain shifted his body weight in the seat. 'How do you mean?'

'We know your old squadron members are being targeted.' Chilcott readjusted himself and cleared his throat. 'But what if one of your own is doing the killing?'

Chamberlain leaned back in his seat. His eyes burning wide. 'What?'

'We have to keep an open mind, Mr Chamberlain. Anything is possible,' Chowdhury said.

'Which one of these is Brian Kershaw?' Chilcott asked tapping the small four-by-six Polaroid image.

Chamberlain gave Chilcott the kind of stare that would cause some others to have the jitters. He looked down at the image and found Kershaw within a second or two. He pressed his finger down upon the soldier sitting on the floor at the far end of the group. He was dressed in local middle-eastern robes, a black ski-mask covered the top half of his face and a sand-coloured shemagh wrapped tightly around his mouth and head. His weapon was across his chest and his legs were folded. He was the only member of the group to be seated. All the others were standing proud for the picture, or draped over the bonnet of a heavily equipped military Land Rover. Kershaw could almost be described as "on the edge" of the photograph, or like a substitute to the first team.

'Which one are you?' Chilcott asked.

Chamberlain tapped the picture again. He was standing between two others, dressed in a similar fashion, nothing making them apart except a difference in height.

'Why did you ask about Brian Kershaw?' Chamberlain asked.

'Only because I met him yesterday.' Chilcott rubbed beneath his nose with the back of his index finger.

'And?'

'And… nothing.' Chilcott was putting on an act, deliberately hamming it up to bait Chamberlain into making some kind of observation.

Chamberlain squinted – it was working.

'He doesn't have any children?' Chilcott continued.

Chamberlain shrugged. 'I don't know. He never spoke of kids.'

'Wife?'

'Dunno, but he got laid plenty.'

'He's a big lad.'

Chamberlain lifted a brow. 'That's what made him popular with the ladies.'

'Was there anyone in "D" Squadron who you didn't get along with?'

He blinked. 'No. We were tight. There's no place for individuals or snowflakes.'

Chilcott scratched the skin between his brows with the nail of his middle finger while keeping a close watch on Chamberlain.

'What are you thinking?' Chamberlain asked him.

'Me? Nothing.'

'Bullshit.'

Chilcott stopped scratching and batted his hand away

dismissively. 'Okay, you got me. Kershaw wasn't what we were expecting.'

'What were you expecting?'

'I dunno – someone like you. Someone like Paul Asher.'

'We're all different.'

'But with the greatest of respect, you both just lost loved ones and were still more amiable than him.'

'We all have our crosses to bear.'

'I'm sure. I'm sure. Anyway, we've traced and made contact with roughly twenty members from your squadron. We're doing what we can to get messages to the families of those others who are still overseas.'

'What are you going to do next?'

Chowdhury intervened. 'We're piecing together the chain of events and evidence. Identifying the similarities with Sammie's case and—'

'Sammie's murder,' Chamberlain corrected firmly. 'It's not a case, it's a murder.'

'I'm not in any way trying to minimise that fact with my terminology. Please accept my apologies, Mr Chamberlain.'

'What similarities?'

'The method used to murder your daughter was the same as in the other attack,' Chilcott said.

'The MO?'

'Yes. The MO was identical. Crushed windpipe. Nothing stolen. No sexual contact. No other obvious motives.' He looked at Chamberlain for a number of seconds.

'And what's going to stop there being a third?' Chamberlain asked, his jaw slack.

'That's a good question,' Chilcott said. 'In all honesty,

we can't answer that until we have more evidence, and more of a motive.'

'Can I speak to Kershaw?' Chamberlain asked.

'Why would you want to do that?'

Chamberlain gave Chilcott a look that left him in no doubt that this was something that was none of his business.

'I wouldn't advise that at this stage,' Chowdhury said. 'Wait for us to complete our enquiries, but by all means you can speak to him after that.'

'How long will that take?'

'It can take…' Chowdhury's voice trailed away as he looked for Chilcott to provide the answer.

'Months,' Chilcott clarified. 'Without a decent lead, these investigations can take months.'

# CHAPTER FIFTEEN

12:12 p.m.

Chilcott answered the call with one hand on the wheel and the other pressed to his ear, much to the distaste of Chowdhury. 'Yep, Chilcott,' he said.

'It's Julie.'

Chilcott steered with his forearms as he fiddled to place the phone onto loud speaker, prodding at the touch screen of his Samsung, while peering up intermittently at the road ahead. He hadn't been back in the department long enough to have set up the Bluetooth connection with the car system.

'Are you okay to speak?' Foster asked.

'Yep, no probs.'

Chilcott glimpsed sideways at Chowdhury who was shaking his head disapprovingly at Chilcott's laissez-faire driving style. He placed the phone down in the drinks holder between them, retook the wheel with both hands and grinned widely at Chowdhury.

'We've had word from Greater Manchester Constabulary.'

'Go on.'

'The wife of Darren Broomfield was murdered seven months ago.'

Chilcott stared ahead. The sound of the rattling diesel engine seemed to grow louder in the silence that followed.

'Hello, Ma'am, it's Jaz,' Chowdhury cut in, giving Chilcott another death stare. 'How was she murdered?'

'She drowned in the bath,' came the instant reply.

'Any forensics?'

'None.' The DCI paused before continuing. 'It's another open-ended case. Broomfield was initially arrested on suspicion of her murder, but later released without charge when no evidence or motive materialised to implicate him.'

'How did the attacker get inside the house?' Chilcott asked.

'Walked straight in. No forced entry. No signs of disturbance. That's why they suspected Broomfield.'

Chilcott drummed the wheel as he considered the update.

'How's it been left, Ma'am?' Chowdhury asked.

'With their murder detectives as an unsolved murder.'

'Do you think they'd be willing to exchange notes?' Chilcott asked finally.

'Possibly. Perhaps you could knock up an email detailing your theory – there may well be more of the Squadron living in their force area.'

'No problem,' Chilcott said. 'We're just coming down the M32. We'll tie up with you back at Central.'

. . .

Back at the station and Chilcott made certain he wasn't followed before ducking into the video suite containing the bank of viewing screens and the technology to examine and secure video evidence. He had with him the numerous CCTV disks from both crime investigations: Glastonbury and Bristol. He checked the room was clear and then locked the door from the inside and wound down the roller blind on the back of the door preventing anyone from seeing him from the outside. He removed the disks and stuck a new large-file memory stick into the computer, copy transferring the extensive trawl of CCTV footage from the Operation Fresco investigation and then repeated the process with the Operation Boundless footage. Although they had super-fast copy technology, Chilcott was still very aware of the time it was taking.

He paced the room with impatience as the final data transferred, checking his watch every few minutes. If he was disturbed, his clandestine plan would be blown out of the water. He knew what he was proposing was unethical and potentially breaching all kinds of data protection law, but his primary focus was on catching a killer, and that had to trump any risk he was taking.

He fished the memory stick from the USB drive and plunged it deep into his trouser pocket. It was late by the time he'd completed his task and most people had gone home for the day, but he sensed the DCI was still lingering somewhere within the building and he found her back in the main office.

'You're still here,' she said. 'Where've you been hiding?'

'Just going over some of the CCTV again. I can't help but think we've missed something.'

'I hear Singleton has been dealt with for voyeurism offences. The filthy bastard.'

'But he's not our man.'

'No.'

Foster noticed Chilcott place a hand in his trouser pocket and keep it there. Her lips twitched. 'What are you doing now?'

'Now?'

'Yes. Now?'

'We can do no more at this time, so I thought I'd call it a day. I've got a fridge full of chilled Bath Ales and I thought I'd spring a couple open.'

Foster lowered her gaze to his trouser pocket once more.

Chilcott removed his hand from his pocket and half-smiled. 'I'll see you in the morning then,' he said.

'Make sure you eat something if you are drinking those beers. I've noticed you haven't eaten anything since you've been back in the office.'

Chilcott lingered on Foster's knowing face before heading off. 'Yes, Mother.'


The clock on the car dash showed 20:09. It was late, but Chilcott had to do this some time and now was as good a time as any. He approached the door and pressed the bell. It was Mrs Chamberlain who came to the door.

'Oh, hello,' she said, slightly startled at seeing Chilcott.

'I'm sorry to disturb you at this late hour, Mrs Chamberlain. I was hoping to catch your husband, just for a brief moment if possible, please?'

She looked purposefully at the rain streaming down

Chilcott's face from his unprotected head. He was wearing a long Columbo-style rain mac, but it didn't have a hood to shelter beneath and he refused to wear a hat.

'Uh… of course… um, please…' She stepped backwards and Chilcott filled the space she'd been occupying.

'Um, I'll just go and fetch Stephen.' She tittered nervously and dipped away into the dry and warmth of their living room.

'Thanks,' he said, but she was already gone.

Chilcott waited just inside the door, aware that water was dripping down from his clothing onto the bristly "Welcome" mat beneath his feet.

Stephen Chamberlain popped a head around the door frame of the lounge and the rest of his body followed a second later. He was chewing.

'I'm so sorry,' Chilcott said. 'I've come at a bad time.'

'No,' Chamberlain answered wiping the back of his hand across his mouth. 'You have something?'

Chilcott hesitated. 'As a matter of fact, I do.'

Chamberlain quickly swallowed whatever was in his mouth.

Chilcott dug a hand into his trouser pocket, removed the memory stick and held it out in a steady hand.

Chamberlain looked down at the small plastic object and then tracked his gaze back up to meet Chilcott's.

'You said you can do things with CCTV; facial recognition, I think you said.'

Chamberlain nodded. 'I did.'

Chilcott offered his hand towards Chamberlain who held out his palm. 'Use this,' Chilcott said dropping the memory stick into the large waiting hand. 'Do whatever you need to do, but don't tell anyone where you got it from. Only speak to me about the results. Do not under any circumstances, tell your FLO or any other cops, especially the DCI that you have this.'

Chamberlain's stare was black. 'What is this?'

'CCTV from the cameras closest to both crime scenes. Three hours before, one hour after. I'm kind of banking on the fact that your guys can do things with this that our guys can't. I'll worry about the legalities as and when I need to. Once you've finished, return the stick to me and do not attempt to copy them.'

Chamberlain studied the stick. 'Understood.' His eyes burned wide with a reinvigorated energy.

Chilcott reached for the door handle and stopped. 'How long?'

Chamberlain reduced the gap between them and ran a clawed hand over his balding scalp.

'Friday?'

'Two days? That'll do me nicely.'

Chilcott reached out, shook Chamberlain by the hand and didn't say another word.

The door closed behind him and Chilcott tilted his face towards the skies feeling the pattering of rain once again upon his skin.

*Well, this is it… shit or bust.*

# CHAPTER SIXTEEN

It was the smell that grabbed Chilcott's attention before the flickering amber glow he could see above the tall-tree lined hedgerow. He knew in an instant what he was looking at and accelerated hard causing his 4x4 to bump and jar off the ragged ruts beneath his wheels. As he broke into the clearing of the field, he saw the full extent of the fire ahead of him. His caravan was well and truly ablaze with flames licking and spitting high into the damp night air.

'Shit. Shit. Shit,' he screamed and brought the Jeep to a shuddering halt and ran helplessly towards the burning carcass of his home. The ferocity of the heat stopped him well short and he covered his face with his hands to shield the scorching air. He then clocked an empty glass canister lying on the floor just inches away from the naked flames. His heart jumped and he ran back to his Jeep and stood on the other side gazing at his caravan through the windows. The rain was falling hard now, but seemed to make no difference to the determination of the blaze.

He watched helplessly for a long moment. There was

absolutely nothing he could do. Had he left the hob burning? Thinking as laterally as possible, he quickly removed his phone and ducked back into the dry of the Jeep. Inside, the temperature was already much hotter than before. He punched 999 into his phone and hurriedly gave his name and location to the call handler, before requesting the fire brigade.

Twenty-seven minutes later Chilcott was standing motionless in the field, staring at the collapsed, smouldering pile of junk that contained his every possession as sirens wailed louder from two approaching fire pumps.

The lead fire officers walked up to Chilcott from behind and put a hand on his shoulder to gain his attention.

'You can kill those fucking horns,' Chilcott said still staring at the remnants of his caravan. 'No one can hear them up here.'

The message got back to the drivers of the large growling vehicles and the sirens were extinguished, but the flashing blue lights remained illuminated.

'Everyone out?' the lead hand asked Chilcott.

'It's just me.' Chilcott's voice was hollow. He noticed the lead officer trying to place him, a puzzled recognition obvious on his face.

'DI Chilcott, Central Major Crime Team,' Chilcott said returning his eyes back to his destroyed, *everything*.

'Yes,' the officer acknowledged. 'That's right. What are you doing here?'

'I… I *lived* here.'

'That was your caravan?' the lead hand asked pointing to what was left of it.

Chilcott turned angrily. 'How the fuck did it take you over half an hour to get here?' he seethed. 'I might have been able to save something.'

'I'm afraid we had difficulty finding your location. You haven't made it easy to be found.'

'That's the way I like it,' Chilcott mumbled, accepting the point.

'I'll send in a couple of the guys to see if we can see what started it. Any ideas?'

Chilcott shook his head. 'I've had a lot on my plate lately. I may have left something on the hob... I just don't know? Shit! I could do without this.'

'Do you have somewhere else you can stay tonight?'

'I dunno,' Chilcott huffed. He hadn't thought about the practical elements of his predicament. 'I guess so. I'm sure I can find someone who'll put me up in the short term.' He immediately had someone in mind, but didn't know how they'd respond.

The fire officer went back over to his team and briefed them as Chilcott wandered back to his Jeep. He took out his phone and pressed it to his ear over the hum of the fire pump generators. The call was answered after a long delay.

'DCI Foster... this had better be good, I was in the middle of a date with Tom Hardy.'

'Can I use your spare room for a few days?' he asked.

'Chilcott?' Her voice sounded clearly disappointed as reality snapped her away in an instant from her fantasy slumber.

'Were you shagging him?'

'What?'

'Tom Hardy. Were you in the middle of shagging him?'

'What?'

'Forget it… look, I need somewhere to stay for a day or two?'

'And you called me? Why not try *Shelter* – I'm sure you'd fit right in.'

'I'm serious. I've nowhere to stay.'

'Have you finally come to some sense about your poxy caravan?'

'Nope. It's currently burning to a crisp.'

Foster sat up. 'Are you kidding me?'

'Wish I was. Came back to find the whole fucking thing up in flames.'

'No way!'

'So, I just need a couple of days to sort something out on a more permanent basis.'

There was a pause of recognition.

'You're being serious.'

'Of course I'm being serious.'

Foster heaved a deep sigh and rolled her eyes. 'Well… I suppose I can—'

'Great. Stick the kettle on, I'll be there in forty minutes… oh, and… thanks.'

Chilcott hung up.

# CHAPTER SEVENTEEN

Thursday 27th February

07:10 a.m.

Foster stared in horror as Chilcott entered the kitchen wearing only off-white boxer shorts, which he was making a display of scratching through. His middle-aged spread hung like slumped blubber over the straining waistband.

'Oh dear God!' she cried out.

'What?'

'We're not married, put something on.'

'You wish.'

Foster sipped from her mug of tea and secretly smiled. They had known one another for almost seventeen years. She had seen Chilcott go through two messy divorces; witnessed him euphoric and seen him desolate, which was the direction he was rapidly headed again now. Despite all that, she couldn't help but admire the way he always seemed to bounce back. He was never down for long; a bit like an ant that just wouldn't squish. But, perhaps more than that, was his aura. The young detectives in training school all knew who Chilcott was even if they'd never met him, let alone seen him. His name was synonymous with success in Avon and Somerset CID. Stories of dramatic rescues, complicated fraud convictions and selfless acts of bravery were all gloriously painted in his name. He was an icon to the newbies, not because of his steadfast values, but because he broke the rules. The new kids seemed to thrive off that. She didn't doubt that at least a third of new recruits were there because of his legend. And secretly, he was her hero too.

'Seriously, Robbie. I don't want to see you parading around like this; I've got to work with you later!'

'Fine. Got a dish towel?'

'You're not putting a dish towel anywhere near that—' her outstretched hand waved vaguely towards his groin area.

'No – I spilt something in my room.'

She shook her head and opened a drawer, tossing a clean folded towel his way. He snatched it out of the air and turned, pulling the cloth of his boxer shorts to one side and giving his bare-arsed cheek a long satisfying scratch – purely for Foster's benefit. He left the room and returned minutes later dressed in yesterday's work clothes and handed her the damp scrunched up dish towel.

'It was only water,' he said.

'It's no problem. You want coffee?'

'Please.'

'Take a seat.'

She watched him drag a stool out from beneath the kitchen island and plop himself down.

'Sleep OK?'

'Better than normal actually.'

'Must be nice to be in a proper bed again?'


Fourteen miles away, Brian Kershaw was looking out through a peephole, but couldn't see who had just banged with determination three times on his door. *Fucking cops*, he thought and moved back into the living room, returning his Glock 19 semi-automatic pistol into a concealed pocket specifically constructed beneath his armchair. As the front door banged louder still, he rolled his eyes and slowly walked back towards the front door.

'Okay, I'm coming,' he called out.

He took another quick peep, but the cops were cunning and still out of view of the small fisheye lens. As he twisted the door handle a weight of force shoved him back off his feet and he fell against the hallway wall. A man came thundering through the doorway with a baseball bat raised above his head and smashed it down into Kershaw's ribs with one almighty blow, forcing all of the air out of his lungs. His sides stung with the splinters of broken bones, but self-preservation-mode kicked in and Kershaw managed to roll away as another furious thrust of the bat narrowly missed his head and sent a small telephone table hurtling through the air as if it was made of balsawood. He scrambled on all fours towards the sitting room, his attacker yelling in incoherent rage in the background. He reached the living room using every drop of adrenalin to get him closer to his goal despite another crushing blow to the back of his knees. They were now both in the same room, his attacker stalking him like a big cat waiting for the final kill. Kershaw sensed the man straddling his buckled legs as he clawed the carpet and heard the whoosh of air as the bat began a high downwards arc. Kershaw's fingertips reached the Velcro flap beneath the armchair and he pulled the weapon free of its housing.

'Police. Put down your weapon,' a voice yelled from somewhere behind, followed by the electric crackle of fifty-thousand volts.

The baseball bat fell to the ground inches from Kershaw's head and as he twisted around he saw his attacker fall face down across his ankles, wires fizzing in his back, his body twitching in spasm.

'Put down the gun,' another loud voice sounded.

Kershaw didn't have time to register that he was pointing his Glock at the police officers before his chest, neck and arm muscles cramped in a millisecond of incapacity. He'd been tasered before but that was during training and he'd been prepared; even able to resist the effects for a few seconds, but not this time. He struggled in vain against the contracting muscles and the dead weight of his attacker lying prone over his ankles. The agony from his broken ribs accentuated the effectiveness of the taser electrodes sticking out of his chest and the weapon fell harmlessly from his finger tips.

# CHAPTER EIGHTEEN

Foster and Chilcott were back in the office staring up at the timeline on the double whiteboard in total silence, deep in their own troubled thoughts.

Suddenly, Chilcott took a marker pen and circled Kershaw's name.

'What are you doing?'

'Think about it – there's only one person in this entire investigation who has got my radar twitching and it's him.'

'He just didn't like you. That's not a crime you know. In fact, I can give you a list of names if you'd like?'

'Har-bloody-har.'

'Seriously though, how the hell are we going to progress this case without a scrap of evidence?'

Chilcott shuffled his feet and sniffed. 'I may have something on the horizon.'

DC Tina Webber entered the briefing room in a hurry.

'Ma'am have you got a moment, please?'

'Yes, Tina?' the DCI said. 'I hope this is important.'

'I'm sorry to interrupt you, Ma'am… ah, Sir… but I thought you should know sooner rather than later—'

'Know what, Tina, we're quite busy here?'

'Gwent police have just arrested Stephen Chamberlain. He's being held at Chepstow Custody Unit.'

'Stephen Chamberlain?' Foster asked with utter surprise. 'Why?'

'GBH with intent.'

'Jesus!' Foster spat. 'What on earth…?'

Chilcott wanted to curl into a ball – he knew exactly what was coming next.

'That's where it gets interesting,' Webber said innocently. 'Officers were sent to an area around seven-thirty this morning after reports of a male being seen in the street with a baseball bat. They arrived just as the male was forcing entry into a property…' she paused for effect. 'It looks like they arrived just in time—'

'Get to the point, Tina,' the DCI pressed.

'Sorry, Ma'am. Uh, Stephen Chamberlain was attacking Brian Kershaw inside his home with the baseball bat, so he got tasered and arrested by the attending officers.'

'Oh my God!'

'It gets worse, Ma'am.'

Foster closed her eyes and pressed her hand to her forehead. 'It gets worse?'

'Kershaw was in possession of a handgun, so he got tasered and arrested too.'

'A handgun?' Foster repeated.

'Yes, Ma'am, a Glock 19 semi-automatic pistol.'

The DCI covered her mouth. 'Why would Chamberlain do that – they were in the same…' she stopped and slowly raked a challenging glare in Chilcott's direction. 'Robbie, what the fuck have you done?'

Chilcott pinched his lips with his fingers and turned to DC Webber. 'Thank you, Tina. That'll be everything, unless you have any other *good* news to pass us?'

DC Webber shook her head, her eyes wide and observant. She lingered on Chilcott's face as she closed the door on her exit.

DCI Foster stood firm, arms folded, challenging Chilcott with fierce eyes. 'Looks like your *horizon* is upon us, Robbie. You'd better talk and this had better be good.'

Chilcott wiped a hand across his face and looked beyond the DCI to the circled name of Kershaw on the whiteboard. He sniffed casually and raised a brow. 'I think we've just found our killer.'

'Did you set this up?'

'Not exactly.'

'Then *exactly* what did you do?'

'I gave Chamberlain a copy of the CCTV from Op Fresco and Op Boundless. I asked him to run it through the military facial recognition software that he mentioned to see if anyone was identified as being at both crime scenes, thereby creating a suspect.' He stared blankly at his boss. 'I think we've just found that answer.'

DCI Foster bared her teeth and took her seat in slow, silent disbelief. She rested her heavy head into her hands.

'Are you trying to send me to an early grave?'

'I didn't tell him to take matters into his own hands—'

The DCI snapped her head around like a striking snake. 'He's a trained fucking killer for fuck's sake, Robbie. He's just lost his daughter. What else would you expect him to do?'

Chilcott scratched behind his ear and looked away.

'Jesus Christ, Robbie! What on earth was going through your mind?'

He dropped his shoulders. 'At least we've identified a suspect.'

'Inadmissible evidence,' Foster seethed.

'I wouldn't go that far—'

'You've breached Data Protection…' Foster flailed her arms wildly. 'What if they'd killed one another?'

'But they didn't.'

'Not through design. It was pure luck those PCs were in the area. We could be looking at a murder with your *stupid* name as an unwitting accomplice.'

Chilcott bit down hard. 'I hadn't anticipated… *this* would occur.'

'No. Clearly not. Chamberlain is going to have to be interviewed about his presence at the address, about why he was beating ten sorts of crap out of Kershaw. What if he spills the beans? You're implicated, Robbie.'

Chilcott didn't speak.

Foster stood up and paced the empty briefing room, shaking her head with disbelief. 'I just…' She glared at Chilcott for what seemed like eternity. 'I get that you want to find the killer. I understand this is more personal to you than anyone else, but not like this.'

'We've finally got progress,' Chilcott continued 'Something that has eluded us for months.'

'And what can we do with it? You've broken the law, Robbie.'

'Interview Kershaw, that's what we can do. Show him the evidence from both scenes. Get a confession—'

'Am I missing something here?' Foster scowled. 'Kershaw is better trained at interrogation than we are. He's a professional in the art of escape and evasion. Do you think he's just going to roll over and tell us he killed Sammie Chamberlain and Jessica Asher?'

'We won't know unless we try. He's fucked in any event, threatening behaviour with a prohibited weapon.'

'That's by-the-by, and any brief worth their salt would argue that situation would never have arisen had he not been forced to defend himself in his own home.'

'Let me see what I can get out of him.'

Foster looked down at the papers Webber had handed to her and sucked in a settling deep breath. 'Well, he's at the Royal Gwent Hospital receiving treatment. He's not in any fit state to be interviewed, thanks to you.'

'Where will he go after that?'

'I don't know, Robbie. I'd be more concerned about how this is going to impact on you.' She paused and sucked in another shuddering breath. 'I really didn't need this.'

Lost in her thoughts for a number of seconds, she fixed a fierce glare at her DI. 'Just get out will you.'

It was several hours later when the DCI called an impromptu briefing with the rest of the team. The rumours had already spread through the office and everyone was sneaking a glance at Chilcott who was sitting, like a good boy, alongside the DCI's chair.

'Okay, everyone,' Foster said to her overtly alert audience. 'I'm sure you have heard about the arrests of Brian Kershaw and Stephen Chamberlain earlier today.' She fixed her eyes on DC Tina Webber who flushed red in the cheeks with the attention. 'As it stands, Mr Chamberlain is helping us with an allegation of GBH with intent and Kershaw for possession of a prohibited weapon.' She paused and cleared her throat. 'Mr Chamberlain was found to be in possession of a series of photographs that suggest Brian Kershaw was at both Op Fresco and Op Boundless murder scenes, and as such,' she spoke louder over the increasing talk in the room, 'DC Phillips will be arresting Kershaw on suspicion of both murders and we will deal with him upon his release from hospital. Kershaw will be transported to Patchway Custody Suite following medical assessment of his injuries and DC Phillips and DC Raymond are currently in Newport awaiting his discharge. I have authorised the collection of intimate and non-intimate swabs. These will be taken by force if necessary and a Support Group have been placed on standby should this be required. Another search team will attend Kershaw's home address and conduct a Section Eighteen search under the powers provided to us by the Police And Criminal Evidence Act.' She looked around the room. 'Any questions?'

Numerous hands lifted high into the air.

'If you are asking about the images found in possession of Stephen Chamberlain, we are looking into the provenance of these and DI Chilcott will have the answers for you when we establish the full details.' She cut him a sideways stare as sharp as broken glass.

Chilcott ignored the provocation and spoke up. 'I'll also

be attending Patchway Custody Suite to conduct the interview of Kershaw alongside Phillips,' Chilcott said.

Foster sniffed loudly. 'Very well,' she said. 'This is a critical period of the investigation. Let's keep it tight and keep informed.' She pressed a button on a hand controller and a mortuary slab image of Sammie Chamberlain came up on the projector screen. Her skin was a pallid shade of duck-egg blue. Her long hair was trained neatly down her shoulders, and even in death a thin white sheet covered her modesty. 'I won't show you the other pictures, unless you don't want to sleep for a week. This is a reminder that our killer is pure evil. Don't be complacent and take nothing for granted.'

# CHAPTER NINETEEN

Friday 28th February

8:30 a.m.

Brian Kershaw woke, sat upright on his thin foam mattress and folded his arms across his ribs. He had refused treatment from the hospital, despite three confirmed broken ribs. No matter how uncomfortable he was feeling at this present moment in time, he'd suffered far worse in the service. For him, the most searing pain was emotional and no medic or painkiller could help him with that. Kershaw lived alone. He had always lived alone. Never married. No children. He'd been the perfect candidate for the Special Forces; no baggage back home; no external weaknesses. He joined the Parachute Regiment back in 1994 and was swiftly identified as a candidate for one of the most elite fighting forces in the world. He was calm and calculating, never rash or reckless.

When he did something, he executed the act with precision and efficiency; that was, until yesterday when he looked into the eyes of his attacker and hesitated. Under normal circumstances, his attacker would be lying dead on his living room floor, a round lodged squarely between the eyes, but these weren't normal circumstances and he'd been surprised by his own vacillation.

The viewing latch of the thick cell door dropped open with a loud clatter of metal and a pair of detention officer eyes peered in through the now open slot.

'Morning, Brian. Do you want some breakfast?'

Kershaw considered saying no just to be spiteful, but he needed his strength if he was going to get through this, so he accepted the offer. 'Sure.'

'Sausage and beans up your street?'

'Whatever comes my way.'

The latch slammed shut and Kershaw sat motionless counting in his head for six minutes, until the door lock clicked and the solid one-inch diameter cylindrical holding bolts retracted from their housing. Kershaw smiled thinly. To his ears, there were only four steel bars keeping him contained.

The door opened inwards with a smooth, greased, weighty motion. Three detention officers and the custody sergeant stood for a beat in the entrance to the doorway. They all knew what Kershaw was; what he used to be and what he was still capable of doing. The sergeant looked to his colleagues who stepped forward with a microwaved plate of food and a hot drink.

'Here you go Brian,' the DO said respectfully, holding out the steaming paper plate at arm's length. A second DO placed the hot drink on the floor just out of Kershaw's reach and handed him a plastic knife and fork to eat his meal.

'Thanks,' Kershaw said looking at each of the officers in turn.

The cell staff stood back and watched Kershaw begin to fork his breakfast and it was clear to all that he was in great physical pain as he winced with each swallowed mouthful.

'There's a couple of detectives here to speak to you,' the desk sergeant said. 'Have your grub, and then we'll let them in.'

Kershaw lowered his knife, but didn't look up from his plate. The sergeant gestured for the detention officers to exit the cell and waited until he was last out and closed the door with a solid thud of thick cold steel.

Kershaw stopped eating and listened as the bolts reengaged before continuing with his meal.

Back at the charge desk, the custody sergeant met with DC Phillips, DC Raymond and an increasingly impatient DI Chilcott who was rapping the desktop with his fingertips.

'He's having his breakfast. You can talk to him after that,' the sergeant said typing an update onto the log of detention on his computer.

'How long's that going to take?' Chilcott asked.

The sergeant finished updating the log and looked up over the screen at Chilcott. 'As long as it takes.'

'Sir.'

'Come again?'

'As long as it takes, *Sir.*'

The sergeant looked at the other two detectives and then returned his gaze back to Chilcott. 'Sorry… *Sir*.'

Chilcott looked at the sergeant's shoulder number and made a mental note. He didn't recall a previous encounter, but that's not to say their paths hadn't crossed in the past.

DC Phillips eased the tension with an interjection. 'How does he come across, sarge – Kershaw, I mean?'

'You know, there's something about him that I cannot help but like.' The sergeant looked at Chilcott with a curled lip. 'He's polite and respectful. It's almost hard to imagine what he's alleged to have done.'

'Isn't that the trick with these psychos– make out you're something you're not. Entice. Entrap,' Raymond offered.

'You had better give me a heads-up of what you are planning to do with him today. He's clearly in a lot of pain.'

'We're going to add to his pain,' Chilcott said bluntly.

Another gentleman in a suit entered the desk area. He was wearing a dark blue pin striped suit over a matching waistcoat and red and black dotted tie. It was the brief.

'I was told my client would be ready by 8 a.m.'

Chilcott swivelled his neck to look at the solicitor.

'You know how it goes,' the custody sergeant said looking back down at his computer screen.

Chilcott felt slightly reassured that the sergeant appeared to take issue with any visitor to his cell block.

'Well, how much longer is it going to take before I can see my client? I've got other things to do you know. Not just wasting my time in here,' the solicitor pushed.

'I'll be sure to let Mr Kershaw know your thoughts,' the sergeant said, still looking down at his monitor.

'I've got commitments in London after this, if you really must know.'

The custody sergeant rested his fists lightly either side of his keyboard and straightened himself up to face the solicitor. 'It's up to you,' he said. 'You can go in there and watch him eat his breakfast and then take a dump, or you can wait in the solicitor's consultation room like most other legal representatives manage to do.' He looked over at Chilcott and smiled falsely. 'Or perhaps, you'd like to talk to these officers about their plans for Mr Kershaw.'

'Are you the investigating officers?'

Chilcott faced the solicitor and offered his hand. 'DI Chilcott, Central Major Crime Investigation Team, and this is DC Phillips, the OIC, and this is DC Raymond. I don't believe we've met before?'

'Yes, good morning. Stephen Bishop – Bishop, Knight and Queensbury Advocates.'

'Sounds like a chess game,' the custody sergeant uttered just loud enough for all to hear.

'Shall we all go through and I'll explain what we propose to do, while it seems we have some time to kill.' Chilcott held out an arm in the direction of the advocate's rooms.

The solicitor cast the desk sergeant a withering stare. 'That sounds reasonable.'

They filed through to the advocate's room where the solicitor and Chilcott took a seat. Phillips and Raymond stood.

The solicitor sat poised with pen on paper. 'Right,' he said. 'I've come in to this blind, I'm covering last minute for one of my staff who has called in sick.'

'Bummer,' Chilcott commented.

'What has my client been arrested for?'

'Possession of a prohibited weapon.'

'Namely?'

'Namely, a Glock 19 handgun and several hundred rounds of ammunition.' Chilcott watched for a reaction from the brief. There wasn't one.

The solicitor maintained a long poker face. 'Is that it?'

'No.'

'No?' The brief rolled his eyes. 'Well?'

'Well… you might want to reconsider your commitments,' Chilcott said blandly.

The solicitor peered at Chilcott humourlessly.

'Murder,' Chilcott said frigidly. 'He is under arrest for murder… times two.'

'Why wasn't I informed of this before?'

'How your company disseminates information isn't my issue. This is a fluid investigation, changing by the minute.'

'Indeed.' The solicitor placed his pen on the pad. 'I'm not sure I can assist Mr Kershaw in that case. I may need to find an alternative lawyer; someone who can offer their unconditional time.'

'Fine. He's not going anywhere and I don't expect we'll have a problem obtaining an extension to the custody time limit.'

'Well, let's not discuss hypothetical issues. Right, I won't take any disclosure from you in case you have to repeat it to a colleague. I need to make a call to the office.'

'Of course, fill your boots.'

# CHAPTER TWENTY

1:16 p.m.

Chilcott didn't do suspect interviews as a rule, unlike on the television when the DCI or DI seem to get waste deep with every single element of an investigation. In fact, the reality was something quite different; the interview team would normally be made up of two highly trained detective constables skilled in the art of the PEACE model of interviewing; a non-confrontational approach to questioning designed to extract information from a suspect in a conversational setting, albeit under video or audio recorded conditions. But this case was different and Chilcott wanted to look into the eyes of the man who had contributed to a failed marriage and a recent life of misery.

Kershaw entered the interview room flanked by his brief, whose commitments in London were obviously curtailed, and two custody detention officers on either side.

Chilcott had persuaded DC Raymond to take a back

seat, and instead, Chilcott was accompanying DC Phillips in the small white soundproofed interview room. Again, unlike on the TV, there was no large glass screen beyond which stood the DCI and other tentative souls; this was just them; two cops, a killer and his brief. A small camera above the door streamed live coverage to DC Raymond who was in charge of the recording equipment, and overseeing the interview and making relevant notes and observations that could be fed directly back to the interview team in real time.

'Please, sit down over there, Mr Kershaw.' DC Phillips said.

The room was set out in a simple formation with two stainless steel seats either side of a single stainless desk with all furniture bolted to the floor to prevent it being used as a weapon, or defensive implement.

Kershaw did as he was told, and Stephen Bishop, his solicitor, took the seat alongside him. Murders were lucrative business for law firms. An investigation could last for years, a trial could last weeks or even months. Chilcott wasn't surprised to see the firm's partner return for the interview, despite all of his self-possessed representation from earlier.

'I understand from your legal representative, Mr Bishop, that you will be providing a prepared statement?' Chilcott said.

'Yes, that's correct,' Mr Bishop said.

Kershaw stared silently, unwaveringly back at Chilcott.

'I'm sure it has been explained to you that we will still be asking questions pertinent to our investigation?' Chilcott told him directly.

'Yes, my client is aware, but he will be electing to make no comment to all questions, as is his legal right.'

'Fine, I just wanted to clear up the situation before we got underway. Brian, a cup of water is there for you. Let us know if you'd like another at any time during this interview.'

Kershaw acknowledged Chilcott with a single nod, but didn't speak. DC Phillips commenced the interview giving the standard caution, date, time and usual legal explanations of the interview process.

'I understand you haven't contacted anyone since you arrived in custody,' she said.

Kershaw's glassy eyes looked back at her with cold emptiness.

'Is there anybody you'd like us to inform on your behalf? A partner maybe?'

He leaned forward and took a sip of water from the styrene cup, placed it back down and sat back in his seat, arms folded.

'Let's get to this prepared statement, shall we,' Chilcott prompted Phillips.

Prepared statements were sometimes a partial confession with mitigating circumstances, or a flat denial, or an attempt at an alibi. Either way, they were usually produced by a solicitor when a police investigation still had some way to go and it was unlikely the suspect would be charged at this particular stage of the investigation. It was a case of: *we're in the game – now show us your cards*, or put another way, *prove it, copper!*

'Yes, I'll read it out,' Bishop said smugly.

*"I, Brian Kershaw would like to assist the police with their investigation by clarifying the following matters regarding the serious allegations made against me. I admit to being in possession of a prohibited weapon and ammunition under the Firearms Act 1968 namely: a*

*Glock 19 rapid-fire pistol and 280 (two hundred and eighty) 9mm jacketed hollow point rounds. However, I have always kept this weapon in a concealed location within my home address and only held it on this occasion on grounds of self-defence and under the threat of grave violence by an unlawful intruder into my home. In relation to the murder offences, I am innocent of these crimes and have nothing further to add in relation to these unfounded allegations."*

Bishop looked up from the page. 'Signed and dated Brian Kershaw, Friday the twenty-eighth of February at twelve forty-seven hours.'

'Is that it?' Chilcott asked.

'That is all my client is willing to offer at this present moment in time, pending further evidence implicating him in these grave and extremely serious crimes.'

'Innocent of these crimes? Do you really think that's enough to prevent you from being charged for these murders?' Chilcott flipped a hand off the top of his head. 'Let's call them what they are shall we. Murders, Mr Kershaw.'

Kershaw looked back at him blankly.

'Okay,' Chilcott said, feeling internal disquiet creeping to the surface. 'I get the silence; you've been trained in RTI; Resistance to Interrogation. I've looked it up on Google – I know the training you have to go through to become an elite SAS soldier. You've no doubt been through torture scenarios: sleep deprivation, naked humiliation, waterboarding even for all I know, but this ain't no *interrogation*, buddy. This ain't no training exercise. We aren't here to steal your secrets or find out where the rest of your squadron is… If you don't play ball, your hard arse is going in the slammer… for life.'

Chilcott saw the muscles in Kershaw's jaw flexing. *Good.*

'What was Stephen Chamberlain doing in your house?'

Kershaw stared at Chilcott with dead eyes. 'Brian Kershaw. Corporal 34781125.'

Chilcott scoffed and leaned forwards on his elbows. 'Stephen Chamberlain… your old Special Forces mucker, your comrade, a fellow "*blade*".'

Kershaw sniffed.

'He thinks you killed his daughter… doesn't he?'

'Brian Kershaw. Corporal 34781125.'

Chilcott fixed a stare on his unmoving subject for a silent moment. 'I think you killed his daughter too. I also think you were fortunate that a passing police response car came to your aid, otherwise we might not be having this conversation.'

Chilcott saw the corner of Kershaw's lip twitching.

'Tell us how long you've known Stephen Chamberlain.'

Kershaw blinked once and turned away.

'It must be quite depressing to know that he believes you killed his daughter. On that subject, you've never had children, have you?'

'I'm not sure the relevance of that question is obvious to me, officer,' the solicitor interjected.

Chilcott shrugged. 'Maybe not. You don't have to answer that one.' He waited a beat. 'We can't *all* have children can we?' He searched deep into Kershaw's eyes. *That wasn't the issue.* Chilcott coughed behind a closed mouth and sank his forehead into a cupped hand. He held the position and spoke down to the table. 'Alright,' he said. 'Tell us where you were on Friday last at between seventeen and nineteen hundred hours.'

His subject didn't move. He blinked once or twice, but nothing more than that.

'I'm afraid my client won't be answering any questions in detail regarding the alleged offences, until we have seen further evidence implicating my client in these crimes.'

Chilcott counted slowly in his head. He had told DC Raymond to knock on the door when the time was right. That time was now. He leaned back and entwined his fingers behind his head. Seconds later, a rat-tat-tat sounded on the door.

'There appears to be someone attempting to gain my attention,' Chilcott announced for the purpose of the video recording equipment. He gave the time, stood up and opened the door. It was DC Raymond. He handed Chilcott a buff A4 envelope. Chilcott thanked Raymond and closed the door again.

'I have just been handed an envelope by Detective Raymond of the Central Major Crime Investigation Team who has been watching the progress of this interview from a remote location.' Chilcott spoke with an authoritative voice. 'This item has an exhibit number of Golf Romeo zero one.' He held it out in full view of Kershaw, the brief and the camera. 'I am removing the contents for all to see. I haven't seen this exhibit until now.' It was true, he hadn't, but he knew what was going to be inside. He lifted the exhibit label and made a point of reading it aloud. 'Images found in possession of Stephen Chamberlain.' Chilcott made an intrigued grunt in the back of his throat and cocked his head towards Kershaw. 'I suppose we'd better see what these are.' He peeled back the yellow and black tape securing the envelope flap and pulled out the contents, leaving them face up on the table in front of him. He brought the top copy towards his face exposing the next image beneath it for twice the effect and slid the top image across the table towards Kershaw and his solicitor.

Kershaw peered down at the colour A4 photograph and the skin around his eyes tightened.

Chilcott picked up the next image. 'Just for the benefit of the recording, these images are date stamped the nineteenth of October two thousand and eighteen.' He looked over the top of the image towards Kershaw. 'That was the date Jessica Asher was murdered in Glastonbury.' He offered the second image to the solicitor. 'This evidence has only just come to my attention. Of course, I'd be happy to pause the interview so that you can consult *fully* with your client.'

'Why wasn't I made aware of these images before now?' Mr Bishop asked, full of bluster and bravado.

'As I said previously, this is a fluid investigation. Evidence is showing up all the time.' Chilcott held back a self-satisfied grin.

'Please stop the interview,' Mr Bishop said looking down at the second image.

'This interview is suspended pending further legal consultation between Mr Kershaw and Mr Bishop.'

Chilcott stood up and exited the room.

# CHAPTER TWENTY-ONE

Two hours later, and they were all back in the interview room. The delay in proceedings had given Chilcott a chance to grab some food and a hot brew. Kershaw's meals were a given – morning, noon and night, but the detectives had to snack and go – that was just the nature of the beast. Chilcott resumed the interview, his fingers entwined, thumb tips gently bouncing off one another as he waited for the other side to speak.

'My client has reviewed his position and is now prepared to answer questions in relation to this investigation,' Bishop announced.

'Sounds like the sensible option,' Chilcott said, his eyes hooded with hatred towards the man sat opposite him.

An awkward silence followed.

Chilcott offered his subject an open palm. 'After you.'

Kershaw sniffed and positioned himself firmly in the seat.

'My client's position hasn't altered,' Bishop said in a low

voice. 'He will be maintaining a not guilty plea in relation to all allegations except possessing the prohibited weapon.'

Chilcott sank against the hard metal back of his seat. *Well, that was a waste of two hours of my life.*

Kershaw then spoke. 'However, I am prepared to give details of my whereabouts at the alleged dates and times of the most recent crime to prove my innocence.'

Chilcott leaned forwards onto the desk and raised both eyebrows to their limits. 'We're listening.'

'I was in Berkshire when the latest murder took place.'

'Berkshire?'

'Berkshire.'

Kershaw's solicitor was scribing everything that was being said verbatim onto his notepad.

'Well then, I suggest you'd better tell us about Berkshire,' Chilcott said with a simple open-ended question designed to encourage Kershaw to provide an unprompted account. He would also predict from the detail in the answer whether or not Kershaw was going to be as willing a participant as he was suggesting.

'I was in Windsor between Thursday the twentieth and Saturday the twenty-second of February. As I'm led to believe, this incident took place on Friday the twenty-first of February at around eighteen-fifty hours.' He looked across at the officers for confirmation of this, for which he got two separate nods.

Chilcott was encouraged by what he'd heard so far. He gestured for Kershaw to continue.

'My train returned to Chepstow Station at eighteen twenty-six hours on Saturday the twenty-second. It was delayed by approximately ten minutes. From there, a taxi cab returned me home shortly before nineteen hundred, where I remained for the remainder of the night.'

'Windsor?' Chilcott asked, circling the word in his day-book. That was a fairly substantial topic to pick apart, but the more detail he could get Kershaw to describe, the more Chilcott could rubbish it and prove his involvement in the murder.

'Yes, Windsor.'

Free recall had shut down as soon as it had begun. Chilcott needed to adopt a different tactic.

'Doing what exactly?' he asked.

'Visiting.'

'Who?'

'The Queen.'

'You were visiting the Queen?'

'Not exactly the Queen, but I knew she was in residence and I wanted to be nearby.'

Chilcott's eyes narrowed to thin slits. 'Why did you want to be nearby the Queen?' Red flags began rising in his mind, only to be lowered again as he reminded himself that Kershaw was spouting utter bollocks in any event.

'She's my sovereign. I wanted to be close. To protect, if necessary.'

'Protect from whom exactly?'

'Any number of nutters out there. It's well known that the Royal Standard flies when the sovereign is in residence.'

*There's only one nutter around here, mate.*

'Tell me about the train.'

'How do you mean?'

'Where did you get it from?'

'Chepstow.'

'What day and time?'

'Thursday the twentieth at approximately thirteen fifty hours.'

'Platform?'

'One.'

'How many changes?'

'Three.'

'Arriving when?'

Kershaw hesitated. He looked up and to the left. 'It was uh....'

Chilcott frowned. That subtle piece of body language meant that Kershaw was accessing the memory part of his brain, or was it all an act? Kershaw would know all about body language and how others could interpret it.

'Um, shortly before seventeen hundred hours. We were a little ahead of schedule.'

Kershaw was providing plenty of detail for Raymond to check as they went along and soon Chilcott would be in a position to blow it out of the water once Raymond came tapping on the interview room door.

'How much did the ticket cost?' Chilcott asked, indulging his subject.

'About forty quid.'

'Return ticket?'

'One way.'

'How did you pay?'

'Cash.'

'At the ticket office in Chepstow?'

'Yes.'

'Do you still have the ticket?'

Kershaw shrugged. 'Doubt it. Once it's used, it's worthless.'

'Unless it's going to help clear your name from a murder rap.'

Kershaw squinted.

'Did you pay for the ticket on the day of departure?'

'Of course.'

'What time?'

His shoulder bobbed and dipped again. 'Around twenty minutes before the train left.'

'Did you keep the receipt?'

Kershaw shook his head. 'That's probably with the ticket.'

'Of course it is,' Chilcott commented dryly.

The squint returned to Kershaw's eye.

'Okay, tell me about Windsor. You were there for two nights – where did you stay?'

'I stayed at a bed and breakfast not far from the town bridge.'

Chilcott had been to Windsor a few times and he was picturing the town bridge as Kershaw spoke.

'Which side of the river was the B&B?'

'Eton High Street side,' Kershaw replied without hesitation.

Eton High Street was the other side of the small Thames river bridge.

'What was it called?'

'The Royal George. It was a pub with accommodation on the first and second floors.'

'Which floor were you on?'

'Second.'

'Room number?'

'Seven.'

'What was your view from the window?'

'The High Street… and the Costa Coffee on the opposite side.'

Chilcott couldn't remember there being a Costa Coffee, but if you were creating a story situated in most UK towns or cities, it was a pretty safe bet and ultimately plausible.

'How did you pay for the room?'

'Cash.'

Chilcott smiled. *Course you did.*

'Did you book it under your name?'

Kershaw looked down at his feet and shifted his weight slightly forwards.

*Interesting.*

'No,' Kershaw supplied. 'I booked it under the name of Jones.'

'That's original.'

Kershaw glared at Chilcott. 'After Lieutenant Colonel H. Jones, a great British war hero.'

'I meant no disrespect, I was just saying…'

Kershaw nodded acceptance of the apology.

'Why not use your real name?'

'They had my money, why should they have my name as well?'

Chilcott pouted. 'That's a fair point. Did you eat at the bed and breakfast?'

'Only breakfast. I'm not paying for something I'm not going to use.'

Chilcott chuckled. 'How about lunch or evening meal?'

'I found a Brasserie beside the town bridge. I ate there.'

'Each day?'

'Yes.'

'What was it called?'

Kershaw wavered for the first time. 'It was some French name. Part of a chain, I believe.'

'You like French food?'

'Who doesn't?'

*My ex-wife, for one*, Chilcott answered silently in his head.

'What would you recommend?'

Kershaw paused before answering. 'The steak.'

Chilcott chuckled inwardly. Another safe answer. He was aware that the SAS used a tactic during hostile interrogations of giving false detailed accounts to send the interviewer off the beaten track. He suspected that was happening now, but he was happy to go along with it. Kershaw was going nowhere and the cops could disprove his story easily.

'Did you book a table?' Chilcott asked.

'No.'

'You just walked in?'

'Yep.'

'Each time?'

'Yep.'

'Where did you sit?'

'A table for two on the far side of the room in front of the bar.'

'Both days?'

'Yep.'

'Were you with anyone else?'

'Just me.'

'What could you see through the windows?'

'I was facing inwards.'

'What colour were the chairs?'

Kershaw paused and a twitch showed itself above his left eye. 'Red.'

*Safe answer for a Brasserie.*

'Who served you?'

'I don't know.'

'Male, female?'

'Female.'

'Uniform of some kind?'

He shrugged and shook his head. 'Black blouse, black trousers.'

*Standard issue.*

'What time would you estimate you ate there?'

'Seventeen-thirty hours.'

'That's precise.'

'That's when I eat.'

'Always?'

'When I can.'

'Did you talk to anyone else at the Brasserie?'

Kershaw cocked his head.

'Any chit-chat, small-talk, anything like that? It must have been lonely being on your own?'

'Not particularly.'

'Not particularly no chit-chat, or it's not particularly lonely being on your own?'

'Both.'

*Where was DC Raymond with that tap on the door? There was enough detail in these answers to blow his account clean out of the water.*

'This has all been very interesting, Mr Kershaw,'

Chilcott mused. 'But how do you account for being in two places at once?' He slid three A4 colour prints from the Operation Boundless CCTV across the table for Kershaw to see once again. 'Because those images clearly show you walking along Whiteladies Road at seventeen-twelve hours on the afternoon of Friday the twenty-first of February.'

Kershaw didn't look at the photographs and kept his head up and forwards towards Chilcott.

'Well?' Chilcott pushed.

'It's not me.'

'Oh come on, I've been doing this job a long time and I've rarely seen more damning evidence.'

'It's. Not. Me.'

Chilcott spluttered a hearty laugh. The brief looked up from his pad for the first time since the interview got going.

'Are you next going to tell me it's a dead ringer?'

Kershaw's eyes flickered in the first show of vulnerability Chilcott had seen from the man. Kershaw wiped beneath his nose with a finger. He'd managed to keep his hands on the table top the entire time, up to this point.

'Yes,' he said.

'Yes, what?'

Kershaw slowly shook his head and his eyes flickered.

'You're staring down the barrel of two murders, sunshine. Two young women, with another police force waiting to speak to you about another. You're never getting out, son—' Chilcott saw moisture building in the man's eyes.

'It wasn't me,' Kershaw repeated at barely a whisper.

'Oh, this is pathetic,' Chilcott commented. 'I've a good mind to march you down to the charge desk myself and put us all out of our misery—'

Kershaw slammed his hands down flat on the desk creating a loud cracking noise. Chilcott was sure he felt the shock wave ripple through the desktop.

'I'd like to call a pause in proceedings,' the solicitor said.

'I think we're done,' Chilcott responded.

'No, we're far from done,' the solicitor answered, 'but my client would benefit from a short break in questioning and further counsel.'

Chilcott rolled his eyes and looked to DC Phillips who had been taking notes throughout the interview.

'Okay. Is ten minutes enough time?' he asked.

The solicitor looked at his client who now had his face buried deep into his hands.

'Twenty may be better.'

# CHAPTER TWENTY-TWO

2:32 p.m.

Chilcott found DC Raymond in the nearby satellite room where he had been following the interview on a TV screen fixed to the wall.

'Why didn't you come in to the interview room and put us out all of our misery? All that shite—'

'Because it's not, boss.'

Chilcott took a half-step backwards. 'What? What do you mean?'

'It all checks out – the train times, the cost of tickets, the B&B, even the Brasserie.' He pointed to a desktop computer. An image of a smart looking restaurant was on the screen, all wooden floors, smart table settings and burgundy-red dining chairs.

Chilcott churned the information over in his mind. 'Still doesn't mean he was there last weekend. He might know the area. Probably stayed at those locations and has an especially good memory for detail. He was highly trained in observation and spatial awareness after all. These SAS guys are like super-humans; hard as nails and smart as a button.'

'I phoned The Royal George, boss – took a gamble and said my name was Brian Jones. They confirmed I was there from Thursday to Saturday. I said I couldn't remember my room number. They told me it was seven. I struck lucky; something was left behind in the room.'

Chilcott slumped back against the wall and stared at his colleague with a slack jaw. Was Kershaw telling the truth? That was impossible, surely. Chilcott had photographs of him in Bristol and Glastonbury. Maybe, Chamberlain had got the wrong date and it was an implausible mistake, but wait, Chilcott had handed him the evidence personally. There was no *mistake*.

'Get him back in the interview room,' Chilcott boomed.

'But it's not twenty—'

'Just do it.'

The solicitor dragged out their return to the eighteenth minute, which only increased Chilcott's resolve and anger. He reminded Kershaw that he was still under caution and gave the time for the benefit of the recording.

'I don't believe in coincidences,' Chilcott said. 'Perhaps I've grown cynical with my time in the job staring at people like you across an interview table. Perhaps I'm just a grumpy old fool who thinks he knows everything. Or maybe, there is no such thing as coincidence and you being in Windsor while a person identical in appearance to your-self is hunting down and killing a young woman in Bristol is just a load of old bollocks.' It was Chilcott's turn to slam the desk.

Kershaw remained passive and unspoken.

Chilcott coughed, clearing his throat and with a dismissive pout said, 'And so, Mr Kershaw. I'm afraid it's down to you to clear this shit up – unless you wish to spend the remaining days of your life behind bars.'

Kershaw scratched through his bushy black beard and dropped his chin to his chest.

*Ahem*, the solicitor prompted his client. 'Tell them.'

Chilcott watched their interaction with interest; the brief knew that whatever Kershaw had to say was in his best interest, but something was holding him back. Silence was the best policy for the officers. There'd be no benefit in disturbing this subtle social interaction. They themselves had already determined the dynamics of the interview without a word being spoken between them. Fleur Phillips was an experienced Tier 3 interviewer – that meant she was more capable than most in this environment. She wasn't being submissive to Chilcott by not asking any questions, she had identified that he had a connection with Kershaw, no matter how fractious it appeared. She, on the other hand, had barely got a glance from the man and knew detailed notes of the interview were just as important as serving up questions. On another day, it might well have been the other way around, but the energy between Chilcott and Kershaw was palpable.

'Tell them what you told me,' the solicitor ordered. 'If you don't…'

Kershaw bit down on his top lip. His eyes came up to meet Chilcott's and he held them in a foreboding gaze.

Chilcott didn't flinch and returned the eyeballing. Kershaw finally succumbed and broke away. He was biting down hard on his lip. He was clearly disturbed by what he needed to say.

Chilcott flashed him a look of understanding. He needed Kershaw to know that he'd read the signs and understood the predicament he was in, and then Kershaw began to speak.

'When I joined twenty-two SAS in two thousand and two, my brother who was in airborne, vowed he would do the same.' Kershaw stopped and scratched slowly at the crown of his head. 'And, he did.' He looked across at Chilcott. 'He joined the regiment in March of two thousand and four and went on to be recruited by the SRR—'

'Sorry, SRR?' Chilcott asked.

'Special Reconnaissance Regiment. Basically covert surveillance and reconnaissance. We were brother and *brother*.' Kershaw began to blink repeatedly and he covered his mouth with the top of a clenched fist.

Any coverage of the mouth during free recall was an involuntary sign that the subject wasn't comfortable with what was being said and could end the flow of information. It was time for Chilcott to intervene. By indulging the *script* of his subject Chilcott hoped to make their connection a little closer. The more comfortable he could make Kershaw, the more likely the chance he'd slip up and seal his fate. Chilcott's voice soothed like an airline pilot talking to his passengers. 'Your brother, is he older or younger?'

Kershaw locked eyes with Chilcott. 'He's dead.'

'I'm sorry.'

Kershaw ran a hand through his hair and gripped the

back of his neck while looking at the neatly stacked A4 images at the corner of the desk beside DC Philips. He dipped his head towards her in gesture to see them again.

Phillips slid them across the table and Kershaw breathed in, his large barrel chest expanding as he brought the images beneath his nose. He wetted his lips and then turned the top image one hundred and eighty degrees and pushed it back towards Chilcott.

'He *was* dead.'

Chilcott squinted not taking his eyes off his man. 'Go on...'

Kershaw ran a tongue around his lips once again and sniffed in with a wet sucking noise. 'We're twins,' he said down to the table. 'Identical.' He paused and shook his head, 'Even the staff at Stirling Lines couldn't tell us apart, so they made my brother shave his head so they knew which one of us they were talking to.'

Chilcott naturally looked at Kershaw's thick dark hair and beard and then down at the top photograph taken from CCTV last Friday on Whiteladies Road. Although "Kershaw" was hooded, it was clear to see that he also had dark hair and thick beard, just like Kershaw had now.

'So what... you're saying *this*...' Chilcott tapped the "Kershaw" on the image. 'Is your dead brother. Is that what you want me to believe?'

'Exactly.'

'I'm sorry,' Chilcott said shaking his head. 'Just to be clear. You are saying the individuals on these images, both in Bristol and Glastonbury, are your *dead* brother?'

'Well he's clearly not fucking dead, is he?' Kershaw bit.

'And why would you think he was?'

Kershaw rubbed his snotty nostrils along the back of his hand. 'Because we left him… wounded. Captured…' His reddening eyes fixed on Chilcott. 'We left him.' His broken voice trailed away.

Chilcott gestured for DC Phillips to take over.

'What is your brother's name, Brian?' she asked softly.

'Barry.'

'When did you last see him?'

'April the sixth, two thousand and ten. The location is classified.'

'That's okay, we don't need to know exactly where you were, but can you give an area or country?'

'Afghanistan.'

Chilcott sat back and stared at his subject with questioning disbelief.

'And you think Barry has returned to Bristol?' Phillips prodded gently.

Kershaw shuffled in his seat.

'Why?' Chilcott asked boldly.

Kershaw closed his eyes for a long moment and then opened them directly on Chilcott.

'He's come back to seek revenge.'

'Revenge… for what?'

'Leaving him.'

# CHAPTER TWENTY-THREE

3:19 p.m.

Chilcott tapped on the already open door and the DCI waved him inside. She was speaking on the phone and it was evident from the content of the heated conversation that she was speaking to the force press officer. She slammed the receiver down and grabbed the sides of her head. 'Argh!" she screamed.

'Problems?'

'Why the hell don't people just do what they've been told?' It was a rhetorical question, she wasn't expecting a reply. 'He's only gone and released Brian Kershaw's name to the press.'

'What?'

'I know... I know.' She slapped the side of her leg in anger. 'Jesus! If a job isn't hard enough we have to deal with cretins like Simon Maxwell.' She sucked in a purposeful breath and held it in as she calmed herself down. 'How did it go?' she eventually asked.

'He's given an alibi.'

'An alibi?'

Chilcott groaned and took a seat. Foster watched him with a critical eye as he lowered his bottom onto the soft blue fabric of the comfy chair.

'Take a seat,' she said.

'Thanks.'

'Well?' Foster asked. 'Are you going to fill me in, or do I have to guess the content of this alibi?'

'I need to go to Windsor.'

'I can't let you go to Windsor. I need you here.'

'It's the only way we can sort this crap out. Kershaw says he was there – he's given exact details of where he stayed; places he had food. If I go, I can either confirm his account or we can expose it as nonsense and then charge him with two counts of murder.'

'A local unit can conduct those enquiries. I believe it's called a good old-fashioned send-to.'

'I've just spent the last two hours of my life staring across the table at that bloke. I know his mannerisms, I know what hand he wipes his nose with, and I even know what table he allegedly sat at for dinner. We involve somebody else to do these enquiries and we're setting ourselves up for error and failure. Failure to the families of our victims and failure in the eyes of the watching public.'

Foster looked back at the phone and her mind switched back two minutes to the conversation she had with that idiot press officer. The thought of Kershaw's name being bandied around the national media was truly cringe-worthy. Her features tightened.

'The B&B is bound to have CCTV,' Chilcott said. 'The Brasserie is bound to have CCTV. Christ! The streets are bound to be stacked with them, it's Windsor!'

'Fine,' she said, still staring incredulously at the desk phone. 'Go up this evening. Stay over if you have to, make your enquiries and be back by lunchtime tomorrow. Kershaw will need an extension of custody time, but with these ongoing enquiries, we'll have no issues nailing that down. I want to be in a position to charge or bail Kershaw by this time tomorrow.'

'I can't guarantee that, Julie.'

'I'm holding a media press conference with DI Chowdhury at 6 p.m. tonight. It'll be benign, but they're not going to be satisfied with that for long. Give me something positive to feed back to our community.'

Chilcott shrugged a shoulder. 'I can't guarantee that either.'

Foster exhaled a long, considered breath and stared at her DI. 'Do you think there's anything in his account?'

Chilcott wiped a slow hand down over his mouth.

'That tells me, yes. I know you can read people better than most, Robbie.'

'That's why I need to satisfy myself that this Windsor story is a load of old bollocks. I have to see it for myself.'

'What about the CCTV?' Foster questioned.

'He says it's not him – he's adamant. Says it's his brother who he believed was dead in Afghanistan.'

Foster scowled.

'I… I have to be honest. His reactions, body language,

and tone of voice… he seems to believe it. I'd almost go as far as saying; he's shitting himself at the thought of his brother being alive. I know he's highly skilled in evasive interrogation techniques, but as it stands, I…' he hesitated, 'well, I'd be inclined to believe he's telling the truth.'

Foster cocked a concerned head.

'Don't get me wrong, he ticks all the right boxes to be our man: his physical ability, location to the crimes, professional links to the victims… on any other day I'd be telling you it's water tight. But I can't. And if it's not him, then someone else is still out there and a danger to society.'

'And if that's the case, we're in a whole world of trouble.'

'I'm going to take the train. Replicate his journey as much as I can.'

'I'll get one of the detectives to drop you down. Do you need to pop back to mine for anything?'

Chilcott looked down at the clothing he'd already been wearing for two days. 'I'll pick something up in Windsor. There's bound to be a Next or M&S where I can get some fresh boxers and a shirt.'

'Put it on expenses.'

'Thanks. I just need to make a call.'

'Fine. Keep me updated.'


DI Chowdhury was out of his office and Chilcott took the opportunity to use his phone. Stephen Chamberlain picked up almost instantly.

'Hi Stephen, this is DI Robbie Chilcott.'

'Oh, hello.'

'You've got yourself into a spot of bother with that stunt.'

'And I'd do it again.'

'Look, I need to ask you a question and I want you to be as honest with me as possible.'

'Okay.'

'Brian Kershaw – does he have a brother who was in the Special Forces in some capacity?'

'No.'

Chilcott breathed a sigh of relief.

'Well…'

'Well?'

'He did.'

'Tell me what he did,'

'Barry was a specialist in intelligence. His unit, the SRR was specialised in covert intelligence gathering. You wouldn't know who they were and if you did, you wouldn't know they were there. They are amongst us, protecting the sovereignty of the nation, or helping to prevent terrorist activity. In Afghanistan they went deep behind enemy lines, often supported by squadrons of twenty-two SAS and other regiments. They fed us the vital information we needed to execute a successful mission. It was an incredibly dangerous role—'

'And that's how Barry Kershaw died?' Chilcott cut in.

Chamberlain stopped speaking.

'Was Barry Kershaw killed in an operation or not?'

'We were deep inside Afghanistan, I'm not permitted to tell you where—'

'I don't need to know any of that. I just need to know if he was killed in an operation?'

'Our mission was to capture Taliban leaders and bring them back to the base.' Chamberlain stopped talking as if casting his mind back to that time.

'What happened?' Chilcott gently prodded.

'Barry was part of the SRR. We were on standby should anything go tits-up with the mission. It did. We were sent in but overrun by the Taliban from all angles. Outnumbered, outgunned, we had to either scrap it out or retreat, but we were taking casualties...' Chamberlain's voice sounded haunted. '...and fatalities. It was fierce. One of the fiercest battles I've experienced. Most of us managed to back up and dig in. If they had flanked us, I don't know if we'd be talking about this today.' There was a long pause. 'We lost four men. Baz was one of them.'

'What did you do?' Chilcott asked.

'As I say, we dug in, held the retreated position and called in air support.'

'And then?'

'We retook the ground, found three of our dead, but Baz Kershaw was gone. We scoured the area for two days, a troop of Paras came in on a Chinook, but he was gone, presumed dead... or worse.'

'I looked him up on Google,' Chilcott said. 'There's nothing about this.'

'That's because it never happened. We weren't there. The mission didn't exist to anyone beyond those involved from the regiment and head shed.'

'Was there anything unusual about Barry?'

'What, apart from being a twin?'

Chilcott closed his eyes. 'Was Brian there that day, during the rescue attempt?'

'Yeah. He took it bad. Not sure he ever got over it.'

'How alike were they, I mean, there are twins and there are identical twins?'

'Spitting image. You couldn't tell them apart at first, they were buggers, constantly playing tricks on us so we made Barry shave his hair off so we could tell them apart.'

Chilcott asked himself the next question in his head before it came out of his mouth, it was a potential game-changer.

'In your opinion, what are the chances of Barry Kershaw still being alive?'

'Barry?' The intonation on the word showed how surprised he would be.

'Hypothetically – you said his body wasn't recovered.'

'That's right.'

'So, is there any possibility he could still be alive?'

Silence followed as Chamberlain considered the question and the possibility.

'Agh, I... I'd be highly surprised, I mean... he'd have to escape or be rescued from wherever he was being held and Special Branch and the ministry would be all over it. This happened over six years ago.'

'What if he didn't inform them that he was still alive?'

'Puh, well, then I guess it's possible. But I can't think for a minute why he'd stay under the radar, he's got family.'

Chilcott felt a chill shoot down his spine. 'Thank you, Stephen. I've got to go now. I'll be in touch again tomorrow. Thanks for the chat.'

Chilcott ended the call.

# CHAPTER TWENTY-FOUR

The train between Bristol and Reading was chock-a-block with passengers. He'd spent the first part of the journey seated alongside a young 'hoody-monster' who stank of weed. That was the trouble these days; a misconception that it was okay to carry the stuff around despite the fact it was still a Class B narcotic and very much against the law to possess. Truth was, thanks to the extensive government cut backs, cops had to prioritise their time and it just wasn't worth getting tied-up with an eighth of marijuana when the control room was sending officers here there and every-where like blue-arsed flies. And as it stood, Chilcott didn't fancy becoming involved himself either, so instead, he removed his wallet pretending to look through receipts and made sure the stoner saw his warrant card. It did the job and almost immediately the youth rose from his seat and gave Chilcott a look like he'd just farted in his soup and he made his way through the standing passengers towards the nearest exit, in spite of the fact they still had forty minutes to the next stop. His new seat companion took the vacant space the moment she realised the youth wasn't coming back and Chilcott was far happier with this arrangement.

Arriving at Windsor and Eton Riverside Station at just before 6 p.m., Chilcott walked a short journey until he was in sight of the magnificent outer West walls of Windsor Castle, lit up spectacularly by bright lights. He looked for the flag pole, the Royal Standard had been replaced by a billowing Union Standard. He felt a pang of disappointment that the Queen was elsewhere. Years before, he'd been on Royal Visit duty as a sergeant when the Queen had visited Wells and Glastonbury. There was something very special about serving Queen and country that only a fellow officer would properly understand. Kershaw understood it.

Checking Google Maps before his departure to refresh his memory of the street names, he soon found the Windsor and Eton town bridge and crossed over towards the Eton side of the River Thames to where Kershaw had suggested he'd been staying. He passed street entertainers doing some sort of high wire juggling act before an enthusiastic circle of clapping and cheering public. Immediately, Chilcott saw the Brasserie beside the river with its welcoming outdoor area and people eating and drinking on the edge of the Thames beneath glowing patio heaters. Opposite the Brasserie, on the corner of two converging roads he saw The Royal George Hotel, and infuriatingly, opposite that on the high street he noticed a Costa Coffee house.

He wandered the streets, not so much like a tourist, but as a curious onlooker taking everything in. It was clear that any high street facing rooms at The Royal George Hotel would overlook the coffee house. Looking up, he hazarded a guess as to which window contained room seven and as he strolled, he identified the obvious CCTV camera locations, which probably belonged to the local council. He was in luck; there were a lot of them, probably due to the royal connection of the town. The high street only small and narrow, had an interesting array of shops in the most beautiful old timber-framed buildings, clearly dating back centuries. He wondered what they were all those years ago, but turned about forcing his historical interests to one side. He had a job to do.

He walked back in the direction of the castle which couldn't be seen from his current location and made along the cobbled streets for The Royal George Hotel.

He entered the building, itself probably a few hundred years old and headed for the small reception desk with an extremely polite and well presented member of staff waiting to greet him with a large welcoming smile.

'Good evening, sir,' she said.

'Hi.'

'Are you staying with us today, sir?'

'How much are the rooms?'

The receptionist held out an arm to the tariff board sitting at the end of the counter top. He read them out in his head; *single room – one-twenty, double – one-sixty*. Chilcott blinked and cried out inwardly. 'Yes, I will, ah thank you. A friend of mine was staying here last weekend actually. I don't know what room he was in, but he said it was particularly pleasant. Would you be able to check the system and see if that room is available, I'd like to stay in that one if I possibly could, please?' He smiled at the receptionist as his mind was screaming, *please be a single room.*

'What were the dates of booking, please, sir?'

'Ah, Thursday the twentieth, checking out on the Saturday the twenty-second, last week.'

'And the name of the booking, please?'

'Jones. His name is Jones.'

'First name?' The receptionist looked up at him expectantly.

'Uh... Fred. I call him, Fred, but his real name's Brian.'

'Yes, we have a Brian Jones on those dates, he was in room seven.'

'That's the one, great. Is it available?'

The receptionist tapped the keyboard with professional efficiency. 'Yes, room seven is available this evening. Would you like me to book you in to that room for tonight, sir?'

'Yes, please.' He looked around the foyer and up at the ceiling line for cameras. A modern-looking dome unit was fixed on the wall behind the reception desk, but there were no other obvious cameras in the reception area. It was probably a management decision not to taint the original features of the building with modern-day CCTV equipment. Quite understandable too.

'Will you require help with any bags, sir?'

'Ah, no, thanks. I've packed light. Thanks anyway.' He was carrying a Marks and Spencer carrier bag containing a newly purchased three-pack of boxer shorts, a plain white stretch T-shirt, a two pack of plain white work shirts, a toothbrush and paste.

'Just the one night, sir?'

'Yes. Thanks.'

The receptionist handed him a form to complete and as she typed details of the booking onto the computer system she asked, 'Are you here for work or pleasure, sir?'

'Ah… a bit of both.'

'Will you be requiring a VAT receipt?'

'No. Thanks.' He dug out his wallet, this time concealing his police warrant card and handed over his Barclaycard.

'That's lovely. The booking is complete. Enjoy your stay with us. Will you be requiring a reservation for the restaurant tonight, sir?'

'Ah, no thanks. I'm meeting friends in the Brasserie across the road.'

'A good choice, sir.'

'Yes… so I've been told.'

# CHAPTER TWENTY-FIVE

Chilcott chose to sit at the back of the room on one of the smaller tables set for two. He pictured Kershaw in his mind and worked out which table he would have selected *if* he had been here. With his specialist training, Chilcott felt sure Kershaw would be like himself and sit looking inward with no chance of any nasty surprises springing up from behind.

'Is that table available?' he asked the young waiter, pointing to the table that he understood Kershaw was describing during the interview.

'Yes, sir. Are you sure you wouldn't want to be seated nearer the window?'

'No. This is fine, thanks.'

The waiter handed Chilcott a menu. 'Any drinks, sir?'

*Too bloody right.* He looked down the wine list and selected a house French Merlot.

'Will that be a small or large glass, sir?'

'The bottle.' *In for a penny, in for a pound.*

The waiter returned minutes later and poured a taster amount into a large bulbous glass. Chilcott went through the motions of tasting, nodding and uttering a pleasing tone, but all he wanted was for the waiter to fill the glass, which he subsequently did. Chilcott ordered rare rib-eye steak with all the trimmings and a garlic bread to start with. He realised he hadn't eaten since the interval in Kershaw's interviews and he was going to make the most of this unexpected pleasure.

He peered around the restaurant, looked at the serving staff, clocked the camera locations and ogled the food plates being delivered to happy-looking customers. If Kershaw was telling the truth, he had good taste, and a bit of spare cash to splash, this food didn't come cheap. Chilcott's mobile phone sounded in his pocket, it was a withheld number but he answered it anyway. 'Yes,' he said without pleasantries.

'It's Julie. We've got the final forensic results from CSI.'

Chilcott sighed. Maybe his time in Windsor was about to come to an abrupt end.

'The attacker was forensically aware.'

Chilcott pressed the phone closer to his ear.

'We have nothing substantial.'

'Nothing whatsoever?'

'Nothing concrete. We've got a partial DNA profile from the victim's coat, but not enough to identify an offender. Just enough to identify that it doesn't belong to Samantha.'

Chilcott tapped the table with his free hand as he thought. Given the location of the attack and the sudden and violent nature of the murder, it was almost implausible to think that no useful forensics had been discovered.

'All we have are the scuff marks in the concrete and a partial boot print to go on.'

'Until we cross-match the print with the boots seized

from Kershaw's address…you never know, we may have a match,' Chilcott said.

'That's already been done. They don't match.'

The waiter returned to the table. 'Your garlic bread, sir.'

*Thank you*, Chilcott mouthed, taking the phone away from his ear for a second as he acknowledged the young man.

'Sounds like your enquiries are progressing well,' Foster said with a patronising tone.

Chilcott shrugged and stuffed a dripping slice of warm bread into his mouth and chomped down as he spoke. 'I'm still researching.'

'Sounds like it!'

'I've got to be honest, this beats slumming it in my shitty caravan with a tin of beans.'

'Don't get used to it – you've got work to do.'

'I'm a veritable coiled spring.'

'I saw *your spring* yesterday morning and it's not all that to shout about.'

'That may be so, but I am working – field work.'

'Have you found the hotel yet?'

'Yes. I'm staying in the same room.'

'Can you see the Costa Coffee house?'

'Yes.'

'The Brasserie?'

'I'm inside it, now.' He tucked another slice of bread into his mouth. 'Really good garlic bread, actually,' he said chewing loudly.

'Didn't your mother ever teach you to eat properly?'

'I thought you were my mother?'

'Seriously, Robbie, what have you discovered?'

'Someone by the name of Brian Jones booked into The Royal George Hotel last Thursday and stayed in room seven.'

'CCTV?'

'I haven't identified myself to the staff yet. I thought I'd enjoy what I can before I'm singled out as a trouble maker.'

'We need CCTV showing Kershaw was, or was not there.'

'I know. Leave that with me.' He took a slurp from his wine glass. 'I think I'll have more luck with this restaurant. I believe I'm seated at the table he described in interview. A camera behind the bar is staring right at me.'

'Good.'

'I'm first going to eat some grub because I'm starving, and then I'll introduce myself to the manager and see what I can dig up.'

'Very well.'

Chilcott fiddled with the stem of his glass as he pondered his next question.

'Has intel thrown anything up about the brother?'

'Nothing. If he's out there, he's a ghost.'

'In more ways than one, according to Kershaw.'

'Indeed. Enjoy your steak and merlot and give me a call the moment you have some progress.'

'How did…?'

'Robbie, I can read you like a book.'


Meal devoured, Chilcott asked if he could see the manager. The poor young waiter looked askance, probably believing Chilcott was going to make a complaint of some kind, but he was a professional young man and did as requested.

A wiry middle-aged man wearing a beige suit approached the table. He held his hands together like he was holding a delicate butterfly between his palms. 'Good evening, sir. I understand you've asked to speak to the manager?'

'Yes, that's right.'

'That's me, Raymond Shaw. Is everything to your satisfaction?' He had a look of surprised concern that suggested to Chilcott that not many people complained to the management. Given the quality of the food and service, he could see why.

'Oh, the food was top notch and your staff are a credit to you,' Chilcott said.

The manager folded in a semi-bow and breathed his obvious relief. 'Thank you, sir,' he said with a preen of the hair at the side of his head. 'Uh... how may I be of assistance to you?'

Chilcott flopped his wallet down on the table and secretively exposed the window flap containing his warrant card. He looked around, giving the manager time to digest the information on the card, but the delay was all for show. He hinged forward and the manager mirrored him.

'That camera,' Chilcott said quietly. 'Is it real or a dummy?'

'Oh, it's real.'

Chilcott made a purposeful one-hundred-and-eighty degree scan of the room. He noticed the manager doing the same. This was fun. He leaned forward just a few more inches. The manager did the same.

'I'm following-up a line of enquiries for a very serious incident,' Chilcott muttered. He locked eyes with the open-mouthed manager. 'I need to see the CCTV on that camera from last weekend, if that's possible?'

The manager frowned for a moment. 'Nothing untoward has happened in here, I can assure you—'

Chilcott twitched his finger and spoke clandestinely. 'I'm not saying it has, but you might be interested to know that a potential murderer had a meal in this restaurant just last week.'

The manager recoiled and stood rigid. 'Hector… get me Hector, please, James.'

The waiter scurried away and returned moments later with another man from behind the scenes of the restaurant. Chilcott looked at them, they were obviously a couple.

'Hector, would you help, um…'

'Detective Inspector Chilcott.'

'Detective Inspector Chilcott access our CCTV from last weekend, please?'

The other man put a hand on the shoulder of the manager, who turned and hurried back out of view.

'Hi Hector, I'm DI Robbie Chilcott.' He shook the man's hand. 'Is that alright if we check?'

'If Ray says so,' he beamed.

'Your steak by the way – spectacular,' Chilcott commented as they walked beyond three tables of other guests and through a door at the side of the bar. The office area was compact but tidy and comfortable.

'Would you like anything?' Hector asked.

'My wine bottle. Is it okay to—'

'Yes, of course. I've been known to have one or two back here myself,' Hector winked.

*I bet you have.*

Within moments a waiter was handing Chilcott the remainder of the bottle and a freshly topped up glass of wine.

'Thank you,' Chilcott said. 'Very kind. Lovely wine by the way.'

'I didn't know you were allowed to drink on duty,' Hector observed.

'I'm not driving anywhere later and I'm not arresting anyone any time soon, so I'll be alright.'

'A perk of being the boss, I suppose?' Hector grinned.

Chilcott smiled.

'Do you know who you are looking for?' Hector asked.

'Yes.'

'I'm quite good with faces, what did he look like?'

Chilcott pouted and considered sharing the description with his new attentive friend. 'Okay. White male, around six feet tall, dark messy hair, so long,' he said holding a hand just beneath his ear. 'A thick dark bushy beard, possibly wearing a long dark baggy knee-length coat, jeans and brown ankle boots.'

'Hmmm,' Hector pondered. 'Anything else?'

'Well, yes actually. He looks a bit… how can I say this without sounding rude?'

'Oh go on, it's just us.' Hector cocked his head and leaned towards Chilcott with a mischievous smile.

'Well, he's got a massive forehead.'

'Yes, I remember him.'

'You do?'

'He wasn't very friendly, but he did tip well.'

'You don't happen to know… did he give a name?'

'No, I don't recall. He was footfall, like you – no booking.'

'What was he doing here?'

'Visiting the Queen. He told me he was visiting the Queen.'

Chilcott sank back in the chair and interlocked his hands behind his head. *Has to be a coincidence.* 'Anything else you can remember about the man?'

'He had steak, like you.'

Chilcott cocked his head. 'Would you remember what time he was here?'

'Which day? He came here two nights running.'

'Either,' Chilcott replied eagerly. 'Either will do.'

'It was early, I'm sure. I wouldn't normally have the time to speak to customers later in the evening as we're usually so rushed off our feet… hmmm, five thirty-ish?' Hector touched his chin. 'Yes, that's probably about right.'

'Can you recall which table?'

'Yes. Your table. He was sat on your table and even on the same chair.'

'You couldn't set this machine to say 5 p.m. last Friday could you… uh, for the camera facing my table?'

Hector took the controls and set the timer to 5 p.m. on Friday the twenty-first of February and left Chilcott to it.

# CHAPTER TWENTY-SIX

Within an hour Chilcott had seen enough. He'd handed Hector a memory stick and requested he burn the footage to take away with him. To all intents and purposes he had just watched Brian Kershaw tucking into a thick rib-eye steak and a couple of French bottled beers. His clothing wasn't the same as in the crime scene CCTV, but that was only to be expected. He couldn't be in both places at once.

He thanked the staff again and set out into the cool evening air and made his way for The Royal George Hotel. On arrival he went straight to the desk and opened his wallet wide for the same receptionist as earlier to see his warrant badge.

'I'm sorry,' he said. 'I should have introduced myself properly before. I'm DI Chilcott from the Avon and Somerset Police Constabulary. I'm investigating a murder in Bristol and I believe a person of interest was staying at this hotel last weekend.'

The young receptionist went a pale shade of grey, offered her apologies, left the chair and kept Chilcott standing alone in the reception area for a good couple of minutes while he heard muffled voices coming from behind a thick stone wall to the side of the desk. He waited a further minute as the voices subsided and then an older woman strode into view.

'Good evening, sir,' she said assertively. 'What exactly did you want from us?'

'I didn't get a chance to say. I'm staying here tonight – room seven. I'm actually in the area investigating a murder that occurred in Bristol last Friday. I have reason to believe a person of interest stayed at this hotel, in room seven.'

'So I've been told.'

'Can I ask how many people have stayed here in room seven since last Friday?'

'I can't give you names for obvious—'

'I don't need names,' Chilcott interrupted.

She punched the keys of the computer. 'Four guests in room seven since then, including you.'

There was little point keeping the pillow cases then. 'I already know he booked in under the name of Jones. Did he leave any credit card details, a contact telephone number maybe?'

The lady behind the desk gave him a wry look.

He held up his hands like he had a gun pointed at him. 'I'm genuine, I promise. I need to confirm the same person we have with us in custody is the person who was here, that's all. Your support may help to release an innocent man.'

They shared a weary standoff.

'How did he pay?' Chilcott asked.

The receptionist looked at the computer and typed a few buttons. 'Cash.' She paused. 'He gave an address. I suppose if you're a police officer, you can have that.' She punched the keys again and gave him the address. It wasn't Brian Kershaw's home address.

Chilcott put the details into his phone. The address didn't register, but the postcode related to an army barracks on Salisbury Plain. He slanted a smile. Kershaw was a slippery customer.

'Thanks. Can I view your CCTV, please?'

'No. You'll need permission from the owners and I'm afraid they are currently in Italy.'

'To be honest,' Chilcott huffed. 'I think I've got enough. Can you think of anything else that might help me identify that Mr Jones is the same person we have in Bristol?'

The younger receptionist peeped her head around the corner of the thick wall.

'Hello again,' Chilcott said upon seeing her face.

'Um, he left something behind in the room. We still have it in lost property.'

Chilcott stepped closer to the desk. The young woman vanished from sight and returned moments later with a tainted brass Zippo lighter. She handed it to Chilcott. 'You can give it back to him if you like.'

'Did he smoke?'

'Nobody is allowed to smoke in the building,' the older woman said.

Chilcott nodded. 'Thanks. I'll hand it back to him and if he says it's not his, I'll pop it into police lost property.'

'Thank you.'

'No. Thank you. I'll head up to my room now. If you think of anything else—'

'Don't worry, we'll tell you,' the older lady anticipated.

He placed the Zippo lighter into a sealed bag, checked the time and headed up to his room.

Next morning, he had breakfast at the hotel, checked out and made his way back to the train station. He saw a British Transport Police officer on the platform and identified himself with a flash of his warrant card. He was fortunate to find the BTP officer and took full advantage of the opportunity. They entered the small station office, where the ex-Met Police Constable was topping up his thirty-year pension with a bit of transport service.

'I need access to your CCTV,' Chilcott said.

'When for?'

'Arrivals last Thursday between 4 and 5 p.m. and the departures last Saturday between 3 and 5 p.m.'

The BTP officer laughed.

'What?'

'Good luck with that, mate.'

'Okay, I've got more specific times I could start with arrivals, fifteen minutes either side of 5 p.m., and departures, fifteen either side of 3 p.m.'

'Platform?'

'For Chepstow.'

'I hope you're not expecting it today.'

'Why not?'

'It's just me in this morning and look at it out there.'

'Just point me in the direction of the machine and I'll go through it. You won't even know I'm here.'

'You know our system?'

'I'm sure I can work it out.'

The BTP officer shrugged. 'You want a drink of something? You're going to be a while.'

'White tea. Two sugars please.'

'Help yourself. The kettle's through the back. Do us a favour and stick a twenty pence piece in the pot for any drinks you have. It's the cutbacks; we don't get drinks supplied any longer.'

'Sure. No problem.'

The BTP officer donned his hat and made for the door. 'The train timetables are in the folder beside the phone. I'll leave you to it – knock yourself out.' He opened the door and stepped out onto the busy platform.

Chilcott looked around the small room and shook his head at the thought of doing a full thirty years' service only to end up in a crappy little office like this. There was no way he'd be doing the same and in less than five years, he'd finally be free from the job.

Starting as he meant to go on, he dropped a pound in the tea fund and settled down in front of the CCTV screen with his first hot brew.

Chilcott realised he had more chance of success if he captured Kershaw's departure than his arrival; he would need to hang around for a spell before taking the train, whereas upon his arrival he'd join the throng of commuters and tourists and exit the station in no time at all. The timetable showed three potential departures that Kershaw could have taken if his estimates in interview were to be believed. Chilcott sipped from his cup and decided to work backwards in blocks of ten minute segments from the latest time possible for him to arrive at Chepstow at around 6.30 p.m. The software was similar to the ones he used back at the Major Crime Investigation Unit and he was soon selecting the departing train at *14:47* hours. With a little fiddling of the controls, Chilcott stopped the footage just as the train was moving away from the platform and selected reverse slow motion. He leaned in close to the TV monitor and watched the public stepping backwards out of the train for the three minutes it remained at the platform. He scanned every face to the best of his abilities, but it wasn't easy watching the footage in this manner. He drew a blank and next selected the *15:07* hour's departure, almost imme-diately noticing a large, solid man leaning against a white painted stanchion with his back to the camera. Chilcott checked the arrival times in Chepstow – this was the train Kershaw was talking about. Estimated arrival at Chepstow was 18:16 hours. He studied his day-book for the notes he had taken from the interview. The times checked out including the delay Kershaw spoke of.

Chilcott sipped from his drink and focused solely on that individual. He had dark hair that was for sure. His build was solid and was of a good height. It was hard to make out the colour of the man's jacket, but it could easily be the same as the one seen in the Brasserie, but Chilcott needed to see his face. The footage rolled slowly in reverse; people walking backwards in front of the stationary man and then Chilcott got what he was waiting for; the man peeled himself away from the metal pillar and for just over a second, he remained in view until he was gone. Chilcott changed the direction to play forwards in super-slow-motion and peered at the corner of the screen. He paused the image as soon as the man came into view and moved forwards in single-framed paused steps. Finally, he had no doubts. It was Brian Kershaw.

. . .

DCI Foster answered her mobile phone after Chilcott failed to get a response from the office phone.

'Julie, it's Robbie. It wasn't Brian Kershaw.'

'Okay,' she answered slowly. 'You'd better talk me through this.'

'I've got him in the hotel. I've got him in the restaurant on Friday evening and now I've got him at the train station at six minutes past three on Saturday – just as he said.'

The DCI fell silent.

'I'm heading back, but we need someone to grill Kershaw about his brother. Get Phillips and Raymond to work on him—'

'I'll speak to Kershaw myself,' Foster said. 'Get back here as soon as you can.'

Chilcott looked down at the timetable. 'I'll be at Temple Meads at twelve forty, ask someone to meet me there.'

# CHAPTER TWENTY-SEVEN

DCI Foster took the unusual step of interviewing Kershaw herself in company with DC Phillips and the legal representative, Mr Bishop. Foster couldn't remember the last time she sat opposite a suspect. An officer in her position was more used to boardrooms and high-level management meetings, but they could be equally as tricky. Introduction and pleasantries over, she got straight to the point.

'Tell me everything you know about Barry Kershaw,' she said. Her body language was strictly no-nonsense.

Kershaw's eyes faltered.

'Where did he live – last known address?'

'Nottingham,' Kershaw offered after a beat. 'He lived in Nottingham. But that was before…'

'Before you and your unit left him in Afghanistan.'

Kershaw's deep set eyes met hers.

'I know everything,' she said bluntly. 'And I know you couldn't save him.'

He looked back at her blankly.

'Where do you think he is now?'

Kershaw stared at a spot on the table half way between them and after several seconds, he shook his head.

'Has he made any contact with you?'

'No,' Kershaw answered without hesitation.

'My colleague, Detective Inspector Chilcott says he has evidence that you were in Windsor at the time of this latest murder. How can I be sure that the person in Windsor is you and not your brother?'

Kershaw looked at the DCI with unnerving deadness in his eyes. 'I was in Windsor.'

Foster sucked in a long considered breath and watched her subject with interest. Nothing about him was telling her a different story.

'Tell me why you think he's killing these young women.'

Kershaw half blinked not enough to close his eyes fully. Perhaps they were trained that way – never leave yourself open to vulnerability, not even for a split-second. Foster could tell that he knew the answer, but instead he shook his head and broke eye contact.

'If you can't provide me with a solid defence for yourself, then we will have no option but to charge you with the murders of Samantha Chamberlain and Jessica Asher.'

'Hold on a minute,' the solicitor interjected. 'You've said yourself that my client was in Windsor at the time of Samantha Chamberlain's murder—'

'Or, it could have been his twin brother.'

'Who you have no trace of and who was officially recorded as deceased by the Ministry of Defence six years ago.'

'He's punishing us,' Kershaw muttered.

All faces turned to him.

'We left him. We didn't rescue him or recover his body. You don't do that in the regiment.'

'So, you're saying he's literally back from the dead, for what… payback?'

Kershaw tilted his head.

'Why would he kill the children of your ex-colleagues?'

'He wants to cause the squadron suffering… just like his.'

Foster mulled over the information for a moment. It was certainly plausible and would be a motive, of sorts, but how much did she believe Kershaw and what were the potential consequences if she let him go?'

'I'm in a dilemma,' she said. 'If I release you on bail, am I putting the public at risk?'

'No,' he replied definitively. 'It wasn't me.'

'When you were arrested, we seized your phone. We've triangulated the coordinates of the phone's location at the time of Samantha Chamberlain's murder. We got this back this morning.' She pulled out a data report from a file and studied it for a moment. 'This shows us that your phone was in fact in the Eton and Windsor area last Friday evening.'

'That's what I've been *trying* to say.'

Foster held up her hand to stop him. 'Your phone was in Windsor. I didn't say you were.'

Kershaw frowned.

'How can I be convinced that you were also there and this isn't some elaborate conspiracy with your brother?'

'I think my client has answered all questions to the best of his abilities. He cannot answer for his brother and you've said yourself that your colleague has proof that my client was in Windsor and Eton at the time of the latest murder. I don't think you have any option other than to release my client immediately, while you continue your investigation.'

Foster bit down and smiled thinly at the solicitor. 'I'm fully aware of the requirements of detention, thank you. I'm going to send you back to your cell while I speak to my colleagues about the best way to manage the way forward. You will not be kept here any longer than is necessary. Do you understand?'

'Yes.'

The solicitor made a deliberate point of peeling up his shirt sleeve to expose his watch face and make a note of the time in his book.

DCI Foster stood up. 'One last thing.'

Kershaw and his solicitor looked at her.

'*If* it is Barry. *If* he is killing these people. How do we find him?'

Kershaw looked at Foster with a glazed numbness. 'You won't find him. He'll find you.'

Foster took a nervous step backwards. 'Interview concluded. Someone take him away.' She opened the door and two detention officers came into the room and escorted Kershaw back to his cell.

Foster was in luck. Chilcott was within cellular range as he travelled back to Bristol by train. She was calling him from her office using the conference facility. DI Chowdhury was standing alongside.

'I've got a decision to make, Robbie. Do we keep Kershaw in the bin on the custody time limits, or release him on bail?'

'I don't think we have a choice,' Chilcott said. 'When you see the footage I've captured up in Windsor, you'll realise we're a bit stuffed. I'll be back in less than half an hour.'

'We don't have that much time to play with. So what would you suggest, Robbie?'

'Release him on pre-charge bail. We'll still have a further twenty-eight days to sort this crap out, one way or another.'

'And what if he goes on to kill someone else?' Chowdhury chipped in. 'I don't particularly want that on my conscience.'

'If we release him, we can return to his address with him and search for the clothing we've seen on the Windsor CCTV. It's not rocket science.'

'And if that isn't there?' Chowdhury was persistent if nothing else.

'We put him on bail conditions of a daily curfew,' Foster suggested. 'We leave it open ended – twenty-four hour doorstep presentation. That way we'll know where he is.'

'And if he doesn't answer the door?'

'Then we put him out as wanted on the Police National Computer. It doesn't matter where he is, if he's stopped, he can be arrested for breaching his bail conditions and brought back here.'

'We can also seize his passport, or put all ports on stand-by,' Chilcott said.

'That's not going to stop him jumping on a small boat and leaving at will,' Chowdhury argued. 'We'd never see him again.'

Foster stared at Chowdhury.

'What? I'm just saying… someone here has to play devil's advocate.'

'Right, I've decided,' Foster said. 'We're going to bail him for a week on condition that he surrenders his passport and is subject to doorstep presentation twenty-four hours per day, except for one and half hours from midday each day to allow him to manage his affairs; go shopping or do whatever he needs to do in town. That gives the armoury time to examine the weapon and ammunition seized from his home and we can tie it all up together at the end.'

'And after that week?' Chowdhury asked.

'We extend the bail if needed.'

'Will his solicitor agree to that?' Chowdhury questioned. 'I mean, that's practically a prison sentence.'

'He'll go for it, or we keep Kershaw in custody today. I know which one Kershaw will opt for. Right, Robbie, come and see me as soon as you arrive back at the nick.'

'Will do.'

The DCI ended the call and tasked Chowdhury to organise the release of Brian Kershaw.


Chilcott's mobile phone rang within moments of the last call ending.

'What did you forget?' he said, expecting to hear the DCI's voice. It wasn't.

'Hello. Is this DI Chilcott?' the male asked.

'Yes, who is this?'

'It's CSI Oliver Trent. I'm calling from the Arson Task Force.'

'Yes, hello. How can I help you?'

'I've been looking into the fire of your caravan and I'd like to ask you some questions about it, if convenient?'

Chilcott looked around at the disinterested faces of the other passengers seated within ear shot. 'I'm currently on a train so my signal may drop, but fire away... pardon the pun.' Chilcott smiled to himself.

'Did you keep liquid fuel stored near to the caravan?'

'No, not that I can think of. I mostly used propane cans. Why what's the problem?'

'The attending fire officers noticed a smell of accelerant, particularly at the rear of the caravan and discovered several scorched patches in the grass away from the main seat of the fire—'

'Accelerant?' Chilcott sat upright. 'You mean the fire was started deliberately?'

'That's how I have become involved, sir. The lead fire officer asked me to investigate the findings and I've also taken a look at the site myself.'

Chilcott stared wide ahead, unblinking. 'Okay...'

'We believe from the speed of the blaze and the considerable heat generated by the fire, that accelerant was used on the main shell of the van as well as underneath.'

Chilcott didn't speak.

'I've notified police control and log and crime reference numbers have been generated.'

Chilcott stared ahead vacantly. 'Thanks.'

'It's not set in stone, but we believe the fire is likely to have been ablaze for around sixty minutes prior to our arrival. I have to ask, sir, under normal circumstances, would you have been home in the caravan at that time?'

Chilcott's mind took him back to that night. He'd

arrived home only twenty minutes or so after the fire was started. It must have been deliberate given the stage the fire had reached by the time he discovered it. He thought about the late finish at Chamberlain's house. 'Yes, I was late off that night, otherwise... '

'I'll be overseeing the investigation from a task force perspective, but will someone from CID be picking up the arson elements?'

'Ye... Uh, yes, more than likely.'

'OK. Unless there are any questions, I'll be in touch again, sir.'

'Uh, no... thank you. Thanks for the call.' Chilcott ended the call and slowly lowered the phone into his lap.

# CHAPTER TWENTY-EIGHT

5:47 p.m.

Kershaw checked the time on his watch. Christ! This was going to be painful if they were going to knock on his door after only a few hours of dropping him back home. He slammed his coffee mug down on the kitchen table, splashing the hot liquid up the back of his hand and stomped towards the unwelcome intrusion. The key was in the back of the door and he unlocked it as he spoke. 'Okay, okay, I'm here,' he called out. 'I'm fucking here.' He confidently swung the door open. 'You can tell that Dete...' He stopped himself short.

Standing in the rain wasn't the police as he'd expected. Standing before him, head bowed low with rain pouring off the dome of a full-face black motorcycle helmet stood a solitary figure in matching black leather motorcycle gear. Kershaw knew in an instant who it was. There was electricity that they shared, along with a blood type.

Barry Kershaw lifted back his head and slowly exposed wild black eyes behind the closed visor. 'You don't appear surprised to see me,' his muffled voice uttered from beneath the helmet.

'I... I... I don't know what to say?'

Barry blinked and looked beyond Kershaw into the hall-way. 'You alone?'

'Ye... yeah.'

The constant pitter-patter of rain bounced off Barry's helmet.

'How... when...' Brian tried to ask.

'That doesn't matter.'

'I... we... thought you were dead. We came back to rescue you—' Barry stopped Brian talking by extending a leather-gloved finger until it touched his lips. It was easier for Brian to say nothing, so he complied.

Barry returned his hand to a deep pocket at the side of his leather jacket.

'How have *you* been?' Barry asked.

'Don't worry about me, what about you? Does Tina-Marie know you're—?'

'Alive?'

Kershaw didn't answer.

'Aren't you going to invite me inside?' Barry asked.

Kershaw looked over his right shoulder into the hallway. 'Of course, sorry,' he said anxiously and turned back to find his brother pointing a Glock 19 semi-automatic pistol with a rock steady grip, directly in the centre of his forehead, a centimetre or two above the level of his eyes. Kershaw had been in these situations before, several times in fact and had always managed to somehow find a way out. Those milliseconds of instinctive reaction had certainly saved his life before, maybe not as many as a cat, but certainly more than once. This time, he was frozen to the spot with a sinking sense of inevitability.

Barry Kershaw didn't wait to pull the trigger. There was no compassionate farewell, or words of ironic meaning. He just had to compress the trigger to the sweet spot by around a tenth of an inch and complete the next part of his mission. The suppressed muzzle barely jerked in his hand and Brian Kershaw crumpled backwards to the floor in a puff of crimson spray, a nine millimetre round punching through his skull and brain with ease. Kershaw dropped where he stood as the echo of one hundred and forty decibels bounced off the hallway walls and escaped into the open air. Although the weapon had been suppressed, the shot fired was still louder than the average clap of thunder and it wouldn't be long before it drew unwanted attention.

Barry Kershaw looked down at his brother lying in a heap, motionless on the floor. He was disappointed not to have seen him twitching. In some ways, he wanted to see his brother suffer, but his death had been instant. He didn't have time to clean up the mess; he did, however, find the casing from the round down by his feet and picked it up. Without stepping beyond the threshold of the doorstep, a gloved hand removed the keys from the back of the door and locked it from the outside. He looked around, left, then right and sniffed the acrid bite of propellant in the air from his weapon, which he concealed once again upon his person. He could hear dogs barking in nearby houses and he swiftly scanned every curtain and drape for movement. Satisfied that he hadn't been compromised, he returned his hands to his pockets and strolled away to his motorcycle waiting in a nearby side road.

Detectives Kazia Arnold and Glen Peters arrived at Kershaw's address and knocked on the door, as directed by the boss. Theirs was the first of the bail checks and they both huddled beneath one umbrella as the rain continued to lash down in vertical rods. They waited ten more seconds and Arnold banged again.

'Surely not,' she said.

'Hold on.'

Glen Peters was a big lad, a tighthead prop for his local rugby team and was often used by the department when they needed a little extra "muscle". He balled his fist and it thundered against the UPVC door. 'There's no way he didn't hear that,' he said.

'Ooh, check you out all butch and everything,' Arnold quipped. They were often crewed together on action teams and enjoyed one another's company. To the outside, they probably appeared to be quite flirtatious with each other, but that was just healthy banter.

They waited a moment more. 'I don't believe it,' Arnold said. 'He's buggered off already.'

'He might be having a crap,' Peters replied, never straying too far away from his favourite form of humour.

'Try again,' Arnold said. 'We're not going anywhere until he opens this door.'

This time, Peters used the butt end of his Mini-Maglight torch and tapped it loudly against the metal flap of the letter box. Dogs started barking in the neighbouring properties.

'Sorry woofers,' Peters apologised.

'What do you think?' Arnold asked. 'Should we call it in?'

'Give it one more try. Can you see through the letter box?'

Arnold lifted the outside metal flap and used the stem of her torch to push the inside flap open and cast a beam inside the darkened premises. She tilted her head to get a better view. 'Oh, shit,' she cried out.

'What?' Peters shouted coming to her side.

'Put the door in,' Arnold shouted urgently, 'he's on the floor and his face is covered in blood.'

Peters rattled the door handle, it was locked. He looked around. 'Step aside, Kaz,' he said and paced several steps backwards. He took a running kick connecting just below the lock. The door moved but didn't breach. These modern UPVC frames were far harder to force than simple wooden framed doors.

'Romeo Alpha one seven four nine,' DC Arnold transmitted anxiously to comms. 'Priority assistance required at 45 Drake Avenue. Male occupant, believed to be Brian Kershaw is unresponsive on the floor inside the property with a significant head injury and large amounts of blood around his face. We are still attempting to gain entry. Romeo Alpha Hotel two-zero do you copy, over?'

DI Chowdhury wasn't listening to his personal radio, but one of the CMCIT team came running into his room and alerted him to the unfolding drama.

'Bollocks,' he yelled. 'Martin, with me,' he said to the detective who had just disturbed his stats inputting – a guilty pleasure that no other cops seemed to get off on. He grabbed his PR and confirmed the message with DC Arnold at the address.

'Get some keys,' he said to DC Martin. 'I'll notify the boss.'

Chowdhury sprinted to the DCI's office and burst in with a token knock at the door. 'Boss. Arnold and Peters have discovered Kershaw unresponsive on the floor of his property. Arnold says he's covered in blood.'

'Oh no! What are the injuries?'

'They're still trying to gain entry, Ma'am. This is all we need – he's only just come out of custody. We're still accountable.'

'That's the least of our problems, Jaz. Where's Chilcott?'

'I dunno.'

'Well find him and tell him to tie up with me ASAP. I'll get on the phone to the FIM and make sure they are monitoring. You go direct to the scene.' She paused. 'I don't like the sound of this. Take control of the situation and preserve all evidence.'

'Yes, boss.'

'Take the big red key and if they're struggling to get inside, force entry. Smash a window, do whatever.'

Chowdhury ran back out of the office with DC Martin following close behind. Foster sank her head into her hands and feared the worst.

# CHAPTER TWENTY-NINE

Saturday 29th February

3:45 p.m.

They travelled in an unmarked car. Chilcott was driving and two detectives flanked Brian Kershaw who was already under instruction to find and hand over the clothing that he took with him to Windsor. He was good to his word and relinquished a jacket and a top identical in appearance to the ones Chilcott had seen on the CCTV.

'Do you smoke?' Chilcott asked Kershaw.

'No.'

'Then why do you need a lighter?'

'Have you got my lighter? I left it at the hotel.'

'The cleaners found it in your room. I can't hand it back yet because we're running forensics on it.'

'What for?'

'Your fingerprints, DNA, that kind of thing. Just a little added safety-net to prove it was you in that hotel room.'

Kershaw bobbed his head in understanding.

'You didn't answer my question. Why do you need a lighter?'

'It's goes with me everywhere. You never know when you might need to make fire to cook or create a distraction.'

Chilcott narrowed his stare. 'Do you all do the same – Special Forces, I mean?'

'I think most practical people do. That little lighter has done some miles, I can tell you.'

'I bet it has.'

Satisfied the officers had secured everything they needed from within the home; Chilcott left Kershaw at the doorstep.

'Expect several knocks per day,' he said. 'It may seem like being a prisoner in your own home, but trust me, it's better than the real thing.'

Kershaw grunted with a nod of understanding.

'Your conditions apply every day until midday next Saturday. You'll hear from us before that time and we'll notify you and your solicitor if we need to extend your bail conditions. Be under no illusion, if we attend and you don't answer the door, you'll be going straight to custody.'

Kershaw tilted his head. 'Understood.'


The DCI had called for a briefing at four. Every officer on the investigation was present including the visual identification officers, researchers, recorders and receivers, analysts and the crime scene manager.

'You have probably already heard that Brian Kershaw has been bailed while we progress the line of enquiries about his brother, Barry – or Baz, as he was known to his regimental colleagues. I've spoken to the Ministry of Defence who confirm that Barry Kershaw was officially recorded as killed in action on January the ninth, two thousand and twelve, though they wouldn't provide any further detail. We *have* to be open-minded that Barry Kershaw is alive and is a suspect in these murders. Don't ask me how he has come back or how he escaped from Afghanistan, I simply don't know and it's not for us to become distracted by these details, however, we must view this as a genuine line of enquiry. In the meantime, I want us to draw up a rota for each day of three and four doorstep checks at differing times, including the hours of darkness and sleep. Our colleagues on uniform can incorporate those checks into their night shifts. Kershaw is aware that we will be door knocking and he will be home. The only exception to this is between the hours of twelve-midday and one thirty in the afternoon. During this time, he is permitted to leave the house and conduct essential living chores and routines. In addition to this, however, I have secured authority between these times for directed surveillance, so even when he is out of the property we will have eyes upon him at all times.'

A hand went up in the audience.

'Yes.'

'Ma'am, what if when we check the address we get no reply?'

'Then the door goes in. We then confirm his absence and we escalate from there. I want this department to conduct the initial checks at the address, until we are satisfied he's compliant and then Gwent officers will take over. The first team of two will check the address immediately following briefing. Sort out between yourselves who will do this and prepare a roster for the next few days. You will do this and you will make the checks at the designated times, is that clear?'

'Ma'am,' twenty-four voices said in unison.

Another hand raised into the air.

'Yes.'

'Ma'am, how realistic is it that the brother is responsible for these murders?'

'What do you think?'

'It doesn't sit well, if I'm honest, Ma'am.'

'None of this sits well. People have died and our job is to prevent further people dying and bring the culprit to justice. I don't know the truth, but we can't hide behind the evidence we've secured from Windsor. Brian Kershaw has been in far worse situations than being a prisoner in his own home. If he is innocent, I'm sure he can take it better than most.'

# CHAPTER THIRTY

By the time Foster and Chilcott arrived on scene, the street had been cordoned off ten houses either side of Kershaw's address. An excitable crowd of locals from the estate were filming and sending live stream footage of the unfolding drama from their mobile phones. Two armed response vehicles parked nose on to one another blocked the road at one end while three District squad cars blocked the other end. DI Chowdhury, DCs Martin, Arnold and Peters were the only officers anywhere near the entrance to the property, other than four firearms officers who had declared the inside of the property safe, and a pair of paramedics who had already pronounced Kershaw deceased at the scene. Kershaw had been shot once in the head. Not so much a murder, as an execution. Death had been instantaneous. Police tape tied around the wing mirrors of parked cars on either side of the road created a makeshift inner cordon to the crime scene.

The four Authorised Firearms Officers were now standing in overt positions at the front of the property holding Heckler and Koch G36s having been authorised by the FIM to deploy the big guns. The Operational Firearms Commander on seeing Foster and Chilcott arrive made a beeline straight for them.

'We've got one male victim with one fatal gunshot wound to the forehead. Your officers tell me you know who the victim is?'

'Yes,' Foster said. 'Brian Kershaw. He is… was, a suspect for the recent murder on St Michael's Hill.'

The OFC gave Foster a knowing look.

'Tell me about it,' she said. 'What's your status?'

'The FIM is awaiting an update, but we need to clear the streets of rubberneckers until we establish the threat level.'

'Agreed,' Foster said. 'Task the uniform officers to increase the outer cordon. We're going to assess the scene and I'll come back to you shortly.'

'Roger that.' The OFC turned about and went back to his officers.

As Foster and Chilcott entered the inner cordon wearing their paper coveralls and shoe-overs, DI Chowdhury provided them with updates. CSI had yet to arrive, but the traffic had been heavy and the police road block was sure to be having a significant impact on the volume of static traffic nearby. DC Arnold was maintaining a major incident log and signed them both into the crime scene.

Chilcott moved to the base of the doorstep, being mindful to stand to one side, preventing the disturbance of any potential forensics. He stared in through the open door at Kershaw's lifeless and crumpled body on the floor of the hallway. It was like looking at someone who had received an instant knock-out punch; legs and arms angled in unnatural positions, his body arched backwards over his heels, only, Kershaw had a dirty great hole in the centre of his forehead between his wide staring eyes.

He peered around the scene. There was the obvious seepage of claret framing Kershaw's head and upper torso, but something was missing from this scenario. He sucked in and imagined the shooting in his mind. He looked up at the deep grey sky. The rain had now stopped, but the ground was still wet under foot. He looked closely into the grooves of the rubber door mat on the inside of the hallway; they were perfectly dry. His eyes keenly scanned the beige carpet at the entrance; it too appeared dry apart from the route the firearms officers used to gain entry; one damp step upon another following the wall line. Chilcott looked back at the corpse. The shooter remained outside on the doorstep, or else Kershaw shot himself – but if that was the case, where was the weapon? An instantly fatal shot as this clearly was would still have the weapon in Kershaw's hand or some-where on the ground nearby, but the AFOs hadn't seized any weapons. He bit down on his bottom lip.

'We need a closer inner cordon,' he shouted across to DCs Peters and Martin. 'We need to preserve the doorstep and hallway.'

DC Martin grabbed a thick roll of police tape and together, they utilised a garden shrub to the left of the front door and the handle of a raid box positioned to the right of the entrance to create a secondary protective area.

'Where are SOCO?' Chilcott asked Chowdhury impatiently.

'They haven't been called Scenes of Crime Officers for

almost fifteen years. It's about time you got with the times,' Chowdhury answered smugly.

'Yeah, whatever. We need a forensic tent at the entrance to the door. The shooter didn't enter the house.'

'CSI are stuck in the road block traffic, they'll be with us shortly,' Chowdhury reported.

Chilcott huffed and looked out along the road far beyond the angled response cars keeping a now sizeable crowd at bay. The strobe lighting of six marked police vehicles created a dramatic backdrop.

He saw the detective looking right at him, but his heart rate stayed steady and unconcerned. His initial plan was to escape and evade, but something brought him back. He was still in his bike gear and helmet and was certain that from this range his identity would remain safe.

'Someone been shanked, bro,' an excited teenage male shouted above the muted voices of others present. 'Fuckin' pigs!' The young hooded teen bumped knuckles with three other hooded youths who began bobbing up and down with exaggerated hand gestures like they were on some sort of gangster rap video.

A female AFO came within feet as she passed the increasingly animated crowd and attempted to move the youths on, but all she got in return was a belligerent torrent of abuse.

'Fuckin' pig. Fuckin' bacon, innit.'

He looked coldly at the youths through his visor. *Disrespectful little fucks. I know what you lads need. A good bit of discipline.* He kept his hand deep inside his pocket, finger poised on the trigger guard, ready to engage in an instant if needed. The cop had a Glock 17 rigged to the outside of her thigh as well as the Carbine in her hands. She was now only inches away, but clearly had no idea who he was. The crowd were becoming agitated, some getting involved and supporting the police officer as the youths continued to spew spiteful anti-police rhetoric. Several other unarmed uniformed officers came running over to assist their colleague.

*Time to retreat.*

He'd seen enough and a second zoomed-in view of the photograph he'd taken just ten minutes earlier on his phone left him confident that he had the registration number of the car driven by the most senior investigating officers. Of course, CID didn't wear a form of identification like the stripes and pips of a uniformed officer, but from the way the others kowtowed when they first arrived, he guessed the woman was in charge and probably a detective chief inspector, because he already knew Chilcott was a DI; an addressed envelope on the small retractable table of his caravan had told him that.

# CHAPTER THIRTY-ONE

9:30 p.m.

A team of detectives gathered back at the station. Kershaw's body was already at the mortuary and one of the detectives was witnessing the expedited post mortem examination. Crime Scene Manager Parsons and his team of forensic officers were still at the scene, the road remained shut off at both entrances to the estate, and a specialist police search unit was conducting a fingertip examination for any signs that would lead them to the weapon or the confirmed identity of the assailant.

DCI Foster wrote *Barry Kershaw* on the white board and addressed the room in a sombre voice. 'This has just become a whole lot more complicated. The IOPC have been notified of Brian Kershaw's death due to his status of being on police bail at the time of his murder and they will be investigating the legalities of his detention and release from our cells. No one person is to blame for this unfortunate and unpreventable death, but I want each and every one of you to cooperate fully with the investigators when they arrive tomorrow.'

'Where are they coming from, Ma'am?' a detective on the front row asked.

'The Independent Office for Police Conduct are based in London, but let's not forget or be distracted from the focus of our investigation, which has to continue regardless of external influences. We now have three linked murders and you must concentrate on solving them all. I am certain the murder of Brian Kershaw is connected to the deaths of the other two girls.' She hesitated and caught Chilcott gazing wistfully towards the window. 'We must identify the suspect, get him off our streets and reassure our community.' She began to stumble over her words as she noticed Chilcott in her peripheral vision fidgeting and rubbing his face, while muttering to himself distractedly. She did her best to proceed over his background mumblings, but gave in and stared at her DI who seemed oblivious to the attention he was drawing upon himself.

'DI Chilcott,' she said.

Every head in the room followed the DCI's point of focus. Chilcott didn't look up from the sheet and continued mumbling incoherently to himself.

'Ahem,' the DCI said louder clearing her throat in a deliberate attempt to grab his attention. 'Robbie,' she said firmly, finally making him look up.

He peered at the boss and then at the faces in the room staring back at him.

'Something you want to share?' Foster asked.

Chilcott frowned and glimpsed again at the sheet of

intelligence in his hands. The DCI gave him an impatient lift of the brow.

He stood from his chair and approached the whiteboard, without answering. He took a marker pen and wrote *ASHER* in bold black letters. Beneath it he wrote *CHAMBERLAIN* and beneath that, he scribed *KERSHAW*. He turned to the DCI. 'He's picking them off in alphabetical order. Look at the names on the list.' He offered Foster the sheet from his hands.

She looked down and read the document in a silent moment and then turned back to her DI. 'Next on the list is Michael Lewis.'

Chilcott held another sheet in the air from the collated intel reports. 'Lewis has a last known address in Heath Halt Road, Cyncoed, Cardiff. We've got to get someone up there.'

'Any intelligence to suggest he has a family?' Foster asked.

'No. Nothing.'

'Detective Phillips,' the DCI said, 'get on to South Wales Police and obtain the name of the on duty force incident manager. Tell them I'll be calling in ten minutes.'

'Ma'am.' DC Phillips left the room with the urgency the situation demanded.

'What else do we know?' she asked Chilcott.

'Well, according to Chamberlain, Lewis is another ex-blade. He left the regiment before Chamberlain.'

'Who's after Lewis?'

'Samual Ling – still in active service. Address in Hereford which makes sense given the SAS base there.'

'Okay, well, he's probably better protected than anyone

right now. Fine, here's the plan. Find out everything possible about all the names on Chilcott's list. If he is correct, the killer is methodically picking them off. We need to know exactly where they live, who is in the family set-up, what they do for jobs, their dependants, their ages, schools they attend, cars they drive... I don't care how you get the information, just get it. I'll notify the FIM in Wales that we need officers to conduct a welfare check at Lewis's address.'

Chilcott stepped forwards to join the DCI. 'I want a minimum of three detectives working on this task. Phone home; tell your loved ones not to wait up. This is going to be a long night.'

'How long does it take to get to Cardiff?' Foster asked openly. 'Anybody know?'

'About an hour by car, traffic permitting, Ma'am,' Detective Dale Woods answered in his strong Welsh accent.

DCI Foster looked at her watch. 'Christ!'

'Woodsy, where are you from, son?' Chilcott asked.

'Rumney, Boss. I used to fish at Roath Park all the time. It's right near Heath Halt Road.'

'So you know the area well?'

'Lived there twenty-six years, before I sold my soul to live on this side of the bridge.'

'Right, you're on the first team heading out there tonight. I need two more volunteers.'

Every hand in the room went up.

Chilcott took a moment to look at his officers. 'Thanks everyone. Unfortunately we can only spare three officers for now, but don't worry, if you are left behind you'll still have an important role to play.' He immediately identified two other officers to go with Woods. 'Get your protective equipment up together; overt body armour, Pava spray, batons and cuffs. Take nothing for granted, Barry Kershaw is a highly trained and extremely dangerous individual.'

The DCI spoke next. 'I'll get on to firearms and agree a tactical plan. We know Barry Kershaw is armed and I'm not letting anyone from my team go unprotected.'

'What about the IOPC, Ma'am?' one of the officers asked.

'They'll just have to sit tight and watch how a real investigation takes place.'

Several officers chuckled.

Foster looked at Chilcott. 'We've just got to hope we're not too late getting to Lewis and his family.'

# CHAPTER THIRTY-TWO

It was gone eleven thirty by the time Chilcott and Foster made it out of the office and now they were back at Foster's home. Instead of coffee, they were sharing a pretty decent bottle of red.

'I appreciate this you know,' Chilcott said. 'The kindness you have shown me.'

'How's it all going with regard to your destroyed belongings?' Foster was happy to be talking about something other than the murders – anything was better than that subject at this time of the night.

'I wasn't insured. I lost the lot. I'm waiting for payday and then I'll pick up a few things and I'll be out of your hair.'

'It's no problem.'

'I'd like to pay you for the food and lodgings—'

'Nonsense. You don't have to do that.'

Chilcott puffed out an exhausted lung full of air and stared vacantly into space.

Foster watched him and took another sip of her wine. 'It has been good to see you back where you belong, Robbie.'

He raised his brows in appreciation at the remark.

'I know your methods can sometimes stray from the norm, but I have to be honest, if you hadn't pulled that CCTV stunt we probably wouldn't be any further forward, and now at least, we have our suspect...' she paused for a considered second, 'even if he is a ghost.'

Chilcott lifted his glass towards hers and they clinked them together. 'Here's to taking a few risks,' he said.

'Indeed, but don't go making a habit out of it.' She watched him a while with interest. He wasn't his usual settled self.

'Something's bothering you, isn't it?'

He ran his tongue around the inside of his lower lip and hid momentarily behind his glass as he took a large gulp of wine.

'What is it?'

Chilcott drew in a long steady breath through his nose until his chest filled to capacity and then forced it back out in a short huff. He scratched the side of his face.

'Come on. Tell me.'

He huffed again and gave in to Foster's persistence. 'Okay – I think Kershaw torched my van.'

Foster's features hardened. 'Go on,' she said leaning forwards.

'When I was talking to Brian Kershaw about his Zippo lighter, he said it was common place for his colleagues to carry something similar – an easy way to make fire.'

Foster shook her head. 'So? That doesn't automatically make them arsonists.'

'He qualified the statement by saying they would use fire to create a distraction, or confuse their enemy.'

'You think Barry Kershaw knew that was your caravan?'

'I do.'

'How would he know, I mean, we had trouble finding it.'

'So did the fire brigade.'

Foster frowned, unsure of his logic.

'I think he's been watching our progress. He'd obviously know the police would investigate the murders right from the time of Operation Fresco. He'd have to know to keep ahead of the game. He's methodical, calculating and precise in his movements. He's probably followed me home without me knowing. He's an expert in covertness. I simply wouldn't have known he was there.'

Foster breathed heavily. 'Why torch the van?'

'A distraction,' Chilcott shrugged. 'Cause confusion. Take my mind off the case. Ruin me a little more than he has already.'

Foster ran a considered hand over her chin and looked nervously to the door.

'But you're a police officer.'

'So? He's got absolutely nothing to lose – he's already dead according to the Ministry and I'm in his way.'

Foster blinked rapidly and looked away. 'If that's the case, then he probably knows where I live too.'

'Probably.'

'Shit. The fire wasn't set to cause a distraction; it was to lead you to me.' She stared at her DI with haunted eyes.

'I'd considered that scenario too,' Chilcott said.

Instinctively, she looked at the windows in turn and quickly stood up and drew the curtains closed.

'It's probably too late for that,' Chilcott said with regret in his voice.

'But how would he know you'd call me?' Foster thought aloud turning back to Chilcott.

He shrugged. 'Who else could I call?'

'But he wouldn't know that.'

'Wouldn't he?'

'Shit,' she spat again and looked frantically for her phone.

'What are you doing?'

'I'm getting the FIM to contact the firearms commander. I want armed response outside my house right now.'

Chilcott pouted. 'Probably wise, if they'll go for it.'

'I'm not going to give them a sodding choice.'

# CHAPTER THIRTY-THREE

Sunday 1st March

9:30 a.m.

The incident room was alive with activity. Every telephone, work station and chair was occupied by an ever growing number of officers progressing their specific tasks with due diligence, so much so, they barely noticed the two po-faced officials flanking the DCI as she showed them through the secure entrance and into her office.

The officers from the Independent Office for Police Conduct were both particularly dour-looking individuals; how you might imagine a tax collector, or a funeral director to look, only more humourless.

'We need the log of custody detention and details of all officers who have had contact or been involved in the Brian Kershaw investigation,' the tall, slim man said.

Foster noted he had a grey pallor, reminiscent of the *Spitting Image* characterisation of ex-Prime Minister, *John Major*. The classic catchphrase of *"More peas, Dear"* kept repeating over and over in her head as the man spoke and she did her best not to break out a smile.

'That is; everyone from the custody staff to the detectives working on the investigation and a detailed explanation of their contact,' the much shorter, but equally stuffy female IOPC officer qualified.

'I can get that to you by the end of Monday,' Foster replied with significantly more animation and urgency to her tone. 'We've got an ongoing situation that unfortunately needs all hands to the pump.'

'Not good enough,' the male officer said. 'That information should have already been made available to us *prior* to our arrival.'

DCI Foster forced a smile veiling her clenched jaw and moved between the two visitors, quietly closing the door to the outside office containing the team of detectives who were thoroughly engrossed in their enquiries. She turned on the spot and stood with her back to the door and her theatrical smile waned.

'We have every intention of cooperating with your investigation. We have nothing to fear and nothing to hide. But you must understand that you have entered a department of the police that does not have the luxury of time. My team are deeply involved in a live situation with a complex series of murders to investigate, and if, at times, my attention is on the job in hand and the welfare of my team, then so be it. Unfortunately for you, right now is one of those times.'

The female investigator scowled threateningly. 'There's

an easy way to remedy that little problem, I can assure you Detective Chief Inspector.'

'Let's just get something straight here, shall we,' Foster bit back. 'You are investigating the death of a police suspect shortly after his release from our custody unit. I get that and I understand the need for that. I wholeheartedly support the requirement for that, but lives are still very much at risk and if you think you can come down here and pull some juris- dictional plug, *you* will certainly be endangering more lives. I pray you understand the significance of that.'

'We'll be the judge of that,' the male investigator said. 'Task someone to take us to the custody suite now would you, please.'

Foster clenched her jaw ready to react, but acknowl- edged that if they were in the custody unit then they weren't going to be under her feet in the operations room. 'Fine,' she said, pretending to reluctantly concede her position. She opened the door and called DI Chowdhury to the office.

'This is Detective Inspector Chowdhury. He will accom- pany you to the custody suite at Patchway where Mr Kershaw was held and he'll provide you with everything you require.'

Chowdhury was about to argue his committed position with the boss, but clearly picking up on the fractious atmosphere in the room he thought better of it.

'I just need ten minutes to sort out my team,' he said to the two officers who were waiting, arms folded.

'We'll come with you,' the male officer said.

'Take your time,' DCI Foster said as they passed her on exit from the office. 'DI Chowdhury here will take care of your every need.'

As they filed out of the room, Chowdhury copped the DCI a look that she acknowledged apologetically and mouthed, *"Sorry"*.

Once they were gone from the incident room, she called Chilcott into the office.

'Keep a low profile, Robbie. When they get wind of how Chamberlain got that CCTV, you're going to be in for a hard time.'

Chilcott shrugged. 'Bring it on. It got us results quicker than anything else we tried.'

'It got us another dead body.'

He scratched behind his head and pouted like a teenager. 'Any update from South Wales?' he asked skilfully changing the subject.

'Woodsy spoke to Lewis's partner briefly last night with DI Slattery from Cardiff Central CID. He says Slattery's good – very much on our side. Jane Lewis confirmed her husband is overseas somewhere, hasn't been home since mid January and isn't due back for another six weeks or so.'

'I thought he was out of the SAS?'

'He is. He's doing some sort of consultancy work with the locals wherever he is in the world.'

'Blimey! What a life.'

'Tell me about it. I feel sorry for the poor woman, for all of them. Can't imagine what it must be like.'

'Any family?'

'Three kids, aged nine to fourteen.'

Chilcott closed his eyes. *Jesus!*

'Slattery has authorised an undercover surveillance team on the house with an ARV unit on rapid standby and the installation of panic alarms.'

'What about the schools?'

'That'll be more difficult to manage, for obvious reasons.'

'Does Jane Lewis work?'

'Receptionist at a local dental practice.'

'Why did it have to be somewhere with public access?'

'Because nowhere in our job descriptions did it mention an easy life.'

'Any indication that Kershaw's been there?'

Foster gave him a stale look. 'Well, she's still alive.'

Chilcott snorted.

'What are Pinky and Perky up to?' he asked referring to the IOPC investigators.

'They've gone over to the custody suite at Patchway with Jaz. Don't worry, it's Sergeant McDaniels on the desk this morning, he'll give them merry hell.'

'God! I feel sorry for them already.' Chilcott grinned as he thought about the reception the two visitors were likely to receive. Custody Sergeant McDaniels was a hard-arsed old sweat from Oban, Western Scotland. He struck fear into the most hardened of officers, and those were the ones he liked. Chilcott didn't fancy being in the shoes of the IOPC officers. 'Any update regarding the media?'

'They're all over Kershaw's murder like a prickly rash. Television, radio, social media, you name it.'

'Shit.'

'Don't worry, Chowdhury's in his element – he's got a Masters degree in media relations, remember?'

'Right up his street then,' Chilcott mumbled.

'Absolutely. No finer officer for the job. I've left him in

charge of handling the press office. He'll be giving an interview later today.'

'Poor sod. Are you staying put to fend off the wolves?'

'No way. We've got a train to catch.'

'A train… we?'

'We're going up to see Kershaw's widow.'

# CHAPTER THIRTY-FOUR

They sat down in the living room opposite the woman who looked about the same age as DCI Foster; forty-eight. Mrs Kershaw had a small frame and apologetic demeanour, probably from everything she'd been through in the years since her husband's death, and now Foster and Chilcott were about to shatter the poor woman's life for a second time.

'I like your house,' Foster said. 'Bright and airy, and I love the way you've designed your photo wall.'

Chilcott sat back and left the small-talk to his boss.

Tina-Marie Kershaw smiled, but didn't offer her own opinion on the observations. The lounge itself was small, but patio doors opened out into a conservatory of similar size with a number of well-tended plants in cheerfully coloured pots giving the space a relaxed and happy feel.

'Where did you say you were from again?' Tina-Marie asked them with caution in her voice.

'Bristol. We both work in the Major Crime Investigation

Department at Bristol. I'm the detective chief inspector and my colleague is one of my inspectors.'

Tina-Marie didn't attempt to hide her bemusement as her eyes widened and a look of uncertainty replaced her questioning features.

'Um, could I be particularly cheeky and ask for a cuppa? It's a very long train journey from Bristol to Nottingham,' Foster said.

Tina-Marie snapped out of her state of distraction. 'Of course, I'm sorry. I should've—'

'No – please. I wouldn't normally ask, only I'm gasping and I don't know when we'll get another chance to have a brew.' She was lying; she wasn't desperate for a drink in the slightest. She had a tea from the buffet car on the final stage of their train journey and Chilcott had a latte, but a cup of tea offers a degree of comfort and a shared connection. And that was something they were going to need if the increasingly untrusting Mrs Barry Kershaw was going to spill any beans about her husband.

She returned to the living room moments later and handed Foster a steaming mug of tea and Chilcott an instant coffee.

'Thanks. That's lovely,' Foster said taking the plain white mug and cupping it in her hands like it was a prize she didn't want to relinquish. She waited as Tina-Marie left the room again and returned soon after with her own cup. Foster smiled and watched over the top of her drink as they both sipped simultaneously. Chilcott silently applauded the DCI's technique.

'You... still haven't said why you're here?' Tina-Marie stuttered.

Foster lowered her drink and placed it on the table between them with a gentle clank of porcelain on glass. 'Barry,' she smiled politely. 'I'm afraid I'm here about Barry.'

'What? I don't—'

'Mrs Kershaw,' Foster said stopping the woman. 'I'm extremely sorry to have to ask this, but, when was the last time you saw your husband?'

'I'm sorry?'

'I'm aware of his military past and the fact he is recorded as deceased.'

'I beg your pardon?'

'Mrs Kershaw. This may seem insensitive and an intrusion on your private life, but we are investigating a series of murders involving your husband's old military unit.'

Tina-Marie's features became hostile and she pinned the DCI with a frosty glare. 'I don't see what any of that has to do with me or my husband.'

Chilcott intervened. 'We're asking you stay vigilant to...' he opened his hands and dipped his chin between them. 'Well, anything out of the ordinary.'

'That's not what she said. *She* asked me when I last saw my husband.'

Foster agreed. 'I did.'

'Why? Why would you ask that knowing the history, as you suggest you do?' Mrs Kershaw's voice was becoming increasingly barbed.

'I'm conducting a valid and important line of enquiries—'

'Are you married?' Tina-Marie cut across Foster.

'No,' Foster said, finding the question slightly uncomfortable to answer especially in the presence of Chilcott.

'Boyfriend. Girlfriend?'

Foster shook her head. 'No, I'm... single.' She half turned in Chilcott's direction. He picked up on it and flashed his eyelids to himself.

Tina-Marie shot the DCI a sharp, stabbing stare. 'Imagine *if you can*, hearing the news that you're never going to see the person you love ever again. And then imagine the pain of having to wait for his body to be repatriated so that he can be buried near to his home and his family.' Her voice wobbled.

Chilcott shifted uncomfortably in his seat. If only she knew the reality. Foster hinged forwards at the waist softly clearing the back of her throat ready to retort.

'And I've had to deal with that every single day for the last six years. My daughter was only seven when Barry...' She looked away and blinked a build up of moisture from her eyes.

'Did you know Brian, Barry's brother?' Chilcott asked.

'Of course I did. They were brothers. Very close brothers.'

The corner of Chilcott's eye twitched. 'He's dead.'

Tina-Marie stopped in her tracks. 'What?' she gasped.

'He was murdered at his home yesterday by the same person who murdered at least two other people connected in some way to your late husband's SAS unit.'

'He was murdered?' Tina-Marie wheezed holding a hand to her wide open mouth.

'Shot once between the eyes,' Foster clarified, putting the metaphorical cherry on the top.

'Oh my God!' Tina-Marie's voice was barely audible despite the utter silence in the room.

The officers allowed her time to digest the news and watched her body wilt.

'When did you last hear from Brian?' Foster asked after a further minute.

'I… ah. Um, I don't know. A year ago, maybe more.'

'You weren't that close to him then?' Chilcott commented.

'We kept in touch once or twice a year, I uh… oh God!'

'I'm sorry we have broken this to you today,' Foster said. 'We understand he had no family…' she lifted the intonation on the word *family* prompting Tina-Marie into an answer.

'No. He was never bothered by all that.' She stared vacantly into the steam rising from her mug.

Chilcott and Foster exchanged a glance and Foster gave him the nod.

'Tina-Marie,' Chilcott said making her look his way, 'we think Barry is alive and we believe he killed Brian, and the daughters of two of his former colleagues.'

If time could stand still, as so many people describe, then this was one of those times. Tina-Marie didn't react at first. It was almost surreal. She just gawped at Chilcott – unmoving – detached from reality – unfeeling. And then her brain reacted to the gravity of his statement. She suddenly slumped back in the chair, her face rapidly changing to aggression. 'I think I want you to leave.' She slammed her cup down firmly on to the coffee table and stood proudly with an outstretched arm. 'Go,' she yelled as tears poured from her eyes. 'Just fucking get out of my house.'

Foster and Chilcott didn't speak. What could they possibly say to comfort this poor woman who clearly wasn't expecting to hear this news. Foster held out a balled-up wad of papers from a nearby tissue box and Tina-Marie snatched it from her outstretched hand and plugged her eyes.

'You're wrong,' she wept. 'He's dead... they...' her lips moved but the words failed to escape from her mouth. Her face contorted as sticky tears entered the corners of her twitching lips. 'We buried him at St Martin's Church...' her voice fell away.

'I know there was a formal funeral, but we have spoken to members of Barry's squadron,' Foster said with calm professionalism. 'And they have confirmed that Barry's body was never... located.'

'No,' Tina-Marie blubbed. 'You're wrong.'

Foster touched the woman's arm and held it there. 'If he is alive, I don't think he's in this area. But I want you to contact me immediately if you see or hear from him. Is that understood?'

Mrs Kershaw didn't answer.

'Tina-Marie, is that okay? Will you call me the moment you have any contact from Barry.'

Her bloodshot eyes bounced around Foster's face and it was hard to establish if anything she was saying was being absorbed.

Foster placed a business card on the coffee table away from the spillage of tea. 'My details are there. I don't mind what time you contact me – day or night.'

'Wha... what... when?'

'I'm sure you've got a million questions whirring around

219

your head at the moment. Is there anyone you can call, anyone who can come over to be with you tonight?'

The crestfallen woman's head jiggled with confusion. 'Why hasn't he…?'

'We can't answer that.'

They stood a moment and watched the fragile walls that she'd built since her husband's death literally fall around her feet like a crumbling sandcastle. It felt wrong to leave her in this state, but in the same token, their presence wasn't helping.

'Call the taxi,' Foster quietly instructed Chilcott and he toddled off to the entrance hallway and gave the number a call.

'Three minutes,' he said returning soon after to the same scene of devastation.

'We'll give you some space to breathe,' Foster said. 'We're heading back to Bristol shortly, but you've got my number should you need it. I can come back any time.'


He was watching them. That's what he did best. That's what he trained so hard to do all those years before. Be patient. Be ruthless. Soldiers were ineffective if they second-guessed each move they made or questioned a command. When it came to killing it was simple; he didn't give it a second-thought. It was his job. It was them or him – a simple enough equation to comprehend, but maybe less so if you'd never faced a situation of finality. He had. And if his own daring escape from Afghan captors ever came to light, he'd be revered as one of the bravest and ruthless of them all. But it wasn't survival that drove him to escape, nor was it for accolades or the temptation of fame and fortune; it was revenge for their betrayal, plain and simple. Betrayal for leaving him to suffer at the hands of his captors. Betrayal at not coming back for him. And now they were all going to suffer pain and agony just the way he had. It hadn't mattered to him that he was taking the lives of innocent people, some as young as his own daughter. It was his right-eous obligation to get even and that was all that mattered. He was surprised at how quickly the police had caught on; he'd anticipated a connection of sorts by the time he'd get to Ling or Newell, given the disconnect in the police constabu-lary communications, but the detective with the caravan was astute. Perhaps it was an error on his part to pick them off the way he had. It was certainly bad luck for him that they shared the same police constabulary area. He was adaptable of course, missions in conflict frequently change in an instant. It was about being flexible in execution without compromising the desired outcome and he still had a way to go before he reached that particular status. He lit a roll up with his Zippo and watched the puff of smoke vanish into the cool night air. The draw on his cigarette was warm to the back of his throat – that was one of the pleasures he missed most in captivity.

He watched as a car pulled up and stopped outside of the address: *his* old address. The driver of the white Toyota Avensis daubed along the side in bold red *"Carl's Taxi"* signage, tapped a small digital display beside the steering wheel and double-tooted on the horn.

The front door opened and he saw a woman wave to the taxi driver who acknowledged her with a nod and a check of his wrist-watch, and then he saw the detective inspector.

The pair waited temporarily at the doorstep and looked back inside the house. He saw them take in the fresh breeze and wrap themselves tighter in their jackets.

He raised his field lenses to zoom in and lip-read as the inspector spoke.

*I think that went quite well, considering…*

Kershaw bit down hard, grinding his molar teeth against one another.

The woman officer who he had already estimated to be a detective chief inspector or possibly even a detective superintendent by the manner in which she was revered by her colleagues including the troublesome DI, jabbed the inspector in the ribs with the point of her elbow and he watched her mouth closely.

*I take no pleasure from that. It's clear we've just opened up a cavernous wound,* she said to the inspector. *Come on, Robbie, let's get home.*

The abrasive grinding noise from his teeth ceased and he fixed his gaze onto his new *mission* as they drove off, oblivious to his presence, no doubts heading towards the rail station.

# CHAPTER THIRTY-FIVE

He waited until the taxi was a minute away and stepped out from the shadows, carefully checking all around, before exposing himself from the thick cover of trees that lined the play park directly opposite his home. Six years, four months and twenty-seven days ago he last walked away from his front door, and that was the last time he saw his wife. After his escape, aided by a ragbag but efficient team of mercenaries, he stayed in the country as he recovered from his wounds. Working cash in hand, no questions asked gun for hire to any organisation willing to pay his rates – he gave no quarter as he systematically scythed down any Taliban stupid enough to cross his path. He knew he was officially killed in action having made a few simple indirect enquiries and he quite liked the freedom which came with that status. But now he was staring at a starker reality – the truth was out and he had to do something about it.

He paced quickly across the road, keen to notice that nobody was around and lifted the black duffle bag from his shoulder, placing it down on the doorstep. Inside, beneath a layer of folded towels, three hundred and fifty grand in clean untraceable notes was bound together along with a simple message on a folded piece of paper; *One day, I hope you'll find it in your heart to understand. B xx*

He rang the doorbell with a gloved finger hearing the shrill tone from inside the door and kept the button pressed for longer than average and swiftly dropped the visor on his crash helmet and sprinted away to the shadow and cover of the trees and his concealed Kawasaki Ninja motorcycle.

The door opened and he saw her. He didn't feel the tug of emotion he thought he might experience – that was good. That would be a weakness. His wife was crying which fuelled his anger and hatred rather than a maternal desire to comfort her. She noticed the bag and hesitated. He deliberately used a bag she was familiar with to prevent the cash getting into the wrong hands if she discarded it where it lay. She looked up suddenly, left and then right; desperate to see the messenger, but she wouldn't see him.

'Barry,' she called out half-heartedly. Her lips moved again, *Barry.* She leant over and took the handle of the bag, raising it from the doorstep. She looked around again and wiped her eyes with her free hand, then stepped backwards and closed the door.

He felt nothing warm or comforting about the situation, but knew he'd done the right thing by his wife. Now, it was time to do the right thing by him. He straddled the powerful bike, ignited the engine and screamed away leaving twenty-three years of memories behind in a plume of exhaust fumes.

---

# CHAPTER THIRTY-SIX

'What's the state of play your end?' Foster asked Chowdhury from the rear of the taxi as it waited at lights, still a good fifteen minutes' drive across town to the train station.

'It's all fine, Ma'am. The IOPC investigators are still here poking around,' he answered in hushed tones. 'They aren't best pleased you broke away to visit Nottingham—'

'That's just tough. How did they get on with dear old McDaniels?'

Chilcott smiled.

'I think he gave them more of a grilling than they gave him to be honest.'

'Good – that's what I like to hear.'

'What about the press release – how's that coming along?'

'Completed. I can email you a copy if you'd like to check it over before it goes out.'

'Good idea. I can read it on my phone. Any other news?'

'No updates from Cardiff or Hereford, I'm afraid, Ma'am.'

'No, that's probably a good thing – shows we're on top of things. Perhaps we should consider the next name on the list?'

'Jerome Middleton,' Chilcott said without hesitation.

'Where is Middleton from again?' she asked either of her DIs.

'Portsmouth, Ma'am,' Chowdhury answered quickest.

'Of course he is – why would I think he'd be anywhere closer to home…'

'Because they are already dead,' Chilcott mumbled.

'It was a rhetorical question, Robbie.' The DCI noticed the taxi driver paying rather too much attention to the conversation than he should have. 'OK, Jaz. Got to go. Keep me updated. Well done.'

'Yes, boss.'

'Perhaps you could meet us at the train station; we'll need a lift back.'

'Of course.'

'I'll give you a heads-up of our arrival time when we get closer.' She ended the call and gave the driver another firm stare.


They pulled up on Station Street and Foster paid the driver and gave him an extra fiver. She'd been careful not to say anything incriminating during her conversation, but cops looked like cops no matter what they wore or where they were. The Avon and Somerset document bag was also a sure-fire giveaway. She hoped the extra five pounds might help prevent loose lips from flapping.

'You want receipt, lady?'

'Yes, I'd better.'

'I make it for twenty-seven quids.'

The official tariff was twenty-two pounds – he'd been kind to include the tip.

'Much appreciated. Thank you for your help.'

'I hope you catch bad man, lady.'

Foster hesitated before taking the handwritten receipt from the driver. She smiled. 'So do I. So do I.'


His Kawasaki Ninja didn't stand out particularly. There was another, newer model in the same parking bay area as his but sporting the traditional lime green fairing, whereas his was predominantly black. A nice-looking red Ducati was next along the bay followed by a poxy little chicken-chaser that looked as if it was better suited to a museum, or scrap yard.

He had guessed correctly where the driver would drop them: it was a toss-up between two set down points, and despite leaving a minute or two after them, he'd still arrived with plenty of time to spare. He was still wearing his helmet and was as inconspicuous as he could be, with a little over ten minutes of free parking still remaining. But that was plenty time enough and he was conscious not to bring unnecessary attention to himself by going a minute over the twenty minutes of free parking.

The female detective looked directly at him and he froze momentarily. And then she continued to scour the immediate vicinity before following the detective inspector along the side road towards the large red-brick entrance to the old Victorian train station. He followed them, careful to appear as matter of fact as possible, using each piece of reflective glass on the parked cars and building windows to take in the maximum detail of his surroundings. They moved inside the building. He was now just feet away. He'd already clocked the double cameras angled down either side of the main entrance – he was being watched, along with every other person coming within ten metres of the building. The detectives walked towards a ticket booth. They hadn't booked two-way tickets. He liked how they rolled. He noted how they had also used the features of their environment to see who may be around them, but he made sure he was just outside of that range.

An elderly man at the front of the queue was having trouble hearing the desk clerk. This was his moment. He closed the gap between them and noticed a station guard clock him from the nearby ticket turnstile. He was no longer inconspicuous; he was a sizeable unit wearing black leathers and a jet black helmet. He came to within inches behind the female detective and quickly dug a blind-sided hand inside his pocket and pulled out a folded note, sliding it into her outer coat pocket without her noticing. He immediately turned and made against the flow of commuters.


Foster sensed movement behind and turned around. She saw a mass of people waiting behind her to be served and other people coming and going, but she didn't see Kershaw.


Foster opened the door to her office and Chilcott and Chowdhury filed in behind. 'Take a seat,' she said as she pulled out the chair behind her desk and sat down, still dressed in the long navy blue anorak she'd travelled in.

'The IOPC aren't happy bunnies at all,' Chowdhury said, taking a seat. His face was taut and stressed.

'Well that's just tough. I'll handle them, don't worry about that. I'm sure you managed to occupy them in my absence.'

Chilcott smirked as he lowered his frame down next to Chowdhury.

'They've now gone for the day; you'll be pleased to hear. They're staying in the Holiday Inn.' He leaned across and handed the DCI a business card. 'They said to call them on your return.'

The DCI slid the card towards her and peered momentarily at it before tossing it to the side. 'How did the press release go?'

Chowdhury lifted his chin – exuding satisfaction. 'It was fine. No problems, thank you.'

'No tricky questions?' Chilcott asked.

'None, that I hadn't already anticipated.'

'Good,' the DCI said. She looked at her watch, it was seventeen minutes to 6 p.m. 'We can all watch you on the news shortly.'

Chowdhury pursed his lips together and rolled his eyes towards Chilcott who gave him a *Clint Eastwood*-type narrow stare. *Are you feeling lucky, Jaz?*

'Anything from Cardiff yet?' Foster asked giving her DIs a once-over.

'Nothing,' Chowdhury replied.

'What's he doing? Do you think he's aware of our operation?' Foster asked.

'Hard to tell, Ma'am,' Chowdhury said.

'Who knows, Julie,' Chilcott countered his voice far more familiar and relaxed.

Foster leaned back against the spring of her chair looked at them both individually and sighed despondently. 'It's about time you two sorted your shit out. We can't afford to have you two scoring points off one another, or seeing who can piss the furthest up the urinal wall—'

'We have individual stalls, not—'

'I don't give a toss what you have, Robbie. This nonsense between you ends right now.'

'Probably sits down anyhow...' Chilcott muttered beneath his breath.

Chowdhury squirmed in his seat as anger built to bursting point.

The DCI drove her hands deep into her pockets and glowered at Chilcott. 'Don't push me, Rob...' She paused and looked down at her left hand, pulling out a folded envelope. 'What's this?' She lifted the envelope in front of her eyes and lowered it onto the table in front of her. 'Either of you know what this is?'

They both shook their heads.

'What is it?' Chilcott asked.

'A sealed envelope.'

'Open it.'

The DCI gave them both a suspicious glance and then slid her finger beneath the flap, removing a handwritten note: *Don't try to stop me. I can no longer be responsible for anyone getting in my way.*

'If this is some kind of sick fucking joke, Robbie—'

'What? I don't know what it is?' he pleaded with open hands.

She tossed the paper through the air in his general direction, the note flipping out of control before falling short onto the floor. 'Right, I've just about had a gut full of your games, Robbie…'

As she spoke, Chilcott picked the crumpled sheet from the floor and read it. He suddenly stood up. 'Where did you get this?'

'Oh, come on. You can drop the act now. It's really not funny and not the slightest bit—'

'Seriously,' he shouted taking Foster by surprise with his strong tone. 'Where did you get this?' His stare was fierce and Foster instantly knew that he wasn't joking.

Her face quickly melted and she rose up from her chair.

'We need to get this to forensics,' Chilcott said urgently. 'It may have his DNA… and the envelope,' he said pointing to the discarded standard white envelope crumpled up on the DCI's desk. 'Quick,' he said to Chowdhury. 'Get me some gloves and forensic bags.'

'Yeah, right,' Chowdhury said dismissively. 'Like I'm gunna—'

'Just get the fucking bag, Jaz,' the DCI snapped.

As Chowdhury scurried out of the door, Chilcott and Foster locked eyes.

'He got close enough to you to plant this on you?' Chilcott questioned aloud.

Foster shook her head. 'He couldn't have. I can't think of a moment when he'd have the chance. We were together the entire time.'

'Shit!' Chilcott spat. 'He's not in Cardiff… he was in Nottingham.'

'His wife!'

'Bollocks!' Chilcott ran for the door. 'I'll get on to Nottingham CID.'

Foster stood rigid staring down at the note. Chowdhury came back through the door wearing a pair of blue latex gloves, holding two clear evidence bags in front of him like a fresh out the box probie at his first drugs raid. 'Where's he going all in a hurry?'

# CHAPTER THIRTY-SEVEN

Chilcott came back into the DCI's office ten minutes later. 'It's okay, she's fine and their daughter's fine too,' he reported.

The DCI was sitting at her desk, arms tight in to her body like a naughty school girl waiting to be reprimanded by the head teacher.

'They've got the house on overt surveillance – an armed response unit is parked right outside and detectives are speaking to Tina-Marie as we speak. He'd be mad to make an attempt to get inside,' Chilcott continued.

'She's okay?' Foster asked with a timid voice.

'Teary, but holding up well, by all accounts. She's obviously made of stern stuff.' He narrowed his stare and noted the fear emanating from his boss. He'd never seen her this way before.

'Hey, come on,' he said squatting down beside her chair, placing his hand on her arm. 'If he was going to hurt you, he'd have done it already.'

'Oh, that makes me feel much better,' she glowered.

'You know what I mean, I'm sorry if it came out…' he stopped talking, seeing her tears. He stood up slightly and put his arm around her shoulders. 'Come on, Julie,' he said calmly. 'We've got protection from the firearms unit. Kershaw can't get to us.'

'He got to you, Rob, and he's got close enough to me to put something in my pocket without me knowing.'

Her tear-ridden eyes didn't lie. He had.

The DCI looked distantly ahead. 'How can we stop him?'

'I don't know yet, but we will.'

'Will we? Do you really believe we can?'

Chilcott didn't answer.

Foster pressed a hand to her forehead. 'This changes everything. How can we be the protectors if he can get to us so easily?' She searched Chilcott's face. 'How can one man cause so much disruption? Christ! This is now a national incident; it's crossing constabulary boundaries, it's the main news story across the channels! This has got far bigger than we can manage.'

Chilcott stood up easing his knees that had been screaming in pain since he squat down next to her. 'We need Chamberlain. We need his connections. We need the military to work with us,' he said.

Foster turned in her chair and stared out of the window into the darkness and the floodlit carpark below. 'You're asking for one of the most secretive military organisations to turn on one of their own, Robbie.'

'One of their own who is targeting and killing his own people, Julie. I don't imagine for one minute their loyalty stretches that far.'

She didn't answer and kept looking outside. 'What if he is out there now? We'd never know. This is a living bloody nightmare.'

The landline broke into life with a shrill ring making them both jump. Foster picked up the receiver and listened to the voice on the other end. She listened for a long moment and locked eyes with Chilcott as she rose from her seat. 'Where?' she asked. She broke away from Chilcott's gaze and looked at her watch. 'When?'

'What is it?'

Foster held a hand up to stop Chilcott interrupting. 'Got contact details?' She waited for the answer. 'Good – email them through to me.'

She gently lowered the receiver and perched herself down on the lip of the desk.

Chilcott didn't ask. He already knew what was coming.

'Middleton's dead.'

'Portsmouth?'

Foster nodded.

'Argh!' Chilcott groaned. 'It's like he's everywhere at the same time. How did Middleton die?'

'Garrotted.'

Chilcott winced.

'They had to peel the wire out of his neck.'

'Where?'

'Home address.'

'We need to be smarter. This is turning into a disaster.'

'Okay.'

'Okay?' Chilcott repeated.

'Let's get Chamberlain back in. This has gone beyond our control. If we can't think like Kershaw then we've no chance of capturing him, he's just too damn slippery.' She puffed out her cheeks in resignation. 'I'll get back on to Special Branch and see what they can do to assist.'

'They may even view it as a terrorist crime and take it on, considering he's targeting military operatives.'

Foster inclined her head and stared back out of the window.


Stephen Chamberlain followed Chilcott through to the main briefing room. He was still displaying the bruises from his confrontation with Brian Kershaw and wasn't expecting to walk into a room filled to the brim with detectives, if he had, he may not have agreed to come. DCI Foster was stood front and centre and greeted him with a handshake and introduced Chamberlain to the assembled detectives.

'We've brought you here, because we can't do this without inside help,' she said. 'So far, we believe that Barry Kershaw is responsible for the murders of five people associated in some way to your old unit, including your daughter, Samantha. He's a step ahead of everything we are doing, so we need to start thinking like him. You know him as well as anyone and you want him captured as much as we do.'

Chamberlain wiped beneath his nose with the back of his thumb and looked at the faces of the officers staring intently his way. 'And if I help you?' he asked turning to Foster.

'Then we'll make sure the judge is fully aware of your invaluable cooperation in helping capture someone who is rapidly becoming one of the most wanted men in the United Kingdom,' she replied stoutly.

'And you'll have the satisfaction of seeking justice... a lawful way,' Chilcott added.

Foster shot him a dumfounded look. If it wasn't for Chilcott, they wouldn't be in this God-awful mess in the first place.

Chamberlain thought for a moment and then asked, 'What do you need?'

Chilcott answered. 'We need you to put yourself in his shoes. Think like him. Act like him. Pre-empt his next moves.' Chilcott shook his head. 'We can't. We don't have your ability or skills to think like the Special Forces. You do.'

Chamberlain bit his lip. 'Okay.'

'Okay,' Chilcott repeated. 'Thank you.'

'On one condition,' Chamberlain said standing taller.

'Go on,' Foster said.

'I do it my way, without the shackles of the law.'

'We can't act above the law—'

'Then you won't catch him.'

'We cannot and will not act in a manner that is above the law,' Foster repeated in no uncertain terms.

Chamberlain shrugged. 'Then you've already lost.'

'Show him the note,' Chilcott said to Foster.

She scratched the side of her face and looked at the collaboration of detectives. 'After briefing,' she said noticing the team reacting with interest to the news they so far hadn't been privy to hearing.

'Okay everyone,' she said. 'You've got your enquiries to continue with—'

'Tell them,' Chilcott spoke loudly over the top of her.

Foster rubbed her face again.

'Tell them. They all need to know.'

Foster eyeballed Chilcott and then looked away. 'I agree,' she whispered. 'But you tell them.'

Chilcott cleared his throat. 'Okay everyone, listen in hard. This is important. This is for your own safety.' He glanced at his boss who was looking down at the floor. 'As you know, my caravan was destroyed by fire earlier this week. We now suspect that Barry Kershaw was responsible and deliberately set it alight.'

Murmurs and gasps of shock rippled through the seated detectives.

'And today…' he paused and checked on his boss again. 'Barry Kershaw came close enough to DCI Foster to place a note inside her coat pocket. We simply didn't know he was there.'

Everyone stared in total horror at the update.

'What did the note say?' an officer in the audience asked.

'It was a threat,' Foster said finally looking up. 'It was a threat to cause harm to anyone who got in his way.'

'That means all of us then?' the same detective said.

'Yes it does,' Chilcott said boldly. 'All of you must take extra vigilant care. Change your routines at home, park somewhere different each night. It will be a pain in the arse, but until we get Kershaw in, we are potentially *all in his way*.'

'He's changed his mission,' Chamberlain announced.

Chilcott, Foster and the entire room hung on those words.

'Meaning?' Chilcott asked.

'Your caravan. The note. He's given warnings, but he won't give them twice.'

Chilcott felt unease building rapidly in the pit of his gut. 'Explain, please,' he asked.

'Assuming no one else has received a note or some kind of sign, he's going for the hierarchy. Cut the head off and the body will fall.' He peered menacingly at the DCI and her DIs. 'He's got a second mission.'

'Jaz,' Chilcott said. 'Anything unusual happened to you or your family?'

'No,' Chowdhury answered, his face displaying clear alarm.

'Good. I think the best practice is to carry on as normal, but be aware.'

'I'm going to speak to the ACC and escalate this with firearms,' Foster said. 'We need twenty-four hour protection when we're outside of this building.'

'He must be staying somewhere, has to be,' Chowdhury said. 'Find out where and we'll have him.'

'No,' Chamberlain corrected the DI. 'He's accustomed to long missions deep behind enemy lines. He won't need a base.'

The detectives fixed their stares upon Chamberlain.

'So what now?' Chilcott asked him.

'You're trying to catch a professional killer,' Chamberlain said. 'And this one has fuck-all to lose – he's already dead.'

'Where do we start?' Chilcott pressed.

'You don't. He's in control.'

'So how the bloody hell are we meant to stop him?' a frustrated Foster bit back.

'*You* change his mission.'

'How exactly?' Chilcott asked.

'You become his main focus and draw him out.'

'What?' Foster said incredulously.

'You'll have more control of the situation by making yourselves the main targets. You've got firearms support, you can almost create the mission for him, that way you can prepare and react proactively.'

None of the detectives spoke.

'You've riled him. That's a good thing. Use it to your advantage.'

The DCI stepped back with a look of utter disgust. 'Are you asking us to be his bait?'

Chamberlain pouted. 'I suppose I am.'

'How,' Chilcott asked.

'Has his name been publicised yet?'

'No. Not his.'

'Do it. Expose him. He's currently operating below the radar. Make it known that he's still alive. Show his face to the public.'

'Jaz,' Chilcott said. 'Can you get on that, buddy?'

'Sure. I can write a press release and disseminate it wherever and whenever.'

'Go national,' Chamberlain said. 'All news channels, TV, radio, daily rags.'

'And then what?' Foster asked.

'We wait.'

'Wait for what?'

'For him to neutralise you.'

# CHAPTER THIRTY-EIGHT

Monday 2nd March

The press release went out as planned and in time for the waking public to see Barry Kershaw's name linked to the murders of the five victims around the country. DI Chowdhury had been provocative enough to tempt Kershaw into some kind of reaction. Just what, remained to be seen.

The DCI had spent the night formulating a tactical plan with the Firearms Commander and Chief Constable and now they were all occupying the largest briefing room at Central, along with the Operational Firearms Commander, his team of AFOs, the most senior ranking duty officer from Bristol, the operational team of detectives and the unprecedented presence of Stephen Chamberlain who was watching from the back of the room.

They had already watched a replay of Jaz Chowdhury speaking to the cameras outside of Force Headquarters and now they were about to receive their orders.

The DCI chaired the briefing with the top brass seated immediately in front of her.

'In my twenty-three years of service I have never had to hold a meeting like this, or even witness one to be honest. We are all gathered here because of the significant threat posed to the public and to us all by Barry Kershaw. You've seen the press release, what many of you don't know is that both DI Chilcott and myself have been targeted by Kershaw in recent days. This is a real and genuine threat. We must all consider our safety and that of our families as our highest priority.' She paused and swallowed deeply. 'Yesterday evening, Chief Constable Maynard, Chief Inspector Planer acting in her role as the strategic firearms commander and myself, drew up a tactical firearms response to the threat level. I will pause in a moment to allow Chief Inspector Planer to brief her team on this, but the nation's eyes are now upon us. What we are proposing,' she said coughing behind closed lips, 'is to draw Kershaw out, and the press release is the first stage of that. We can only assume that he will see it. What we must hope is that he feels compelled to react and that's where you come in to this complicated and unparalleled operation.' She looked at Chilcott seated alongside the strategic firearms commander. 'Those of us in direct line of danger will be required to wear covert protective armour at all times when outside of secure police environments and our homes have been installed with panic alarms for added security. Firearms ARVs have been tasked to provide regular patrols in the areas most at risk and they have been authorised to deploy their assault rifles at the start of each shift, until the threat level is reduced. I would ask for your patience and professionalism during this time. You are not permitted to divulge the details to anyone outside of this room. That is paramount to all of our safety.' She clicked a button on the overhead projector control and an image of Barry Kershaw in his service days came up on the screen. 'Take a good look,' she said. 'This man is lethal. He is trained to Special Forces levels of escape, evasion and survival. He has particular skills in covert surveillance and intelligence gathering. We don't know how or when he escaped captivity by the Taliban. We can only assume he suffered greatly and we cannot anticipate the degradation of his mental health. He is systematically destroying the lives of the special air service squadron who he appears to blame for his capture and subsequent lack of rescue. He has already killed SAS soldiers and family members. We must view Kershaw as deranged, highly unpredictable and an extremely dangerous individual.' She saw Stephen Chamberlain shifting on his feet at the back of the room. 'I'd like to personally thank Stephen Chamberlain who is with us at this briefing today, for his cooperation and insight into Kershaw's mind. Some of you won't know, but Mr Chamberlain's daughter was the third victim of Kershaw that we know of.'

Heads turned and peered Chamberlain's way.

'Although Mr Chamberlain is no longer in active service, he served alongside Kershaw and was present during his capture. Treat Mr Chamberlain with the utmost respect and listen to what he has to say. It may save your lives.'

She looked over the heads and Chamberlain mouthed his thanks.

'Right, I'll now hand over to Chief Inspector Planer who will provide the detailed tactical plan for the firearms response.' Foster walked forwards and sat between Chilcott and Chowdhury.

As the SFC addressed the room, Chilcott leaned across Foster. 'Rousing,' he said. 'I think you've put the shits up everyone with that speech.'

Foster faced him with a blank expression. 'Not least me, Rob. Not least me.'

# CHAPTER THIRTY-NINE

6:20 p.m.

Foster and Chilcott left the Major Crime Unit in the DCI's car as planned. She waved to the guard seated in the glass-walled security office and he released the barrier to allow them free. They were dressed in covert body armour beneath their regular-looking clothes. Anyone could tell they were wearing them if they were within arm's length, but to everyone else they were just regular detectives heading home after another long day at the office.

She followed the usual route from Feeder Road and they chatted as normal. But nothing felt normal about this journey and their acting ability was being severely tested. Chilcott had been in sticky situations in the past, but nothing compared to this. No amount of witty banter was going to get him out of this particular scenario, should it all go wrong.

Instead of heeding Kershaw's advice, Foster had deliberately put herself and Chilcott in the firing line, quite literally. Little was known about Kershaw's accessibility to firearms. He was certainly in possession of a 9mm handgun, according to the forensic report on his brother's fatal wound, the armoury suggesting he used a Glock 19, being a widely used weapon of choice for the Special Forces. How he got the weapon was anyone's guess. He was still clearly well connected and able to fund his own personal arsenal of weaponry, but what else did he have? He was known to be a dead-eye shot with a rifle, excelling in this discipline along with most others, according to his training report dutifully supplied by Special Branch who were in close liaison with the Ministry of Defence over the increasingly delicate "situation", as they termed it.

They didn't know if the car had been bugged and had to assume that it had, so their conversation was generally benign; what Chilcott fancied for tea, when he was moving out and other topics of this ilk.

It took them longer than normal to reach home. A small collision on the M32 had caused a nauseatingly slow delay to their progress. Chilcott had secretly even questioned whether Kershaw had set it up for some tactical reason, and wondered if Foster had considered the same. If she had, she wasn't showing it.

Their progress was being monitored at the control centre at HQ. Foster's car had been secreted with a tracker and detectives were dotted in strategic positions ready to launch drones should the need arise. Quebec ninety-nine, the force Eurocopter was also on standby, but would only be used in the event of a significant incident. There was only one helicopter for the entire force and the chances of a call out to an ongoing burglary, car pursuit, high risk missing person or any manner of other demanding jobs was high.

Foster pulled in outside of her home and they exited the car in silence. Chilcott felt an urge to turn about and search the immediate vicinity, but forced himself against this. They had been briefed to look nervous, no issues there – that was coming naturally enough, but it was essential they didn't go too overboard.

Control centre knew they were home and the second part of the operation kicked in. Covert ARVs were instructed to take up strategic positions within a quick strike range of the house. Overt ARVs had been cruising the street several times that day, but they weren't coming now, not for the next couple of hours at least. They chose the times deliberately; when the firearms crews would be vying for their refs break and a bite to eat – a time when they were at their most vulnerable. If Kershaw had done his homework, which he surely would have done, he would know the routines of the officers.

Foster stopped at the doorstep and looked down at one of the potted plants positioned either side of the entrance. It had been moved and the telltale ring of dirt could be seen just off centre.

'That's odd,' she said.

'What is it?'

'The flower pot – it's been moved.'

Chilcott's chest sank to his belly and he turned around. Cars continued to pass at a sedate twenty miles per hour.

Foster dug out her keys and unlocked the door.

'Careful,' Chilcott whispered. 'Let me go first.'

Foster stepped aside and Chilcott walked through the

doorway. The hall was dark, so he flicked on the light. He looked down at the floor for signs of damp feet, but there was nothing. He listened for a moment and then beckoned Foster to come inside.

'Jesus, Rob, I'm on eggshells here.'

'Tell me about it.'

They'd been briefed not to disclose the operation just in case Kershaw had found a way to tap into their conversations.

'Cuppa?' Foster asked.

'Sure.'

She went through to the kitchen and stopped abruptly. 'Rob… Robbie,' she said more urgently.

'Yeah, what is it…' he joined her in the kitchen and stopped alongside her.

Lying on the breakfast bar was an A3 sheet of paper with a hierarchal family tree of the officers who worked in the Major Crime Unit, including their dates of birth. Foster's name was at the top, Chilcott and Chowdhury's underneath, and beneath them the names of the sergeants and constables.

'He's been here,' Foster breathed.

A chilled shiver shot down Chilcott's back and rocked him to his feet. He looked closer at the sheet of paper. 'He's put an address beneath Jaz's name.'

Foster stepped forwards to take a closer look. 'Shit, that is his address.' She quickly removed her phone desperately scrolling through the list of contacts until she got him.

'Jaz, it's Julie. Are you home?'

'Yeah, I'm just cooking for the kids. What's up?'

'Lock your doors, stay away from the windows and don't let anyone outside.'

'What's going on?'

'I'm redirecting the firearms teams to your address. He knows where you live.'

Chowdhury didn't speak, but Foster could hear panic in his breathing.

'It's okay. It's okay – Chilcott's on the phone to the FIM right now. We'll have someone to you shortly. Just stay put.'

'Oh no,' Chowdhury said quietly.

'Have you got any body armour with you?'

'My bo… no… it's at work.'

'Okay, don't worry, the ARVs are on their way.'

'How do you know this?'

'That doesn't matter right now, just keep your family safe and make sure your phone is fully charged.'

'Is he coming for me?'

'It looks that way. We'll get a local response car to you ASAP.'

'Okay.'

'Jaz, it'll be alright. Just stay close to your family and we'll be to you as soon as we can.'

'What do I tell them?'

'I don't know, think of something.'

He didn't respond.

'Jaz, I've got to go. Keep your phone on standby.'

'I will,' his timid voice replied.

Foster put the phone down and called the FIM herself confirming the changes to the operation.

'I'm just going to check upstairs,' Chilcott said as Foster continued updating the force incident manager.

Chilcott looked at the deep soft pile in the dark beige carpet on each stair tread. There were no marks or distinguishable footprints, so he stepped cautiously upwards, his eyes trained above, his heart pounding like a freight train. He got to the top and entered the first room. His body was like a block of ice, frozen with fear. The room was clear. He moved on to Foster's room – there was nothing out of the ordinary, and finally he walked to his room and looked around from the doorway. It looked just as he'd left it. He stepped inside and stared down at the bed. A lump was beneath the duvet rising noticeably up from the centre of the bed. His breathing became shallow and he grasped the corner of the cover tossing it back with a sharp tug. It was his pyjamas. His head pounded with the adrenalin surge and he turned and went back downstairs.

Foster was still on the phone. Chilcott checked the front door was locked and closed all the front-facing curtains on the ground level.

'Right,' Foster said coming into the living room. 'Forensics are on the way over here and the ARVs have been reassigned to Jaz's home address.'

'How long before they get there?'

'Seven or eight minutes. They're going Code One.'

Chilcott rubbed his mouth. 'Are all the ARVs going?'

'Yes. Until we can secure Jaz and his family then they're going to remove them to a safe place.'

Chilcott's face dropped and he questioned his own mind.

'Are you okay?' Foster asked.

'What if *this* was part of his plan, create a diversion; remove the threat of the ARVs.'

'How do you mean?'

'It's right we must protect Jaz and his family, but what if Kershaw isn't there... what if he's still here... somewhere out there.' He pointed outside.

The dawn of recognition painted the DCI's face. 'Oh shit!'

Chilcott got on his phone to the operational firearm commander, currently hotfooting it towards Jaz Chowdhury's home address.

'Jimbo, it's Chilcott. We've made a mistake. We need one of your units to return to us and take us away with Chowdhury and his family.'

'Alright, boss,' OFC James Wicks replied over the din of wailing sirens. 'I'll turn back Flannery and Hooper to pick you up. You can stay with them while we secure DI Chowdhury and his family.'

'Thanks, mate. Appreciate it.'

'Give us a few minutes and we'll be there.'

'Understood.' Chilcott ended the call.

'Get a few things together. We can't stay here tonight, not until Kershaw's out of the picture.'

'How long have we got?'

'A few minutes.'

Foster nodded and made her way quickly up the stairs throwing a few toiletries, underwear and comfortable clothing into a travel bag. Chilcott didn't have to worry about that, he was practically wearing his worldly possessions.

Several minutes later and the door bell sounded.

Chilcott went to the window and peeked through the curtains outside. 'It's them.'

'Who is it?' Foster asked through the closed door still careful to double-check.

'AFO Hooper, Ma'am,' the answer came from the far side of the door.

Chilcott went across. 'That's them.'

Foster opened the door and saw two fully-kitted AFOs standing on the doorstep, each sporting a Heckler & Koch G36 assault rifle across their chests.

'Are you two a sight for sore eyes? Please, come inside,' she said.

'Ma'am,' they acknowledged and stepped in.

Foster turned and began to walk back through the hallway. Suddenly a *thwacking* sound filled the room followed by the instant felling of AFO Hooper onto the hallway floor in screams of agony. Foster turned and saw the officer clutching his knee, blood spurting out through his fingertips. AFO Flannery took immediate evasive action and took a position of cover further inside the kitchen.

'Get back out of view,' she shouted. 'Get back, Ma'am.'

Chilcott ran across to Foster and bundled her to the floor and they scrambled behind the kitchen wall.

Screams of pain and terror from Hooper filled the entire house. Flannery pressed her emergency button and screamed down the Airwave radio to comms. 'Oscar Foxtrot Six One One, priority. We're taking fire. Officer down. Officer down. Immediate back up required.'

'Hoops, are you okay?' Flannery called out. 'Can you crawl to cover?'

'He's taken out my fucking knee cap,' Hooper squealed.

'Try crawling to me,' Flannery directed.

'We need to close the door,' Chilcott shouted over Hooper's cries. 'He must be out there with a rifle.'

'I didn't even hear the shot,' Foster said all of a panic.

'He's using a suppressor,' Flannery said. 'Hoops, can you get to the door and close it?'

'Argh, argh,' Hooper continued to scream whilst curled up tightly trying to keep his knee together with his bloody hands.

'Chase the back up!' Foster ordered AFO Flannery.

'Oscar Foxtrot Six One One, priority,' Flannery shouted down her Airwave radio. 'Oscar Foxtrot Two Two Eight Three has been shot. Immediate back up required.'

'Roger,' the calming voice of comms came. 'Units are en route to your location. Take cover and await their arrival. Medical assistance has been requested.'

'Roger,' Flannery noted. 'Approach with extreme caution. The target's location is line of sight of the front door, repeat, line of sight of the front door.'

'What's out there?' Flannery asked DCI Foster. 'What features?'

'Um,' the DCI fumbled over her words. 'It's open common land, uh... a small wooded area a hundred yards or so away and that's it.'

'That's where he is.' Flannery got back onto her radio. 'He's in the trees, over.'

'We've got to get that front door closed,' Chilcott said desperately, 'and get Hooper away.'

'Hoops,' Flannery shouted, 'can you get to the door?'

Amidst the tears of agony, Hooper began to pull himself around until he was facing the outside, his hand reaching out for the edge of the door. A slick of crimson blood left a snail trail behind him. Just as he touched the wooden edge of the door, another *thwack* zipped through the air and Hooper slumped motionless on the floor. His cries of agony immediately extinguished.

'Hoops?' Flannery called out inching her face around the edge of the kitchen doorway. 'Hoops?'

Hooper was unresponsive.

'Oh my God!' Foster said at barely a whisper. 'Is he dead?'

'Hoops. Hoops... Hooper,' Flannery called out, but still no reply. 'I have to see.'

'No,' Foster said looking deeply into the fiery young eyes of the brave constable. 'Don't go out there, he'll shoot you too.'

'I can't leave him.' She pressed the transmit button on her radio. 'Oscar Foxtrot Six One One, how long for that back up,' she shouted.

'ETA three minutes, Six One One, over,' comms replied.

'That's two minutes too long,' she replied, her voice shaking and desperate. 'I think Hoops is dead.'

The sound of the transmit button at the other end clicked, but no words came through.

'Did you copy?' Flannery called, almost crying as she spoke.

There was another elongated silence before comms responded.

'Copied. The FIM is monitoring.'

# CHAPTER FORTY

Three minutes might well have been three hours the way they were feeling right then. The front door was still open, nothing could be seen beyond the black void of the night and they were still huddled tightly behind the wall of the kitchen doorway.

'What do we do?' Foster asked anxiously.

'We sit tight,' AFO Flannery answered.

'But what if he's around the back now, looking right in at us through the window?'

They all looked out through the large kitchen window.

'Shit,' Flannery cursed. 'Is there anywhere away from the windows that we can get to easily?'

'I uh…'

'Come on think.'

'No… n… nowhere.' Just as the DCI spoke, a *thwack* zipped through the air and the dishwasher door splintered with the impact of another high velocity round.

'He's still out front,' Chilcott said. 'Let's stay put for now.'

'Agreed,' Flannery said.

The faint sound of howling sirens grew in the far distance. Flannery peeked around the doorframe and snuck her head back quickly again. She repeated the move several times and then turned to the detectives. 'Stay right here, I'm checking on Hoops.'

She crawled out from behind the wall and belly-shuffled along the carpet towards her colleague. She crawled up his legs towards his face. He'd taken a direct hit below the level of his protective helmet. If the perp was still out there, Flannery was surely a goner too. She looked up out through the door, waiting for her lights to go out, but they didn't. She could see the telltale blue strobe lighting of her fast-approaching colleagues and quickly got to her feet as the first two BMW X5 armoured vehicles screeched to a sudden halt immediately outside of the door. Almost immediately four AFOs scrambled from their cars, two pointing their carbines out towards the tree line while the others ran into the house.

Chilcott took the opportunity to run.

'Where are you going?' Foster shouted.

'I'm doing my bit,' he replied racing out through the kitchen door.

AFO Flannery tried to pull him back, but he broke free of her grasp. Chilcott ran beyond the defensive line of AFOs taking cover behind the X5s and continued into the dark open space.

'I'm here, Kershaw,' he shouted, his arms wide welcoming a response from Kershaw.

'What the hell's he doing?' Flannery shouted.

Foster sat back on her heels, her body numb as she

watched her DI surely running to his death. 'He's drawing him out,' she answered as silent tears rolled down her cheeks.

'Look for the muzzle flash,' Flannery shouted to her crew mates as she joined alongside them waiting for that millisecond of light to give away the shooter's location.

Kershaw lifted his head from the scope for a fleeting second as he watched the detective inspector break through the protective line that the firearms officers had just created, and run in his general direction like a demented lemming. The strobe lights from the vehicles bounced off the vegetation that surrounded him, but he was well covered. He had to admire the misguided bravery of the detective. He was sacrificing himself to prevent the others from being killed, but the woman would be next… after him. There was no other way. He lowered his eye once more to the telescopic sight and prepared his breathing for his next target. At no more than eighty metres' distance, accuracy wasn't going to be an issue.

The detective was in the cross hairs, but he was a moving target, reducing the distance between them all the time. He was shouting something, but Kershaw couldn't clearly make it out and he wasn't bothered about listening in any event. He removed his finger from the trigger guard and prepared the next shot.

Foster dragged herself outside and hid down low between two of the officers using the large 4x4 as cover.

'Get back inside,' one of the AFOs shouted at her angrily. 'Get back inside and close the door, you're putting us all at risk.'

'That's my DI out there. Can you see him?'

Flannery scrambled behind her colleagues. 'You can't stay out here, Ma'am. It's too dangerous.'

'But Robbie…'

'He's doing us a favour; he's going to expose the shooter's position.'

'If he shoots.'

'Come on, Ma'am,' Flannery said grabbing Foster by the scruff of her suit jacket, bundling her unceremoniously back towards the house.

Suddenly, a shot rang out, echoing as it bounced off the building walls. Flannery instinctively hit the deck with the DCI still attached to her grasp and she lay on top of her superior officer. 'Is everyone okay,' she yelled and received positive feedback from her four colleagues.

A second loud shot followed the first and everyone ducked low again for cover.

As each of the AFOs returned their status, Foster began to weep uncontrollably on the floor.

'Did you get the location,' Flannery asked her team mates, but three of the AFOs were already mobile and closing down the distance to the target.

'Let's get you inside,' Flannery said, still acting as a human shield between the DCI and Kershaw's line of sight.

They scurried into the building and hastily closed the door. 'You must stay with me, Ma'am.'

Foster shook nervously.

The Airwave radio on Flannery's body armour beeped

into action. 'Closing in on target position,' came the transmitted update.

'Chilcott,' Foster wept into her hands.

Flannery returned transmission. 'Report on the condition of DI Chilcott, over.'

They didn't respond.

Foster sank her head and curled up into a ball.


The officers came in at an ever narrowing angle. He couldn't shoot at one without the other AFOs having an advantageous position to fire back. Up ahead of them, the silhouette of a body lay face down on the floor, and just a few metres further back they saw a man facing them.

'Armed police. Drop to your knees and place your hands on your head,' one of the officers shouted swiftly closing in. 'Drop to your knees or we'll fire,' he yelled.

The man did as requested and his knees sank into the cold, soft turf. He slowly interlocked his fingers behind his head and waited for the first firearms officer to reach him.

He was forced face down onto the ground and his hands were quickly speed-cuffed up his back. He was searched where he laid, a knee from the second officer pinning his shoulder firmly to the ground. The third officer training his G36 at point blank range on the prisoner. A fourth and fifth AFO joined them and went across to the body lying on the ground. After a quick inspection, they gave comms a report via the radio.

'One fatality,' an officer reported. 'And one suspect in custody.'

Foster heard the update through Flannery's Airwave and

she crumpled onto the floor.

'Are you staying here?' Flannery asked. 'I need to join my colleagues.'

'No,' Foster wept. 'I need to see…' she couldn't bring herself to say his name.


By the time Foster and Flannery reached the other firearms officers, they had already gained full control of the scene. A commotion was going on around the detained suspect, but Foster only saw the motionless outstretched legs sticking out of the shrubbery in the dark night air. She took several steps forwards and then an uncontrollable urge rose up from her feet and she vomited onto the floor.

AFO Flannery came to her aid. 'Are you okay, Ma'am? Would you like to sit down?'

Foster doubled in two as a second surge of vomit cascaded around her feet. She spat out the remnants and wiped her mouth and nose with a tissue from her pocket.

'Are you okay, Julie?' a familiar voice asked from behind.

Foster stopped spitting and stood bolt upright.

'Eaten something dodgy?'

She turned and saw Chilcott's face.

'You bastard,' she shouted raining her fists down onto his chest. 'I thought you were dead.'

'Oh… sorry to disappoint you.' He looked into her pooling eyes and took her by the hand.

'Don't you ever do that again,' Foster spluttered, somewhere between laughter and tears.

'Kershaw's dead,' Chilcott announced.

They both looked at the stationary legs and Foster's

questioning head turned to the melee a few metres away.

'If that's Kershaw, then who…?'

Stephen Chamberlain stared down at his daughter's murderer with the kind of satisfaction only someone in his position could feel. The AFOs were being robust with him, as well they might, considering he'd just put two rounds into Kershaw; the first in the groin and the other through his skull. He stood like a rag doll, as he was rough-handled by the officers, but his eyes didn't stray from the prostrate body lying before him.

Chilcott observed him with a tragic irony. He may well have just saved their lives, but his own and that of his wife were now truly shattered.

The OFC came across to Foster and Chilcott. 'We'll take him to Patchway and then it's over to you guys.'

'Sure,' Chilcott said on behalf of Foster who was still regaining her composure. 'Thanks for your help, Jimbo.'

'No worries. I'll get the guys to write this up as soon as.'

'Cheers.'

Chilcott watched the AFOs thrust Chamberlain into the back of a marked prisoner transport van and drive away, lights blazing.

The CSIs were clicking away with their cameras and although it seemed a done deal, Kershaw's death would have to be treated like every other murder.

'Shall we go and check out your gaff?' he asked Foster who nodded silently.

They began to trudge back towards Foster's home, the street now alive with emergency vehicles and nosy onlookers. A forensic tent was already erected at the front of Foster's house, protecting the body of AFO Hooper. Officers in white paper suits were coming and going and the first media broadcast van was setting their position to live beam the extraordinary first pictures from the scene.

Chilcott put his arm around his boss and pulled her close. 'You okay, Julie?'

She looked disbelievingly towards her home.

Chilcott took out his phone and dialled Jaz Chowdhury.

'Hello Jaz,' he said. 'It's Chilcott. Are you and the family safe?'

'Yeah, we're fine, thanks. How about you guys?'

'We're okay. You want to meet me at Julie's place; we've got a bit to do down here.'

'Of course...' he hesitated. 'I heard Barry Kershaw's dead.'

'Yeah... Stephen shot him... saved our lives in the process.'

Chowdhury was silent for a beat. 'I heard that you did a brave thing. I listened to everything unfolding through the AFOs Airwave radio.'

'I did a stupid thing.'

'Maybe you did.'

Chilcott heaved a deep sigh and looked around at the mass of activity. Foster was standing motionless in front of the white forensic tent – a stark reminder of the danger they had faced and the gravity of the situation.

'I hope it's over, Jaz,' he said soberly. 'No more death.'

'It sounds like it is.'

Chilcott pinched a smile and he saw a paramedic approaching him, being directed by AFO Flannery.

'I've gotta go, mate. We'll see you here soon.'

He ended the call and put a smile on for the others.

# CHAPTER FORTY-ONE

They decided that the office was the best place for them to be. Foster's home was a no-go area while CSM Parsons and his team did their thing, and Chowdhury was satisfied that with the threat over, his family could return to their home. The three of them sat facing one another in the boss's office, each clutching a hot steaming brew.

Chilcott could see in Foster's face just how much the last few hours had knocked her confidence.

'So,' he said, 'who's going to interview Chamberlain?'

'It can't be us,' Foster said. 'We'll have to take a back seat from here on in. We're too involved ourselves to make fair or impartial decisions.'

Chilcott took a sip of his drink. 'He's got good mitigation.'

Foster raked her eyes towards him. 'He still unlawfully killed someone.'

'It seems unfair,' Chowdhury offered. 'Him killing Kershaw probably saved lives.'

'I agree,' Foster said. 'Without doubt, it did, but he wasn't authorised to take matters into his own hands.'

Chilcott turned away and bit his bottom lip.

'Rob?'

'There must be something we can do for him?'

'Let the wheels of justice turn. You saw his face; he got what he wanted.'

'Can't help thinking about his wife – she's lost them both, one way or another.'

Foster nodded slowly, but her eyes refused to look away from her DI.

'How did you know?' she asked Chilcott.

He shook his head. 'Know what?'

'How did you know Chamberlain would be there?'

A minuscule twitch in the corner of his eye told her she was onto him.

'I didn't.'

'You knew by running into the open, you'd create enough of a distraction to allow Chamberlain to take his opportunity.'

Chilcott slurped loudly from his mug. 'Don't know what you're talking about?'

She studied him.

'I know you, Rob, and I know you take gambles.'

He dipped his head and flashed his eyes at Chowdhury.

'If anything saved us out there tonight, it was your actions.'

'I entirely agree,' Chowdhury said.

'If Chamberlain hadn't got to Kershaw first and you were… well, the AFOs would have had him.'

'Why didn't they shoot back when they heard the two shots?' Chowdhury asked.

'Because I was out there,' Chilcott said. 'They saw the location from Chamberlain's muzzle flash. It's that simple.'

'I'm going to put something to the chief about your actions tonight, Robbie. I can't guarantee anything will—'

'I don't want anything from him.'

'What do you want then?'

He looked at Chowdhury for a long moment.

'I want to come back here full-time. This is where I need to be. Around the people that make a difference.'

Foster pulled a face and glanced Chowdhury's way.

'Let me work alongside Jaz. I know I've been an arsehole, but… if you'd both have me, I'd like to come back.'

Foster caught Chowdhury's eyes and saw them smiling.

'Let me consider it,' she said.

'How long?'

Foster sniffed and looked out through the glass-walled office into the incident room. It was really only down to Chilcott's *unique* methods that they'd brought a swift end to the killings.

'Jaz,' she said. 'What do you think?'

He smiled subtly. 'Well, he's still got a bit to learn, but I guess we could use an extra pair of hands around the place.'

Chilcott clenched his fist and landed it softly on Chowdhury's shoulder in a playful display of upset.

'Fine.'

'Fine?' Chilcott repeated.

'I'll make a case to the detective chief superintendent to reinstate you full-time.'

Chilcott exhaled loudly with relief and sank his head forwards. 'Thank you,' he whispered.

'Just one thing.'

'Sure, you name it.'

'Get yourself somewhere to live pretty damn quick, I don't know how much more I can take of seeing you parading around my home in your boxer shorts.'

---

Keep reading for a preview of the latest DI Chilcott novel, ***Death Do Us Part***.

# DEATH DO US PART

A DI CHILCOTT MYSTERY
BOOK TWO

# PROLOGUE

Friday August 13<sup>th</sup>

7:02 p.m.

The couple walked side-by-side in a purposeful silence until they reached the edge of the jetty. They paused for a beat and looked at each other.

'Permission to board,' she called out breezily.

Jane Hicks looked out from the cabin and saw a smiling Debbie Baxter standing at the edge of the walkway, holding a "token" bottle of something white in her hands. Her husband, Walter, stood flaccidly at her side, but he was anything but smiling.

'Please do,' Jane said, coming towards them with an outstretched arm to help the glamorous younger woman step across from the wooden jetty and onto the open-plan stern of her boat. She took the bottle of wine with a polite smile and an 'Ah, that's sweet of you', but she didn't bother to look at the label. Turning to Walter, she extended a thin, measured smile, but instead of offering her arm in the same manner she had to his wife, Jane simply turned her back and made towards the inside with Debbie's arm looped inside her own.

'Well, if it isn't our fun-loving neighbours,' the other host, Trevor Hicks, boomed with dramatic gusto as he joined them on the deck from within the cabin of his plush, forty-five-foot Princess cruiser. He gave Debbie a welcoming wink and extended an upward nod to Walter, who didn't reciprocate any form of greeting of his own. Trevor had with him a customary glass of champagne sloshing inside a tall crystal flute.

'Ah, that's… kind of you,' he said, taking the bottle of gifted wine from Jane in his free hand. 'Can I offer either of you a glass of fizz to help get the party started?'

'That would be lovely,' Debbie said. 'Thank you so much.'

'I'll have one glass of *that* wine, please,' Walter replied with an upturned lip, referring to the donated bottle in Trevor's left hand.

'One glass of fizz and one…', Trevor made a point of bringing the bottle to his face for a closer inspection of the label, '… Chilean Chardonnay.' He caught Jane with a mischievous glint of the eye, and he grinned insincerely at Walter.

'Coming right up, sir,' he said with a subservient bow.

Stopping at the sliding cabin doors, he turned. 'Are you sure I can't tempt you with a vintage Dom Pérignon, Walter? It's rather nice, you know. Who knows, it might even help you relax?'

'So I see from your empties on the jetty. I assume they will be gone by the morning.'

'Of course, dear Walter – ever the environmentalist.'

Trevor winked at his wife; the wind-up had begun.

'No,' Walter answered. 'One glass of Chardonnay will be adequate. Thank you.'

Trevor beamed a broad smile, his bleached white teeth catching the fading light of the dropping sunset. He shot a final glance at his wife and stepped back into the cabin, party music and laughter escaping from the open doors.

'Well,' Jane said. 'Shall we join the others inside?'

'Who else is here?' Debbie asked with apparent interest.

Walter cast her a dour stare.

'We've got *Gekko*, *Master and Commander*, *Stainer*, *The Captain*, oh, and their better halves, of course.' She giggled, and Debbie joined in her amusement.

'Quite a gathering,' Walter commented just as the immediately recognisable and penetratingly high-pitched laughter of *Gekko's* wife – Rosemary Collins – escaped through the gap left in the door by Trevor who had just announced the arrival of the latest guests.

'Why must Trevor give everyone nicknames?' Walter asked.

Jane just smiled. *Wait until you hear yours.* She was pretty sure Walter had no idea he was widely known in this tight-knit marina community as, *The Serial Killer* due to his cold, dead-eyed stare.

Seeing a mark of recognition in Debbie's eye, it seemed apparent that she was also "in" on the joke.

It was Trevor's passion to have as much fun in life as possible, and if that meant upsetting a few people along the way with his wicked yet priceless sense of humour, then so be it.

Jane prized the doors wider for them all to pass through, and the ambient, soothing rhythms of a *Chilled Ibiza* classic greeted them.

'Here you go, Debs. Enjoy that, my love,' Trevor said, bounding towards her with a brimming flute of lively, top-end champagne.

'Walter,' he said in sad contrast and handed Walter a yellow plastic beaker containing his tepid Chardonnay. 'Can't be too careful.'

Walter peered down disapprovingly at his alternative drinking vessel, setting Rosemary into further fits of hysterics at his expense, but Trevor hadn't quite finished with him yet.

'They always say you have to watch the quiet ones… don't they, Walter?'

Walter looked back at his host with utter disdain and the blatant, unapologetic hatred he had for the man.

The Hicks' lived a lavish lifestyle. Their boat was by no means the most expensive on the marina, but their passion for life couldn't be matched. *Generosity* was a noun that came nowhere near describing their unparalleled hospitality levels. Eight unopened bottles of vintage Dom Pérignon champagne chilled inside individual ice buckets on the side of the galley. They would probably only go through half that amount tonight, but it was the thought that counted for their valued friends.

Trevor lowered the music volume and stepped into the middle of the lounge area.

'So, now we're all here,' he roared, holding his glass aloft. 'Here's to the end of summer, and may we all enjoy calm waters and distant horizons.'

'Calm waters and distant horizons,' everyone except Walter repeated as they joined Trevor in a lofty toast of their glasses.

'So,' Trevor said playfully to Debbie. 'We're all putting our keys into the pot later. You up for a little fun tonight?'

'I'm game for anything,' Debbie giggled, giving Trevor a gentle prod in the ribs with the point of her elbow.

'We'll be doing no such thing,' Walter said.

'It's okay, Walter,' Jane said. 'He's only joking. Ignore him. You know what he's like.'

'Yeah, we don't need keys – none of us are driving,' Trevor roared, clinking glasses with several of the other guests, including Debbie.

'Are you still enjoying marina life here?' Tim Collins, also known as *Gekko* after the character *Gordon Gekko* in the film *Wall Street*, asked Debbie as she took a seat on the crescent-shaped cream leather sofa beside him.

Tim was a retired City banker of almost thirty-five years, hence the nickname. He and his wife had always planned to spend their twilight years beside the ocean.

'I love it, thank you.' She glanced around the room and caught the smiles and welcomes of other guests.

'How long's it been now?' Tim quizzed. 'Since you both first pitched up here?'

Debbie looked across the cramped saloon towards her husband, standing by himself close to the outer doors.

'It's been nearly fourteen months now.'

'And I understand the sale of your house in Pensford went through?'

'Yes. In fact, it was faultless.'

'Blimey! Just as well Stainer wasn't handling it; you'd still be there at Christmas.'

Ben Staines was a local property agent and had quite an impressive portfolio of premises, but he also came with a reputation as a bit of a shit magnet. If anything could go wrong in Ben's world, it generally did.

'I heard that, *Gekko*,' Ben replied from across the room and balled a playful fist in Tim's direction.

'He's only jealous,' Tim whispered, grabbing Debbie's partially empty glass from in front of her in one smooth motion. 'I'm sure he just wants to sit next to the most beautiful woman on the marina... instead of me.'

'Aww,' Debbie cooed and knocked his arm playfully with the back of her hand. 'You're just saying that to be nice to me.'

'Debs is ready for a top-up,' Tim called out to Trevor, holding out the champagne flute in an outstretched arm towards the host.

'Oh... no really, I'd... I'd better not.'

Trevor dutifully came to Debbie's side and, barely taking his eyes away from hers, he skilfully filled the glass, treating every drop of the champagne with reverent respect.

'Ooh, thanks. But I really can't get—'

'It's no crime to live a little,' Trevor replied, handing her the refilled crystal glass flute.

Across the room, Walter was watching her with the eyes of a hawk, a miserable one at that.

Trevor navigated the guests with the bottle of champagne until he was opposite Walter. Trevor took pride in his hosting skills, and Walter's disconnection with the rest of the party was glaringly apparent and at odds with what Trevor would have desired.

'So, what did you say you did for a living before retiring?' Trevor asked Walter to engage and include him in the party.

'I didn't.'

Trevor stepped back in a theatrical display of defensiveness.

'Okay,' he said, holding up his hands, one containing the nearly full bottle of Don Pérignon, the other his glass flute. 'Then pray do tell us, Walter, what did you do for a living? How can you afford that beautiful yacht of yours?'

Walter's eyes tracked Trevor's without deviation. The rest of the guests hushed to near silence. All they could hear now were the relaxed tones of *Café del Mar* playing softly in the background.

'I worked for the Ministry of Defence.'

'Ah, a *James Bond-type*, I bet?' Trevor jested. 'Quiet and mysterious. Got your licence to kill and all that?' He beamed broadly to his audience, much to the delight of Rosemary, who was well on her way to a serious hangover in the morning.

Walter didn't reply and kept his eyes trained on his much younger host, who appeared to be deriding much comedic mileage at his expense.

'He was a draughtsman,' Debbie whispered to Tim. 'He worked in the drawing office.'

'I won't tell anyone if you don't?' Tim reassured her.

She giggled softly and sipped from her glass.

'Nibbles anyone?' Jane asked, producing a large silver platter of prepared canapés, fresh peeled prawns, dressed crab, and savoury snacks. The warm smell of samosas filled the saloon. 'We've got meat and veggie options,' she said, taking a bite from the first delicious-looking morsel nearest to her. Years of corporate and private entertainment had shown her this was the best way to break the ice when it came to eating at parties – scoff something first yourself. And after all, she'd spent four hours of the day making the stuff, so the last thing she wanted was for everyone to stand around politely staring at the plate of food while waiting for someone else to make the first move. Sure enough, Rosemary stepped forward, took a dish from the stack on the side and took one of everything on offer.

'Top-up anyone?' Trevor asked, holding the freshly-opened bottle of champagne aloft, before heading directly for Rosemary and topping up her glass to the brim, even though she hadn't answered.

'Anyone else?' he asked, catching Walter's disapproving frown from across the room. He lowered the bottle and quietly walked over to him.

'Come on, Walter,' he said gently. 'Just one little glass of fizz? No one wants to see you alone here tonight.'

'I'm not alone. I'm with my wife.'

Trevor twitched a brow and looked back over to where Debbie was surrounded by all the other men on the small half-moon sofa.

'We've got a busy day tomorrow, and I want to be compos mentis,' Walter said.

'Ooh, that sounds interesting. What are you up to tomorrow then?'

Walter didn't answer immediately. He peered at Trevor with a dubious mistrust.

'We're picking up a new boat,' Debbie shouted from across the way. 'We can't wait. It's wonderful.' She looked at her husband's disapproving glare and then ducked down as if hiding behind her glass.

Trevor turned back to Walter, whose facial expression hadn't altered.

'So I see,' Trevor said. 'Walter looks positively gripped with excitement.'

Walter narrowed his gaze.

'Where are you picking the new boat up from, Walter?' Trevor asked.

'Salcombe Marina.'

'Salcombe? That's a beautiful location but a long way to go for a boat. Are you transporting it by land?'

'No, we're sailing.'

'You're sailing to Salcombe! What about the predicted winds over the next few days? I've heard it's going to get pretty messy out there.'

'You don't need to worry about me.'

Trevor scratched the side of his temple. 'I'm not.' He turned back towards the half-moon sofa. 'But Debs, on the other hand.'

'You don't need to be concerned about my wife either.'

'Okay,' Trevor said, holding his hands up in submission and taking a step or two further backwards. 'I was just trying to be helpful.'

'Are you causing problems again, Trevor?' Ben called over playfully from the sofa.

'Not me… not me.'

Trevor turned his back on Walter. 'I think I need a top-up.'

'Tell me about this trip of yours tomorrow,' Tim asked Debbie. 'What boat are you getting?'

'It's a new *Amel Sixty*.'

'New?'

Debbie nodded.

'My god! What's that… one point four, one point five million?'

'Something like that. I leave Walter to do the negotiating.'

She took a moment to catch the eye of her husband and smiled across to him.

'What are you doing with your existing yacht?'

'It's already traded. We arrive at Salcombe, do a hand-over, and then return on *Death Do Us Part*.'

Tim nearly spat his drink across the table as he reacted to the new boat's name.

'That's an interesting choice of name. Don't you think that could be tempting the fate of the Sea Gods? You know what they say?'

'I chose the name. I think it's perfect.'

'Well, then who am I to disagree? What time are you planning to leave? The tides are early tomorrow.'

'We're heading off by seven-thirty at the latest and plan to make a late stop-over somewhere in Cornwall. We'll then do the final stretch to Salcombe, probably arriving late on Sunday.'

'Have you seen the forecast? Have you been on a trip in weather like that before?'

'Yes, I used to work as crew on large commercial yachts. And Walter and I have sailed to the Channel Islands and France numerous times, so this should be fairly straight forward.'

'When do you think you'll be back in your swish new boat?'

'Possibly next weekend, weather permitting. We are going to spend a few days in Salcombe. I love it there; it's just so beautiful on a summer's day.' Debbie sipped from her glass and glanced at her husband. He was paying her undivided attention from across the room.

'Just keep a close eye on that weather,' Tim suggested, like a father to his daughter. 'It's due to change late on tomorrow with a front moving in from the west.'

Noticing her concerned frown, he quickly backtracked. 'Uh… but you never know with the English weather.' He smiled and finished his glass of champagne.

'Your wife seems to be enjoying herself,' Debbie commented as she looked over to Rosemary, who was fussing over spillage of champagne on the sheepskin rug.

'Oh, she's never long without a glass in her hand. She must have thought all her Christmases had come at once when Trevor and Jane moored up next to us three years ago.'

'They do like a party, don't they?'

'Every weekend, and most days in between. They're still young enough to enjoy life while they can.'

He looked over conspiratorially at Trevor, who was "playing down" Rosemary's little drinks accident.

'I do wish they'd give it a rest sometimes, though. It would be nice to come down here occasionally and enjoy the peace and tranquillity, which is why we bought the boat in the first place.'

'How long have you lived here full-time?' Debbie asked.

'We started visiting at weekends and then gradually built up to living here permanently around two years ago; once we got to know a few people around the marina – you know how it goes.'

'Yes, I know what you mean. Walter lives here full-time, and I do try to be here as much as possible, but I sometimes also stay away with friends.'

'Yes, I've seen you coming and going.' He gave Debbie a knowing lift of the eyebrow.

She flashed a smile and then covered her mouth with her glass and glanced sideways at her husband.

'I'm going to check up on Rosemary. Good luck with your voyage tomorrow.' Tim touched the top of her arm and then slid his legs away from under the table to join his increasingly tipsy wife.

Debbie wasn't alone for long. Dave Reynolds approached and took the recently vacated and still warm seat alongside her. He waited for Walter to look away in another direction before speaking.

'Hi Debs, how are you doing?'

'I'm good.'

'So, it's tomorrow?'

She nodded and looked down gingerly.

'That's great,' he said.

Her eyes darted up and around his face. 'Yes… yes, it is.'

The rugged, thirty-one-year-old heir to a multi-million-pound fortune looked anxiously towards Walter, who was fending off the attentions of an increasingly amorous Rosemary Collins.

'Okay, you two?' Trevor said, bounding over towards them with another opened bottle of champagne. 'Who's ready for a top-up?'

Dave put a hand over the top of his glass. 'I think I may go onto the brandies, Trev. Too much of this, and I'll be anyone's.' He looked sideways at Debbie, who recoiled with blushing coyness.

'I think I'll join you in that, Dave,' Trevor said as he refilled Debbie's flute with bubbly.

'Let that be the last one,' a stern voice came from across the table. Walter was now standing just feet away from Debbie with his arms firmly folded.

'Hello, Walter,' Dave said. 'I hear you are off to collect your new boat in the morning.'

'Only if *she* stops drinking.'

'Oh, she's just having—'

'Just having what?'

'I was just going to say… Debs is enjoying a couple of drinks, that all. She's not coming to any harm.'

Walter moved towards his wife in a determined fashion. 'Well, then maybe it's time I put an end to that.'

Dave quickly turned towards Debs. She was curled up on the seat beside him.

Instinctively, he reached out and pulled at Walter's arm. 'I'm sure Debs is old enough to decide for herself.'

'Get your fucking hand off me.'

Time, sound and movement stopped in an instant.

Walter's face was tight with fury.

'Come on,' he shouted, shooting out a hand and taking a fist full of Debbie's white blouse. 'It's time to go.'

He yanked her towards him, thrusting Debbie's body forwards against the table.

'Hey, watch it, you prick,' Dave yelled, reaching out for Debbie's arm.

Walter clamped eyes on the younger man while still holding Debbie by a balled fist of material.

'Stay out of my business,' he seethed through gritted teeth.

Dave swung his legs out from beneath the table and fronted up to Baxter toe-to-toe as Tim and others attempted to claw him back from the confrontation.

'I said watch it,' Dave replied, taking hold of Walter's wrist in a firm and uncompromising grip.

'You'd better let go, son,' Walter said, looking down at Dave's hand. 'You can't afford to be up on charges of assault.'

Dave hesitated for a second and then released his grip.

'Walter,' Trevor called out as he came back up to the saloon from the toilets. 'Where are you going? You've only just turned up. We haven't sorted out the wife-swap yet.'

Jane prodded Trevor in the ribs with her elbow and silenced him.

All background chatter had ceased, and eyes were trained on Walter and his wife.

'I'm sorry, Walter,' Trevor backtracked. 'I was only joking about the wife-swap.'

'Yes, that's all you do,' Walter spat as he pulled Debbie closer towards him with considerable force.

'Go easy,' Dave shouted, bouncing his chest off Walter's shoulder.

Walter pointed a rigid finger towards him. 'You keep your bloody nose out of our business, and I'll keep mine out of yours.'

He twisted the strap of Debbie's handbag, slung over a shoulder, and dragged her behind him towards the exit like he was leading a donkey.

Everyone watched him, rooted to the spot.

He turned around at the exit. 'Thank you for the…' He looked around at the stunned faces peering back at him and paused on Trevor's gawking face. '…hospitality.'

He led the way through the sliding doors with an uncomplaining Debbie still connected by her bag strap. Dave tried to follow, but Tim stopped him.

'Don't get involved, son.'

'But he can't do that.'

'Bloody hell,' Trevor cussed. 'What an obnoxious little shit. He's only gone and ruined the party.'

'Do you think we should check if Debs is okay?' Rosemary slurred to her husband.

'We'll leave soon,' Tim said. 'We're moored close to them. We'll hear if anything else happens and if it does, I'll call the police.'

'You'll do that?' Dave said. 'Call the police if he continues?'

'Yes, yes, absolutely.'

'I don't know. I think we should check Debs is okay,' Dave said.

'Leave it, Dave. Some things are best not getting caught up in.'

'Why on earth is she with him?' Jane said. 'There is absolutely nothing appealing about that man whatsoever.'

Trevor stepped outside onto the decking, but Walter and his wife were already out of sight.

'Money,' Tim said to Jane. 'There can be no other reason. She's with him for the money.'

# CHAPTER 1

Wednesday 1$^{st}$ September

10:17 a.m.

As he checked the ongoing and fresh Storm Log reports of each reported crime in the various districts that his department covered, veteran Detective Inspector Robbie Chilcott stared wistfully at his computer screen. Chilcott had been on duty at the Bristol Central Major Crime Investigation Team since 7 a.m. He was starting to suffer the light-headed effects from a caffeine overdose resulting from excruciating inactivity and general malaise. He slowly ran a hand through his receding hairline and dragged it with a crackle across his two-day-old silvery stubble before cupping his head in his hand. It wasn't unusual for his department to have barren periods when serious crime abated for a day or two, but this had been a ball-achingly dull couple of weeks.

The murder detectives of the CMCIT had plenty to do. The department was carrying three investigations in preparation for Crown Court trials, including two separate gang stabbings and the coroner's investigation into the death of Barry Kershaw, an investigation that made a significant impact on the department and, on a personal note, took Chilcott to the edge and back. The Independent Office for Police Complaints were also still involved, sniffing around like a pesky dog and causing the team, especially Chilcott, a notable degree of grief. They were particularly interested in Chilcott's methods, something that made him stand out from his peers. He didn't do things intentionally maverick, but unfortunately for him, it often just turned out that way. He was unique in how he saw crime, but probably more problematic for him was the distinctive way he tackled it. After nearly three decades of service, Chilcott had crafted an inimitable style of crime-fighting. To some, he was a legend. To others, including his direct line supervisor, Detective Chief Inspector Julie Foster, he was never more than one unconventional decision away from bringing down the entire department.

It wasn't that Chilcott was bored as such – this still beats the hell out of general response work or dealing with the repetitive types of jobs his counterparts in district CID had to manage. And it wasn't that he hoped for more murders, perish the thought, but he needed *something* to keep him focussed, driven and away from the hounds of the IOPC.

A *tap*, *tap*, *tap* on the door broke his lethargic stupor.

Detective Inspector Jasjit Chowdhury was standing in the open doorway. A sharp-dresser whose cologne entered a room before he did, Chowdhury's appearance was the polar opposite to Chilcott, who could get three days out of the same shirt and generally smelt of Febreze. Chowdhury was

Chilcott's equivalent. They shared the DI responsibilities of the department, often running concurrent investigations with the same pooled team of detectives between them. Chowdhury was young and keen. A corporate man. A "yes" man. Management liked him; he would never give them sleepless nights.

Chilcott wasn't proud of the fact, but he'd lost his cool when Chowdhury was selected for the DI position at BCMCIT ahead of him. He'd struck the young detective and served a temporary suspension from the department as a result. But now he was back, and they were together, Chilcott had the chance to right his wrongs.

'Hey, Jaz,' Chilcott mumbled. 'How are you doing, mate?'

Jaz Chowdhury approached Chilcott, waving a sheet of A4 paper held out in front of him. 'Not sure how you're fixed?' he said.

Chilcott waved a heavy hand over the top of his sparse desk. 'Snowed under, as you can see.'

'I've been made aware of a job that might interest you?'

Chilcott frowned and looked back at the ongoing call logs. Had he missed something?

'If you're not free, then I can run it by—'

Chilcott leaned over and snatched the sheet of paper from Chowdhury's loose grasp. 'Let me see that.'

He read the typed report for a few seconds, his frown deepening with each paragraph.

Chowdhury stood back and silently watched his counterpart taking onboard the information.

'What's this crap?' Chilcott said, wafting the sheet of paper through the air like it was meaningless twaddle.

'Looks like a job for the CMCIT,' Chowdhury said.

'Really?' Chilcott asked incredulously and handed the now crumpled report back to his colleague.

'Looks like a complete crock of shite to me. I know I want something to keep me occupied, but I'm not that desperate.'

Chowdhury looked down at the report with bemusement.

'How can you say that, it's a high risk missing person?'

'So?'

'So, it's something that needs proper investigation.'

'By the suits on district. This isn't a major crime issue. Never was, never will be.'

Chowdhury shrugged. 'DCI Foster seems to think it is.'

Chilcott paused and stared disapprovingly at Chowdhury.

'Let me see that again.'

He hinged forwards and snatched the report back, dropping it onto his desk beneath his gaze. He rested his head in his hands as he read the document once more, but this time, with a keener eye.

Finished, he slid the paper back to the side of his desk but didn't pass comment.

'Well?' Chowdhury said after ten seconds of silence.

'I'll make some enquiries.'

'So, I can leave that with you?'

'That's what I said, didn't I?'

Chowdhury bowed with sarcastic reverence and backed respectfully out of the room.

Chilcott waited until he was certain Chowdhury had gone and then stared out through the window at the three-quarters-filled staff car park below. It was the tail-end of the holiday season for officers with young families. He didn't begrudge them their time off; they were a tight unit, and holidays were necessary for the soul. If only he'd followed the same sage advice those years ago, perhaps he'd have a better relationship with his own daughters… and still have a wife. The fact was, he now lived alone, and work was both his poison and his crutch. The months of self-isolation following Jaz Chowdhury's surprise promotion to the BCMCIT had hit Chilcott hard. Living in a grubby caravan beneath the flight path of landing aircraft had dented his ego and confidence. But now, six months on since returning to the department, he was getting closer to his old self, and that pinch of investigative desire was keeping him awake at night.

He sighed deeply and searched the papers for a contact number.

'Sergeant Pottersley, Portishead Police Station,' the zealous reply came.

'Hello, Sergeant. This is Detective Inspector Robbie Chilcott, Central Major Crime Investigation Team.'

'Oh, hello, sir.'

'Is it convenient for you to speak right now?'

'Yes – yes, absolutely. Ah, how can I help you, sir?'

'I've just been handed your report on the high-risk missing person from Portishead Marina.'

'Yes, that's right. Debbie Baxter.'

'Yeah…' Chilcott's voice tailed away. 'What can you tell me about the job, and what raises the threshold for CMCIT to investigate this over a district department?'

'I did receive approval from your DCI—'

'Yes, yes, but it's now in my lap, and I want to know why?'

'Well, it's an odd one, really.'

'I can see that.' Chilcott's tone was less than cordial.

'The report was made by a third party, not the MISPER's husband—'

'Well, what does the husband have to say about his missing wife?'

'That's the interesting part; he's a real odd-ball. Very defensive and states his wife is visiting her sister in north Wales.'

'Has that been confirmed?'

'No… we-uh… we haven't found any details about a sister in north Wales, or anywhere come to that.'

Chilcott rolled his eyes. 'Okay. Was he asked for an address?'

'Um, no… I don't think so. We have run all other relevant checks on both the subject and her husband, Walter Baxter, but neither come up on the radar.'

'It says here that she's been missing for eleven days,' Chilcott said.

'Yes, sir.'

'Well, why don't we have more information than this?'

'It was only reported to police four days ago… on day seven.'

'Yes, I got my O-Level in mathematics, Sergeant.'

'Sorry, I didn't mean to—'

'So, back to my original question – why does this warrant my team looking into this?'

The sergeant hesitated, and Chilcott heard him clearing his throat away from the mouthpiece.

Chilcott raised both eyebrows with impatient reticence.

'I've got a hunch,' the sergeant finally offered.

'You've got a hunch?'

'Yes, I can't prove anything, but—'

'But?'

'The husband is hiding something.'

Chilcott didn't answer.

'The husband is hiding something; he has to be.'

Chilcott huffed loudly into the mouthpiece and turned with glazed eyes out of the window.

The sergeant didn't say anything immediately. Perhaps he was sussing on the fact that he was wasting Chilcott's time.

'I'd really like you to investigate this, sir,' he finally plucked up the courage to say.

'Would you?'

'If anyone can get through the tough exterior skin of this bloke, it's you, sir.'

Chilcott half-smiled. A little flattery went down well from time to time. He puffed out air through his lips, making them flutter with a sound like a wet fart.

'Okay, I'll entertain your imagination. Tell me about him.'

'I know this is going to sound odd—'

*You have no idea?*

'But he looks like a serial killer.'

Chilcott closed his eyes.

'Did you just say, *"He looks like a serial killer?"*'

'I did, sir. And you'd know what I meant if you saw him.'

'How long have you been in the job, Sergeant?'

'Me? Sixteen years.'

'And what do you recall about your training days, right back to when your policing career began?'

'Never to judge someone on their appearance alone?'

'Never judge someone on their appearance alone, that's right. And what have you just done?'

'It's not—'

'Come on… what have you just told me, and what have you just done?'

'But you have to see him.'

'I'll be the judge of that.'

The sergeant didn't answer.

'Where is he now, this… husband?'

'On his boat.'

'At Portishead Marina?'

'Yes.'

'Does he live on his boat?'

'Yes, I think he does.'

'Is it a *big* boat?'

'It's a sailing yacht, sir.'

'Is it a *big* sailing yacht?'

'Fairly big – I don't know anything about sailing, so I—'

'And neither do I, Sergeant. So why isn't a CID detective investigating this instead of a homicide detective?'

'You will have to ask the DCI, sir. I can't answer that.'

Chilcott nodded and cast his gaze once again out of the window into the car park.

'I will,' he uttered wearily. 'Don't worry. I will.'

# CHAPTER 2

10:42 a.m.

'This job you've got me on, Julie,' Chilcott said, waltzing straight into the DCI's office.

'Do come in,' DCI Julie Foster said sarcastically. 'I'm not busy with anything.'

DCI Foster and Chilcott went back years. He trusted her as one of only a few people who truly understood what made him tick. To him, she was more than his supervisor; she was his friend.

Chilcott tossed the case paper onto her desk.

'It's bullshit.'

Foster peered up at him with the disdain his disruptive and insubordinate entrance deserved.

'You don't like it?' she asked.

'Crock of shite, if you ask me.'

'I don't believe a thirty-one-year-old female missing for eleven days is a *crock of shite*, as you so eloquently put it.'

'I get that, but why us? Are we not snowed under

enough with the shortage of staff and the backlog of cases? We should only be dealing with the serious stuff.'

Foster removed the reading glasses from the tip of her nose, folded them slowly and placed them carefully onto the desk in front of her.

'Sit down,' she said.

Chilcott rolled his eyes but did as she told him.

'Since you've been back with us, you've barely taken a day off, Robbie. What with the Fresco murders—'

'Neither of us has.'

The DCI waved his comment aside.

'That may well be the case, but I'm in charge of this department. You aren't, and your welfare is on my shoulders. This is a nice little job you can get your teeth into and have a change of scenery at the same time.'

'I don't want a change of scenery.'

The DCI stood up and pushed the door closed.

'Rob, I've watched how the Fresco killings affected you. It's gone deep. I get that, and I understand the Herculean effort you put into that case.'

He glanced at her and then looked away. Operation Fresco was a case that had plagued and tormented Chilcott as his only unsolved murder. Fourteen fruitless months he spent hunting the faceless killer of an innocent 17-year-old girl. The case cost him his marriage, his home and his self-respect. But then *"Fresco"*, as the department had nicknamed the killer, murdered again, and Chilcott grasped his chance for redemption. He got justice, but, in the process, it nearly cost Chilcott his life.

'This job is a perfect way for you to put all that stress

behind you. A nice, gentle case by the sea. How could you possibly want to turn that down?'

Chilcott pinched his lips tightly between his fingers and caught her eye again.

'What do I know about boats?'

'You might not know anything about boats, but you sure as hell know how to close out a murder enquiry.'

'Who mentioned murder? This is just a missing person case, isn't it?'

The DCI smiled thinly and gave Chilcott a knowing once over.

'You know Jaz and I can handle the department. We were coping just fine before you returned from exile.'

'It's a detective constable job, not a case for a DI who should be here directing serious investigations. I can't remember the last time I got my hands dirty on a poxy MISPER case. I had eleven years of that crap on district.'

The DCI returned to her seat and unfolded her spectacles, placing them back into position on the tip of her nose.

'Fine, I'll give the gig to Jaz then. I'm sure he could use a break too.'

'Hold on,' Chilcott said with an outstretched arm. 'If I take it, I don't want it to be seen as charity or some kind of *light-duty*.'

'It's not, and it won't.'

'What resources will I have?'

'You can have one DC to do the *dirty work*, as you call it. I'll leave you alone to manage and progress the case as you see fit, and you can report back to me as and when you have any results.'

'But I'm still based here?'

'Look,' Foster said, turning her chair to face him. 'This isn't a way of trying to get rid of you if that's what you're thinking? We've only just got you back! There's an office at Portishead HQ. You can use that. It's an old admin office, fully kitted out with everything you'll need. I use it when I'm there. You can use that, or you can deploy from here. It's your choice.'

'I want Fleur Phillips then.'

'No can do. Fleur is tied up with the Operation Fresco case. The coroner has put a tight deadline on that file, and I can't spare her for this—'

'Go on, say it...'

Foster's face softened, and she gave Chilcott a wry squint of the eye. 'This case, I was going to say.'

Chilcott groaned.

'Okay, I'll take Richie Allen.'

'He's yours.'

'Just like that?'

'Just like that.'

Chilcott looked around the boss's room and wiped a finger beneath his nose.

'Do you want to break the news to DC Allen, or shall I?' Foster asked.

'I'll tell him,' Chilcott said, taking back the case paper from Foster's desk.

'Keep me appraised.'

'I'll have this sorted by this time tomorrow; you'll see.'

He made for the door but paused at the exit.

'Hey,' he said, turning with a slight smile. 'Thanks for thinking of me.'

Detective Constable Richie Allen was a well-liked member of the team. A favourite with the ladies in the department, he was a bright, sharp-witted officer with a liking for brightly-coloured ties and wearing shoes with no socks, as was the way with the young'uns these days. Chilcott had only known him for the six months since his return to the department, and DC Allen had less than one year's major crime investigation experience, but he was dogged in his style and was a keen thief-taker. Only thirty-seven and single, Chilcott had taken an instant liking to Allen, who, in turn, seemed to know a great deal about Chilcott's achievements and some of his less than illustrious antics.

'Allen,' Chilcott said, passing DC Allen's desk and continuing towards his office. 'A word, please?'

DC Allen looked up over the top of his work station and rose gingerly from his chair. He followed Chilcott and timidly tapped his knuckle on the door to his DI's office.

'Come in, Richie. Take a seat.'

DC Allen stepped guardedly into the office and lowered himself onto one of the soft blue chairs, his bottom only just perched on the end.

'How are your crimes looking, son?' Chilcott asked.

'Um, I'm pretty much on top of them, boss. I'm sorry if any are dragging. I'll ensure I—'

'Give me numbers. How many cases are you juggling?'

'Five ongoing investigations, sir, not including the Powlett fraud.'

'I'm taking you off the Powlett fraud.'

'Why… what have I done?'

'You haven't done anything wrong. I need a detective to work on a case with me, and I chose you.'

'Oh… thank you, sir.'

'Don't worry about your existing workload; we'll be back to normal in no time. Just tie up any loose ends you had planned for the rest of this week.'

'Okay, boss, that's no problem. Uh, when do we start?'

'As soon as you're ready.'

'I can be ready by the end of play today,' DC Allen beamed enthusiastically. 'Thanks for having faith in me, sir.'

Chilcott looked blankly for a second at his young, keen colleague.

'I'm going to be honest – I wanted Fleur Phillips, but she's unavailable. This is a good opportunity, son. Do as I say and not as I do, and we'll get along famously.'

# CHAPTER 3

Thursday 2nd September

08:44 a.m.

Portishead Marina on the north-western fringe of Bristol was a recently modernised and improved marina. Unusually, the water was landlocked by large barriers similar in appearance to double canal lock gates. The vista was an impressive sight with luxury high-rise apartments encasing row upon row of pleasure craft from one side of the marina to the other. The place felt like it was dripping with money.

'What's first, boss? Are we going to speak to the MISPER's husband?' DC Allen asked as they strode along the frontage of restaurants and cafés.

'No, we're not. We already know he's suggesting his wife is with her sister. I think before we chat to him, we should speak to the marina manager; introduce ourselves and get a lay of the land, or water, as the case may be.'

He stopped beside an empty outside table and looked inside the large plate glass window of the nice-looking café.

'But first, we're going to have a brew. Let's just sit back and people watch for a while.'

DC Allen looked puzzled.

Chilcott peered up at the breaking clouds in the sky and positioned a metal chair to make the most of the warmth on his face.

'This'll do lovely,' he said, crossing his outstretched feet before him.

DC Allen followed suit and sat down on the opposite side. He looked around for a moment. 'Not many people to watch, boss.'

'Just trust me.'

A waitress joined them outside and sprayed the metal table top with a heady sanitizer-fuelled spray.

'Are you eating with us today, gentlemen?' she asked.

'Just drinks, thanks,' Chilcott said.

'Would you like the wine list, sir?'

Chilcott scratched the top of his head and smiled at the girl. 'I would… but we'll just have coffees, for now, thanks.'

They gave their orders, and Chilcott sat back against his seat and took in the surroundings. There was no denying it; this was a picturesque and entirely relaxing location. DCI Foster had indeed done him a favour.

'Do you know anything about boats, Richie?'

'Me? No, nothing, boss. Other than they make me feel sick when I'm on one.'

Chilcott smiled. He knew that feeling only too well.

'This is how we learn. We observe. We blend in. We watch.'

'And drink,' DC Allen quipped.

'There's always time for coffee. Rule one of the detective's handbook.'

Coffee done, they headed for the marina manager's office situated at the sea-bound mouth of the marina. More like an elevated viewing platform than an office, the operation was similar to a scaled-down air traffic control tower. Introductions at the door over, the manager, Simon Dupont-Avery, took them up to the control room, boasting an impressive bank of closed-circuit TV monitors and communications equipment.

Chilcott nodded satisfaction as he looked around the small glass-walled room.

'What a nice job you have.'

'It's a delightful job, enabling all these lovely people to enjoy their time at the marina,' Mr Dupont-Avery replied. 'Do you gentlemen sail?'

'No... I wouldn't know the front from the back,' Chilcott quipped, giving DC Allen a little wink.

'The bow from the stern,' Dupont-Avery corrected in a teacher-like tone.

Chilcott waved a dismissive hand back at him. 'See, that's exactly what I was saying.'

'I saw you earlier at Le Parisien, having coffee. Is this your first time here at the marina?'

*So much for blending in.*

Chilcott nodded and looked around the office again at the modern technological equipment.

'Yeah, it's our first time, in a work capacity anyhow. This must be one of the most crime-free places in Bristol?'

'I'd like to think so. We certainly try to keep it that way.'

'Do you keep records of who is staying on the marina at any one time?' DC Allen asked.

'Yes, of course, you can't just turn up. Demand for berths is high since we updated the marina facilities. People come from far and wide to moor their boats with us.'

'And what about daily movements?' Chilcott asked.

'The Bristol Channel is challenging, even for the most experienced of sailors. The tidal range is the second highest in the world, somewhere between twelve and fourteen metres. Subsequently, that means many of these vessels are limited to when they can get out to the open water. For safety's sake, we log requests to leave and return to the marina, as we have to manually open and close the marina gates to allow egress and access, but we don't do anything else with those records. That would be like big brother watching, and we wouldn't want that.'

'Perish the thought,' Chilcott muttered as he leaned in closer to a bank of small, coloured HD TV monitors.

'How long do you keep the mooring records for?' DC Allen asked.

Chilcott looked up from the screens and gave his colleague an approving nod.

Dupont-Avery moved towards the window with a confident swagger.

'For as long as you like. We have records dating back to 2011, but again I stress, purely for archive purposes.'

'We only need this year. Got that, have you?' Chilcott asked.

'Yes, of course.'

Chilcott beamed a smile.

'I'm sorry. You still haven't said why you are here. You said you were…' Dupont-Avery curled his lip and peered towards Chilcott. '…murder detectives.'

Chilcott didn't answer and asked a question of his own instead.

'Got a good grasp of things here, though, haven't you? You know, who comes, who goes?'

'Well, I wouldn't say—'

'You noticed us.'

Chilcott stared at the man with a no-nonsense determination of someone who wasn't about to be placated with managerial gibberish.

Dupont-Avery shook his head.

'I'm sorry… I…?'

'You noticed us over there at the coffee shop.' Chilcott pointed over to the corner of the building line to the side entrance of the café.

'You can't see the tables from here, so how did you notice us? Was it the cameras?'

'I first noticed you when you walked towards the gangway beneath us.'

He pointed down to the walkway at the top of the lock gates.

'What made us stand out?'

Dupont-Avery chuckled. 'Well, neither of you are dressed for the ocean.'

'That's good,' Chilcott said. 'It's good to be vigilant, especially in this day and age.'

Dupont-Avery hesitated. '…You… still haven't said why you are here?'

Chilcott tossed DC Allen a theatrical look of surprise. 'Haven't we?'

'No. You haven't.'

Chilcott opened the pages of his daybook and thumbed through, even though he knew the name he was searching for.

'Debbie Baxter, she's one of your locals, is she?' Chilcott smiled.

'Yes, Debbie and her husband have been with us for about a year now.'

'So…?' Chilcott said, inching towards the glass-walled observation point. 'Which is their boat?' He immediately turned and watched Dupont-Avery. There was no searching of a computer database or handy desk-top manifest, and he came alongside Chilcott.

'It's at the end of row seven, at bay ten.' Dupont-Avery pointed out into the marina. '*Death Do Us Part,*' he said with a whimsical intonation.

'Death Do Us Part? Is that the name of the boat?'

'Yes.'

'What sort of a name is that?'

'Granted, it's an unusual name for a boat, but we see all sorts here. We only stipulate that there is no profanity or innuendo in a vessel's naming. We have families living on the water and in the apartments, as well as thousands of visitors each year. It wouldn't do to have such words displayed, and we must uphold a certain quality of life here.'

'Which one is it?' Chilcott said, leaning his head closer to the glass. 'They all look the same to me.'

'Oh, it's a beauty. A two thousand and twenty, Amel

Sixty. It's the only one here; in fact, it is possibly only one of several in the UK at this present moment in time.'

Chilcott showed his ignorance of the subject with a shrug.

'It's a beautiful craft, wonderfully made,' Dupont-Avery continued.

'Amel Sixty – sixty feet long, by any chance?'

'Yes, that's correct.'

Chilcott grasped DC Allen's shoulder with his firm grip. 'See, Richie. I said I'd get this sailing malarkey in no time at all.'

Dupont-Avery blinked slowly.

'So, let's say, you know, for argument's sake, I wanted to splash out some of my pension in a few years' time for one of those bad boys – what would it set me back?'

Dupont-Avery's lips twitched, and he attempted not to break into an impertinent smile.

'I'd suggest you'd need a little more than a police pension, Detective. Though one has to admit, one wouldn't know what that was.'

'Try one.'

'Well…' Dupont-Avery said, staring fancifully towards the far away yacht at the end of jetty seven. 'I'd suggest *that* Amel Sixty would most certainly be in the region of seven figures.'

'A million quid?'

Dupont-Avery faced Chilcott with a superior; *you can't afford this lifestyle* kind of look. 'That's correct.'

'Their boat cost them a million quid?' Chilcott's eyebrows were nearly touching his fading hairline.

'Yes, it's now possibly one of the most expensive yachts we have here.'

'Holy shit,' Chilcott breathed and looked out of the window once again. 'Can you take us down there? I'd love to see what a million quid's worth of boat looks like. Wouldn't you, Richie?'

DC Allen was watching his supervisor with the kind of awe reserved for kids meeting their football heroes. 'Um, yes… of course I would.'

'They are down there, right?' Chilcott asked Dupont-Avery. 'Mr and Mrs Baxter?'

'Well, I haven't seen Debbie for a while now.'

Chilcott pursed his lips and held them protruding as he turned to his colleague. 'What's that?' he asked, seeking clarification.

'I've seen a lot of Walter, but not of Debbie.'

'Since?'

Dupont-Avery adjusted his rimless glasses higher up his nose.

'Since the twenty-first of August.'

'The twenty-first of August?' Chilcott repeated to DC Allen, who jotted the date in his daybook.

'What happened on the twenty-first of August?'

'*Death Do Us Part* moored here for the first time.'

Chilcott scowled. 'I thought you said they'd been here for over a year?'

'I did, but *Death Do Us Part* is a new yacht to the Baxter family and has only been here since the twenty-first of August. They departed the marina on August the fourteenth with their previous yacht, *AWoL*, and returned in *Death Do Us Part*.'

'Absent without leave?' DC Allen asked.

'Another Way of Life.'

Chilcott was staring out of the window once again.

'And was Mrs Baxter here when *Death Do Us Part* arrived on the twenty-first?' he asked.

Another quick touch of the specs, and Dupont-Avery shrugged. 'I assume so.'

'Assume so?'

'I don't recall seeing her as they passed through the lock, and I know I haven't seen her around the marina since. She normally frequents Le Parisien on a Tuesday at around eleven-thirty...' He stopped himself upon seeing Chilcott staring inquisitively back at him.

'But you saw her leave on *AWoL* when they left the marina?'

'Yes, absolutely, I was controlling the lock gates. I do believe Mrs Baxter waved to me as they departed. She's such a joyous individual.'

Chilcott and DC Allen shared a silent moment.

Chilcott stepped slowly towards Dupont-Avery. 'I'm not expecting you to know this,' he said, baiting the marina manager, who appeared to have an all-seeing and all-knowing knowledge of his patron's movements. 'But, do you know where they picked their new boat up from?'

'Yes, I do.'

Chilcott's eyes widened in anticipation of the answer.

'They were sailing to Cornwall or south Devon depending on their progress and then collecting their new yacht from Salcombe, south Devon, before making the return journey back here.'

Chilcott ran a hand down over his face.

'So, just to be clear, you last saw Debbie on the day she left here but did not see her return, and you haven't seen her since.'

'That's correct.'

Dupont-Avery's expression grew quizzical. 'But I wouldn't expect to see her. She's at her sister's, is she not?'

Chilcott sniffed the air. 'You tell me.'

# HOW WAS DEAD RINGER?

I would be grateful if you could leave an honest review.

I love to hear feedback and reviews help other readers take a chance on a new author for the first time.

It need only take a moment of your time and be as short as you like.

Visit my Goodreads page at James D. Mortain,
or my Amazon author page at James D Mortain.

Thank you!

# FREE EBOOK

## THE NIGHT SHIFT

Join my *CRIME SCENE TEAM* and receive the compelling short story prequel to the *Detective Deans Mystery* trilogy for FREE.

By signing to join my *CRIME SCENE TEAM*, you will receive your gift plus occasional news and updates related to my writing.

Don't just be a reader; become part of the team!
Visit www.jamesdmortain.com for more information.

# BOOKS IN ORDER

## DETECTIVE DEANS SERIES

### STORM LOG-0505
eBook/Paperback/Audio

### DEAD BY DESIGN
eBook/Paperback/Audio

### THE BONE HILL
eBook/Paperback/Audio

---

## DI CHILCOTT SERIES

### DEAD RINGER
eBook/Paperback/Audio

## *DEATH DO US PART*
eBook/Paperback/Audio coming soon

## *A WHISPER OF EVIL*
Coming in all formats late 2021

# ACKNOWLEDGEMENTS

As always, I am indebted to many people who have helped me create this book. For their specialist knowledge of both the military and the police services, I'd like to thank: James Hermon, Richard Kitchener, Phil Croll and RJ Price. For their valuable input, having read the raw version of this book (and not consigned it to the bin), I'd like to thank: Terry Galbraith, Jane Hampson and Michael Kavanagh. To my fantastic editor, Debz Hobbs-Wyatt, who is a joy to work with – long may you rip my work to shreds. For two competition winners whose prize was to see their names as characters in this book, I'd like to thank: Julie Foster and Fleur Phillips for the use of their names. And to a returning competition winner whose character saw a promotion, I'd like to thank Nathan Parsons. A huge thank you to the many people who make up my *Advance Reader Team* – your ability to identify the most minor niggles is outstanding, and I am blessed to have you on my team. If you are a new reader of my writing, thank you so much for taking a chance on me.

ACKNOWLEDGEMENTS

And to my returning readers, you guys are simply the best! Your loyal and continued support keeps me motivated during the many late and lonely nights at the computer.

# ABOUT THE AUTHOR

Photograph Copyright of Mick Kavanagh Photography.

Former British CID Detective turned crime fiction writer James brings thrilling action and gritty authenticity to his writing through years of police experience. Originally from Bath, England, James now lives in North Devon with his family.

James still has a 'normal' day job but is happiest creating fictional mystery and mayhem. He is currently completing book 3 of the DI Robbie Chilcott series, due for release later in 2021.

Don't miss the latest releases by following James on Amazon, Bookbub and Goodreads.

You can connect with James on social media or by visiting his website at www.jamesdmortain.com.

Please send any emails to jdm@manverspublishing.com.

facebook.com/jamesdmortain

twitter.com/@jamesdmortain

instagram.com/jamesmortain

Made in United States
Orlando, FL
21 October 2022

23712698R00198